Miss Read, or in real life Dora Saint, was a school teacher by profession who started writing after the Second World War, beginning with light essays written for *Punch* and other journals. She then wrote on educational and country matters and worked as a scriptwriter for the BBC. Miss Read was married to a schoolmaster for sixty-four years until his death in 2004, and they have one daughter.

In the 1998 New Year Honours list Miss Read was awarded an MBE for her services to literature. She is the author of many immensely popular books, including two autobiographical works, but it is her novels of English rural life for which she is best known. The first of these, *Village School*, was published in 1955, and Miss Read continued to write about the fictitious villages of Fairacre and Thrush Green until her retirement in 1996. She lives in Berkshire.

Over the Gate

INCLUDING

The Fairacre Festival

* * *

Miss Read

Illustrated by J. S. Goodall

An Orion paperback
Over the Gate first published in Great Britain in 1964
by Michael Joseph Ltd
The Fairacre Festival first published in Great Britain in 1968
by Michael Joseph Ltd
This paperback edition published in 2007
by Orion Books Ltd
Orion House, 5 Upper St Martin's Lane,
London WC2H 9EA

3 5 7 9 10 8 6 4

A CIP catalogue record for this book
is available from the British Library.

ISBN 978 0 7528 8231 4

Typeset at The Spartan Press Ltd,
Lymington, Hants
Printed in Great Britain by Clays Ltd, St Ives plc

The Orion Publishing Group's policy is to use papers that
are natural, renewable and recyclable products and
made from wood grown in sustainable forests. The logging
and manufacturing processes are expected to conform to
the environmental regulations of the country of origin.

www.orionbooks.co.uk

Over the Gate

For
Kit and Ivor
with love

CONTENTS

* * *

1. The Portrait

If you walk down the village street of Fairacre you will come before long to The Beetle and Wedge on the left-hand side. It is a long, low public house, sturdily built of brick and flint, and so attractive to the eye that it is easy to miss the narrow lane which runs between its side and the three cottages, also of brick and flint, which stand next to it.

This lane leads to the downs which shelter our village from the north-east wind. It begins, fairly respectably, with a tarred and gravelled surface, but after a quarter of a mile such refinement ends; the road narrows suddenly, the tarmac finishes, and only a muddy track makes its way uphill to peter out eventually on the windy slopes high above the village.

Here, where the hard surface ends and the rutted lane begins, stands a pair of dour grey houses which bear no resemblance to the cheerful brick-and-thatch architecture of most of Fairacre. They are faced with grey cement which has fallen off, here and there, leaving several scabrous patches. Each has a steep gable terminating in a formidable spike, and the roofs are of cold grey slate. Even on a day of shimmering heat, when the small blue butterflies of the chalk downs hover in the still gardens before them, these two houses present a chilly visage to the passer-by.

They were built in the latter half of Queen Victoria's reign by a well-to-do retired ironmonger from Caxley. At the same time he had built a larger and more imposing residence in the village street for his own use. This was called Jasmine Villa and boasted a black and white tiled path, an ornate verandah of iron trelliswork, and was magnificently out of keeping with the modest dwellings nearby.

Laburnum Villas, as the two were called, had housed the ironmonger's aged mother and two spinster sisters in one, and a married couple with two sons, all of whom worked for the family, in the other.

When I first took up the headship of Fairacre village school, some years ago, the property belonged to a descendant of the ironmonger's, and was pathetically shabby. The owner lived in Caxley, but Jasmine Villa became familiar to me, inside and out, for the tenant, Mrs Pratt, played the church organ and sometimes invited me in to hear one of my pupils practising his solo part in an anthem. At one time too she let a room to one of the school staff so that I became well acquainted with the chill of the late ironmonger's drawing-room and the gloom of his stairway.

But Laburnum Villas remained a mystery. The windows of one were shrouded in dirty lace, and inside, I heard, dwelt an old lady of ninety, who supped innumerable cups of strong tea and dozed between whiles. The tea was made when she rose in the morning and the pot kept hot on the hob all day, the kettle steaming comfortably beside it, ready for refilling. Sometimes, when the children and I walked past on our way to the downs, I thought of that somnolent room murmurous with the humming of the kettle, the gentle snoring of the old lady and the purring of her great black cat which was sometimes to be seen sitting in the window sunning itself.

Next door seemed a little livelier. The windows were clean, the curtains fresh, and a trim lawn sloped down to the front gate. Occasionally we saw a middle-aged man and woman working in the garden, but we rarely met them in the village street, a bare two hundred yards away. They seemed to lead a retired life tucked away from the main street of Fairacre and, like all curious country people, I was interested to hear more about them from Mrs Pringle, the school caretaker.

8

'A very respectable pair,' was Mrs Pringle's dictum when I asked. This was high praise from my curmudgeonly school cleaner and she must have noticed my surprise.

'I always speaks fair of folks when I can,' continued Mrs Pringle self-righteously, putting down her dustpan and settling herself on the front desk for a good gossip. The desk groaned under her thirteen stone but knew better than to let the lady down. 'There's mighty few these days as can be spoke fair of in Fairacre – a proper lazy, shiftless, godless, money-grubbing lot as they be. As I said to Mr Pringle only last night: "If this is the age of flatulence," I says, "then there's something in being poor but honest!" '

'But tell me about Laburnum Villas,' I urged, steering Mrs Pringle back to the point. Once launched on a sea of invective she will sail on for hours, as well I know. The great clock on the wall, ticking ponderously, already said ten minutes to nine, and very soon the children would be called in from the playground.

'Well, these Hursts,' said Mrs Pringle dismissively, 'have only been here two or three years, but before that the Fletchers were there. As nice a family as ever come to Fairacre,' boomed Mrs Pringle, warming to her theme, 'despite their old grandad being a byword in Caxley for pinching things he never had no need of off the market stalls. A real affliction he was to them – everlasting having his name in the *Caxley Chronicle* for all to see.'

'But the Hursts –' I persisted, one eye on the clock.

'Highly respectable,' replied Mrs Pringle, inclining her head graciously. 'Chapel-goers, but none the worse for that, I daresay.' The parish church of St Patrick's has Mrs Pringle's support and the choir stalls there reverberate to her powerful contralto lowing, so that this was magnanimous indeed.

'Both been in good service,' continued the lady, 'and was with Sir Edmund over Springbourne way for donkey's years. When the old gentleman passed on, they went to one of his

9

relations, I seem to recall. Some long way away it was. Let me think.'

There was a pause while Mrs Pringle frowned with concentration. New Zealand, I thought, or the Argentine, perhaps. The sound of children's voices stirred my conscience and I rose from behind my desk.

'Leicester!' said she triumphantly. 'I knew I'd get it in the end! That's right, it was Leicester they went to.'

At this point a small girl appeared dramatically between us. 'Please, miss, Ernie made me give him half of my toffee bar and now his tooth's come out in it,' she gabbled agitatedly, 'and what's more he says it's all my fault.'

'Rubbish!' I said, advancing to the door. 'It's nothing more or less than rough justice.'

'I was about to tell you,' boomed Mrs Pringle's voice behind me, heavy with outraged dignity.

'Sorry!' I called back above the rising din. 'It'll have to wait!'

Slowly, Mrs Pringle collected her paraphernalia together and limped heavily from the room, her back expressing outrage in every sturdy line. Mrs Pringle's bad leg 'flares up', as she puts it, whenever anything goes wrong. It looked as though I should have to wait some time before she would be in a fit state to tell me more about the mysterious Hursts.

But, before long, I had occasion to call at Laburnum Villas. The leg of a small brass trivet came off in Mrs Pringle's massive hand whilst she was polishing it. As she explained: 'When things are let get that filthy, they needs a bit of purchase put on them.' It was apparent that the purchase this time had been too much for my elderly trivet. I looked at it sadly.

'I'd take it to Fred Hurst,' advised Mrs Pringle. 'I daresay Mr Willet would have a go if he had a soldering iron, but he hasn't, so there you are.'

'How do you know Mr Hurst has one?' I asked.

'Because he fixed the twiddly-bits up to the chapel pulpit real lovely,' replied Mrs Pringle proudly. 'Mr Lamb told me at the Post Office, and what's more he says he likes doing soldering jobs any time he's asked.'

I must have looked a little diffident for Mrs Pringle's normal bellow rose to a crescendo of hearty encouragement.

'You pop down after school and see him,' she advised. 'Better than taking it to Caxley. You won't see it again this side of Christmas if it gets in there.'

There was some truth in this remark. Urged by Mrs Pringle's exhortations and my own curiosity I decided to walk down the lane after tea carrying my trivet with me.

It was one of those bell-like May evenings described by Edmund Blunden. A sharp shower had left the village street glistening and the bushes and trees quivering with bright drops. Now, bathed in evening sunlight, the village sparkled. Scent rose from the wallflowers and polyanthuses in the cottage gardens, and blackbirds scolded from the plumed lilac bushes. Our village of Fairacre is no lovelier than many others. We have rats as well as roses in our back gardens, scoundrels as well as stalwarts ploughing our fields, and plenty of damp and dirt hidden behind the winsome exteriors of our older cottages. But at times it is not only home to us but heaven, too, and this was just such an occasion.

As I waited in the porch, cradling the trivet, I wondered if there would be the usual delay in answering a country front door. A back door is usually open, or quickly answered, but I knew from experience that rusty bolts and heavy chains are often involved in front-door transactions in Fairacre. Only on formal occasions do we call at front doors, but this, I felt, was one of them.

To my surprise, the door opened quickly and quietly, showing an elegant white-painted hall and staircase. Mrs Hurst greeted me politely.

'I wondered if your husband –' I began diffidently.

'Come in,' she smiled, and I followed her into the drawing-room on the right-hand side of the corridor. The sight that greeted me was so unexpected that I almost gasped. Instead of the gloomy interior which I had imagined would match Laburnum Villas' unlovely exterior I found a long light room with a large window at each end, one overlooking the front, and the other the back garden. The walls were papered with a white-striped paper and the woodwork was white to match. At the windows hung long velvet curtains in deep blue, faded but beautiful, and a square carpet echoed the colour. Each piece of furniture was fine and old, shining with daily polishing by a loving hand.

But by far the most dominating feature of the room was a large portrait in oils of a black-haired man dressed in clothes of the early nineteenth century. It was not a handsome face, but it showed strength of character and kindliness. Surrounded by an ornate wide gold frame it glowed warmly above the white marble fireplace.

'What a lovely room!' I exclaimed.

'I'm glad you like it,' replied Mrs Hurst. 'My husband and I got nearly everything here at sales. We go whenever we can. It makes a day out and we both like nice things. Our landlord let us have the wall down between these two rooms, so that it's made one good long one, which is a better shape than before, and much lighter too.'

I nodded appreciatively.

'Sit down, do,' she continued. 'I'll get Fred. We live at the back mostly, and I'll tell him you're here.'

I waited in an elegant round armchair with a walnut rim running round its back, and gazed at this amazing room. What a contrast it was, I thought, to Mrs Pratt's counterpart at Jasmine Villa! There the room was crowded with a conglomeration of furniture, from bamboo to bog oak, each hideous piece bearing an equally hideous collection of malformed pottery. That was, to my mind, the most distracting room in

Fairacre, whereas this was perhaps the most tranquil one I had yet encountered.

Fred Hurst returned with his wife. He was short while she was tall, rosy while she was pale, and certainly more inclined to gossip than his dignified wife. He examined my trivet carefully.

'Nice little piece,' he said admiringly. 'A good hundred years old. I can mend it so as you'll never know it was broken.'

He told me that he could get it done in a week, and we talked generally about our gardens and the weather for a little while before I rose to go.

'I envy you this room,' I said truthfully. 'The school house has tiny rooms and furniture always looks so much better with plenty of space for it.'

'Pictures, too,' added Fred Hurst. He pointed to the portrait. 'One of my ancestors,' he continued.

I heard Mrs Hurst draw in her breath sharply.

'Fred!' she said warningly.

Her husband looked momentarily uncomfortable, then moved towards me with hand outstretched. 'We mustn't keep you, Miss Read,' he said politely. 'I'll do my best with the trivet.'

I made my farewells, promised to return in a week, and walked to the gate. There I turned to wave to Mrs Hurst who stood regally still upon her doorstep. She wore upon her pale face such an expression of stony distaste that I forbore to raise my hand, but set off soberly for home.

What in the world, I asked myself in astonishment, had happened in those few minutes to make Mrs Hurst look like that?

A week later, in some trepidation, I called again. Somewhat to my relief, only Fred Hurst was at home. He took me into the charming drawing-room again and lifted my mended trivet from a low table. The repair had been neatly done. It was clear that he was a clever workman.

'My wife's gone down to the shop,' he said. 'She'll be sorry to miss you.'

I murmured something polite and began to look in my purse for the modest half-crown which was all that he charged for his job.

'She doesn't see many people, living down here,' he went on. 'Bit quiet for her, I think, though she don't complain. I'm the one that likes company more, you know. Take after my old great-great-grandad here.'

He waved proudly at the portrait. The dark painted eyes seemed to follow us about the room.

'A very handsome portrait,' I commented.

'A fine old party,' agreed Fred Hurst, smiling at him. 'Had a tidy bit of money too, which none of us saw, I may say. Ran through it at the card table, my dad told me, and spent what was left on liquor. They do say, some people, that he had some pretty wild parties, but you don't have to believe all you hear.'

It was quite apparent that Fred Hurst's ancestor had a very soft place in his descendant's heart. He spoke of his weaknesses with indulgence, and almost with envy, it seemed to me. Certainly he was fascinated by the portrait, returning its inscrutable gaze with an expression of lively regard.

I could hear the sound of someone moving about in the kitchen, but Mr Hurst, engrossed as he was, seemed unaware of it.

'I should like to think that I took after him in some ways,' he continued boisterously. 'He got a good deal out of life, one way and another, did my old great-great-grandad.'

The door opened and Mrs Hurst swept into the room like a chilly wind.

'That'll do, Fred,' she said quenchingly. 'Miss Read don't want to hear all those old tales.' She bent down to pick an imaginary piece of fluff from the carpet. I could have sworn that she wanted to avoid my eyes.

'Your husband has mended my trivet beautifully,' I said
hastily. 'I was just going.'

'I'll come to the gate with you,' said Mrs Hurst more gently.

We made our way down the sloping path to the little
lane.

'My husband enjoys a bit of company,' she said, over the
gate. 'I'm afraid he gets carried away at times. He dearly likes
an audience.' She sounded apologetic and her normally pale
face was suffused with pink, but whether with shame for her

own tartness to him or with some secret anger, I could not tell. Ah well, I thought, as I returned to the school house, people are kittle-cattle, as Mr Willet is fond of reminding me.

'A pack of lies,' announced Mrs Pringle forthrightly when I mentioned Mr Hurst's portrait. 'That's no more his great-great-grandad than the Duke of Wellington!'

'Fred Hurst should know!' I pointed out mildly. I knew that this was the best way of provoking Mrs Pringle to further tirades and waited for the explosion.

'And so he does!' boomed Mrs Pringle, her three chins wobbling self-righteously. 'He knows quite well it's a pack of lies he's telling – that's when he stops to consider, which he don't. That poor wife of his,' went on the lady, raising hands and eyes heavenward, 'what she has to put up with nobody knows! Such a god-fearing pillar of truth as she is too! Them as really knows 'em, Miss Read, will tell you what that poor soul suffers with his everlasting taradiddles.'

'Perhaps he embroiders things to annoy her,' I suggested. 'Six of one and a half-dozen of the other, so to speak.'

'Top and bottom of it is that he don't fairly know truth, from lies,' asserted Mrs Pringle, brows beetling. 'This picture, for instance, everyone knows was bought at Ted Purdy's sale three years back. It's all of a piece with Fred Hurst's goings-on to say it's a relation. He starts in fun, maybe, but after a time or two he gets to believe it.'

'If people know that, then there's not much harm done,' I replied.

Mrs Pringle drew an outraged breath so deeply and with such volume that her stout corsets creaked with the strain.

'Not much harm done?' she echoed. 'There's such a thing as mortal sin, which is what plain lying is, and his poor wife knows it. My brother-in-law worked at Sir Edmund's when the Hursts was there and you should hear what went on between the two. Had a breakdown that poor soul did once, all on account of Fred Hurst's lies. "What'll become of you when you stand before your Maker, Fred Hurst?" she cried at him in the middle of a rabbit pie! My brother-in-law saw what harm lying does all right. And to the innocent, what's more! To the innocent!'

Mrs Pringle thrust her belligerent countenance close to mine and I was obliged to retreat.

'Yes, of course,' I agreed hastily. 'You are quite right, Mrs Pringle.'

Mrs Pringle sailed triumphantly towards the school kitchen with no trace of a limp. Victory always works wonders with Mrs Pringle's bad leg.

In the weeks that followed I heard other people's accounts of the tension which existed between volatile Fred Hurst and his strictly truthful wife. It was this one regrettable trait evidently in the man's character which caused unhappiness to Mrs Hurst. In all other ways they were a devoted couple.

'I reckons they're both to be pitied,' said Mr Willet, our school caretaker one afternoon. He was busy at the never-ending job of sweeping the coke into its proper pile at one end of the playground. Thirty children can spread a ton of coke over an incredibly large area simply by running up and down it. Mr Willet and I do what we can by exhortation, threats and occasional cuffs, but it does not seem to lessen his time wielding a stout broom. Now he rested upon it, blowing out his ragged grey moustache as he contemplated the idiosyncracies of his neighbours.

'They've both got a fault, see?' he went on. 'He tells fibs. She's too strict about it. But she ain't so much to blame really when you know how she was brought up. Her ol' dad was a Tartar. Speak-when-you're-spoken-to, Dad's-always-right sort of chap. Used to beat the livin' daylights out o' them kids of his. She's still afeared that Fred'll burn in hell-fire because of his whoppers. I calls it a tragedy, when you come to think of it.'

He returned to his sweeping, and I to my classroom. I was to remember his words later.

Time passed and the autumn term was more than half gone. The weather had been rough and wet, and the village badly smitten with influenza. Our classes were small and there were very few families which had escaped the plague. Fred Hurst was one of the worst hit, Mrs Pringle told me.

It was some months since the incident of the trivet and I had forgotten the Hursts in the press of daily affairs. Suddenly I remembered that lovely room, the portrait, and the passions it aroused.

'Very poorly indeed,' announced Mrs Pringle, with lugubrious satisfaction. 'Doctor's been twice this week and Ted Prince says Fred's fallen away to a thread of what he was.'

'Let's hope he'll soon get over it,' I answered briskly, making light of Mrs Pringle's dark news. One gets used to believing a tenth of all that one hears in a village. To believe everything would be to sink beneath the sheer weight of all that is thrust upon one. Seeing my mood Mrs Pringle swept out, her leg dragging slightly.

At the end of that week I set off for Caxley. It was a grey day, with the downs covered in thick mist. The trees dripped sadly along the road to the market town, and the wet pavements were even more depressing. My business done, I was about to drive home again when I saw Mrs Hurst waiting at the bus stop. She was clutching a medicine bottle, and her face was drawn and white.

She climbed in gratefully, and I asked after her husband. She answered in a voice choked with suppressed tears.

'He's so bad, miss, I don't think he'll see the month out. Doctor don't say much, but I know he thinks the same.'

I tried to express my shock and sympathy. So Mrs Pringle had been right, I thought, with secret remorse.

'There seems no help anywhere,' went on the poor woman.

She seemed glad to talk to someone and I drove slowly to give her time. 'I pray, of course,' she said, almost perfunctorily. 'We was all brought up very strict that way by my father. He was a lay preacher, and a great one for us speaking the truth. Not above using the strap on us children, girls as well as boys, and once, I remember, he made me wash my mouth out with carbolic soap because he said I hadn't told the truth. He was wrong that time, but it didn't make no difference to dad. He was a man that always knew best.'

She sighed very sadly and the bottle trembled in her fingers.

'He never took to Fred, nor Fred to him, but there's no doubt my dad was right. There's laws laid down to be kept and them that sin against them must answer for it. "As ye sow, so shall ye reap," it says in the Bible, and no one can get over that one.'

She seemed to be talking to herself and I could do nothing but make comforting noises.

'Fred's the best husband in the world,' she continued, staring through the rain-spattered windscreen with unseeing eyes, 'but he's got his failings, like the rest of us. He don't seem to know fact from fancy, and sometimes I tremble to think what he's storing up for himself. I've reasoned with him – I've told him straight – I've always tried to set him an example –'

Her voice quivered and she fell silent. We drove down the village street between the shining puddles and turned into the lane leading to the misty downs. I stopped the car outside Laburnum Villas. It was suddenly very quiet. Somewhere nearby a rivulet of rainwater trickled along unseen, hidden by the dead autumn grasses.

'You see,' said Mrs Hurst, 'I've never told a lie in my life. I can't do it – not brought up as I was. It's made a lot of trouble between Fred and me, but it's the way I am. You can't change a thing like that.'

She scrubbed at her eyes fiercely with the back of her hand, then opened the door.

'Can I come and see him?' I asked impulsively. She nodded, her face expressionless.

I followed her up the steep wet path to the forlorn house. Its ugly exterior, blotched with damp, was more hideous than ever. Inside, in the lovely room, Fred Hurst lay asleep on a bed which had been brought from upstairs. He faced the portrait above the mantelpiece.

The sleeping man woke as we entered and tried to struggle up, but weakness prevented him. I was aghast at the change in him. It was apparent that he had very little time to live. His eyes wandered vaguely about the room, and his breathing was painful to hear. His wife crossed quickly to his side and took his hand. Her face softened as she gazed on him.

'Fred dear, it's me. And I've brought Miss Read to see you,' she said gently.

A flicker passed across his face and the dull eyes rolled in my direction.

'Come to see me?' he asked slowly. 'Me, or my great –' he took a shuddering breath, 'or my great-great-grandad? He is my kin, ain't he, my love?'

There was a terrible urgency in the hoarse voice as he turned to his wife. Across his wasted body her eyes met mine. They had become dark and dilated as though they looked upon hell itself, but her voice rang out defiantly.

'Of course he's your kin,' she cried, tightening her grip on his hand. 'Miss Read can see the likeness, can't you?'

I responded to the challenge.

'A strong family likeness,' I lied unfalteringly, and felt no regret.

2. STRANGE, BUT TRUE?

Poor Fred Hurst died a fortnight before Christmas, and Mr Willet, who is sexton of St Patrick's as well as caretaker of Fairacre school, had the melancholy task of digging his grave. We could hear the ring of his spade as it met sundry flints embedded in the chalk only a foot or so below the surface of the soil.

It was a dark grey December afternoon outside, but within the classroom was warmth, colour and a cheerful hum as the children made Christmas cards. Above their bent heads swung the paper chains they had made. Here and there a pendent star circled slowly in the keen cross draughts which play constantly between the Gothic windows at each end of the school building. A fir branch, cut from the Vicarage garden, leant in a corner giving out its sweet resinous breath as it awaited its metamorphosis into a glittering Christmas tree.

Crayons stuttered like machine guns as snow scenes were created. Reindeer, with colossal antlers which took up far too much room, tottered on legs – inevitably short – across the paper. Robins, fat as footballs, stood on tiptoe; Father Christmas, all boots and whiskers, appeared on every side at once; holly, Christmas puddings, bells and stars flowed from busy fingers throughout the afternoon. And every now and then, during the rare quiet pauses in their activity, we could hear the distant sound of Mr Willet at work, in the desolate solitude of an empty grave.

The winter afternoon was merging into twilight when the

21

children shouted and skipped their way homeward from Fair-acre village school. Mr Willet, coming from the churchyard next door, propped his spade against the lych gate and paused to light his pipe. In the murk, his wrinkled countenance was illumined, standing out against the dark background like a Rembrandt portrait. Hands cupped over the bowl of his pipe, he squinted sideways at me.

'Finished your day, I s'pose,' he commented. 'Nice work being a school teacher,' he added mischievously.

'What about you?' I retorted.

Mr Willet flung back his head and blew a fragrant blue cloud into the mist around him. 'Got your plaguey coke to sweep up now I've dug poor old Fred's last bed,' he answered equably. He reached for the spade with a massive muddy hand.

'My kettle's on,' I said. 'Come and have a cup of tea before you start again.'

'Well now,' said my caretaker, eyes brightening, 'I don't mind if I do, Miss Read. I'm fair shrammed. Grave-digging be mortal clammy work this weather.'

We strolled back together, across the empty playground, to the school house.

'Here, I can't come in like this!' protested Mr Willet at the kitchen door. 'All cagged up with mud! What'll old Mrs Pringle say when she comes to wash your floor?'

'No more than she says every week. This house is the dirtiest in the village, so she tells me.'

'Miserable ol' faggot!' Mr Willet smiled indulgently. 'How she do love a good moan! Still, this mud's a bit much, I will say. Give us a bit of newspaper and I'll 'ave it under me boots.'

We settled in the warm kitchen, the tea tray between us on the table. We were both tired and cold, and sipped the tea gratefully. It was good to have company and Mr Willet always has something new to impart. He did not fail me on this occasion.

'Poor old Fred Hurst,' he mused, stirring his cup

thoughtfully. 'I've got him right at the end of a row next to the old bit of the churchyard. Funny thing, he's lying aside Sally Gray. Two fanciful ones together there, I reckons.'

'Sally Gray?'

At the querying tone of my voice, the spoon's rotation stopped suddenly. Mr Willet looked at me in astonishment.

'You don't tell me you ain't heard of Sally Gray! Been here all this time and missed Sally?'

I nodded apologetically, and pushed the fruit cake across to him to atone for my short-comings. Mr Willet waved it aside, his eyes wide with amazement.

'Can't hardly credit it. She's about the most famous person in Fairacre. Why, come to think of it, we had a young chap down from some magazine or other writing a bit about her. Before your time, no doubt. Nice enough chap he seemed, although he had a beard.'

Mr Willet checked himself, blew out his own thick walrus moustache, and resumed his tale.

'Well, *beard*, I calls it. 'Twasn't hardly that. More like one of those pan cleaners, the bristly ones, and much the same colour. For two pins I'd have advised him to have it off, but you knows how touchy young fellers get about their bits of whisker, and I was allus one for peace. "Civility costs nothing," my old ma used to say. She were full of useful sayings.'

I began to see where Mr Willet got his own fund of maxims. No matter what the occasion, tragic or farcical, our caretaker-cum-sexton at Fairacre always has some snippet of homely wisdom to fit the case.

'And what did he write?' I prompted, edging him back towards the subject.

'Nest to nothin', when it come to it!' Mr Willet was disgusted. 'I thought at the time, watching him put down these 'ere twiddles and dots and dashes and that –'

'Shorthand,' I interpolated.

'Maybe,' said Mr Willet dismissively, 'but I thought at the

time, as I were saying, that he'd never make head nor tail of that rigmarole, and I bet you a quid that's just what happened. You know why?' Mr Willet raised his teaspoon threateningly. 'After us talking to 'im best part of a January afternoon, up the churchyard there, with an east wind fit to cut the liver and lights out of you, all 'e 'ad to show for it was a measly little bit in the corner of a page. And most of that was a picture of the gravestone, what you could make out through the fog, that is. Proper disappointing it was.'

'Which paper?' I asked.

'Some fiddle-faddling thing they brings out the other side of the county. Not worth looking at. All about flowers, and old ruins and history and that. Waste of time really, and not a patch on the *Caxley Chronicle*.' Mr Willet drained his cup and set it carefully down on the saucer. 'Well, must be off to me coke-sweeping, I s'pose.' He began to push back his chair.

'Not yet,' I begged. 'You haven't told me a word about Sally Gray.'

'Well, now –' began Mr Willet, weakening. 'I daresay the coke'd keep till morning, and it don't seem hardly right that you don't know nothing about our Sally.'

He watched me refill his cup without demur, rearranged his muddy boots on the newspaper and settled, with evident relish, to his task of enlightenment.

Sally Gray, Mr Willet told me, died a good ten years or more before he was born, in 1890 to be exact, and as her gravestone bore testimony, 'in her 63rd year'. Consequently, as he pointed out, he was not speaking at first hand, although he could vouch for this strange story, for his mother and grandmother had both heard it from Sally's own lips during her last illness.

Evidently she had always been 'a funny little party', to quote Mr Willet. She was the only child of elderly parents and was brought up in the end cottage of Tyler's Row. Her father was a carter, her mother took in washing, and the child grew up used to hard work and little reward for great labour. Nevertheless, she was happy enough, although the other children in the village found her prim and shy and tended to tease her. She was small of stature, so that she was called 'Mouse' by the boys, and dressed in cut-me-downs of her mother's which gave her a ludicrous dowdiness which invited the ridicule of the girls. No doubt her primness and shyness were the outcome of this treatment.

Her greatest joy was in reading, which she mastered at an early age. Books were scarce, but tattered volumes cast out from the vicarage nursery came her way and gave her endless pleasure. Sometimes a newspaper became available and she read the account of Victoria's coronation to her parents, to their wonder and pride.

When she was twelve or so she entered into service at the Parrs, a well-to-do family who lived in a Queen Anne house at the end of the village. She was quick and neat, obedient and dutiful, and gave satisfaction to the mistress of the house and, more important still, to the housekeeper who ruled the staff with a rod of iron. She lived in as a matter of course, although only five minutes' trot from her own home, but was often allowed to slip along the village street to see her family. Sometimes the cook gave her a bowlful of dripping, or a stout marrow-bone for the stock pot, to eke out the meagre commons of the Grays' diet. Sally was always careful to hide these titbits under her cloak, safe from the eyes of the housekeeper or village gossips who might be encountered on the brief journey.

Time passed. Housemaids came and went at the Parrs' house, but Sally remained. Girls who had worked beside her, dusting, brushing stair carpets, carrying interminable cans of hot water to bedrooms, married and left. They showed their fat offspring to Sally in the fullness of time, and commiserated with her about her state of spinsterhood. Sally did not appear to mind. She was as spry and nimble as ever, although a few grey hairs now mingled with the dark ones, and she continued to trot briskly about Fairacre.

One bitterly cold winter, the two old Grays fell desperately ill, and Sally asked leave to sleep at home and to work part-time at the Parrs. Mrs Parr, who was an autocratic person, did not care for the idea. By now, Sally was senior housemaid. It was she who carried in the early morning tea, pulled back the heavy curtains on their massive brass rings, and announced the weather conditions prevailing to her comatose mistress. She disliked the thought of someone else taking on these duties and told Sally that she must 'give it much consideration'. However, Mrs Parr knew full well that if she wished to keep Sally in her service then there must be some slackening of the reins whilst the old people were in need, and graciously gave her consent. 'But understand,' added the lady severely, 'you are to bring in the morning tea whenever it is *humanly possible*.' Sally promised, obedient as ever, to do all in her power.

For the next few months she scurried between the great house and the little thatched cottage and more often than not was early enough to take up the tea to her mistress and prepare her for the return to consciousness.

One summer morning, just before seven o'clock, she hastened by the dew-spangled shrubbery and was amazed to see the doctor's carriage outside the front door. In the kitchen a woebegone staff, sketchily dressed and with hair in curlers, poured forth the dramatic news. The master was dead! A heart attack, said the doctor, and mistress must be kept lying down to get over it!

Within a month poor Mr Parr was buried, his widow was settled in France, and his son was directing the decoration and alteration of his heritage. To Sally's stupefaction she found that she had been left the fabulous sum of one hundred pounds by her late employer. Young Mr Parr took her into Caxley and deposited it for her in the safety of a bank.

The village was agog with the news. Sally's parents were

beyond understanding her good fortune. Their days and nights were spent in fitful dozing, hovering between life and death, stirring occasionally to sup a bowl of gruel before sliding down thankfully upon the pillows again. In the thick of harvest time, as Fairacre folk sweated beneath a blazing sun, they slipped away within three days of each other and were buried together not far from Mr Parr's newly-erected marble angel.

Although she mourned her parents sincerely, there was no doubt that Sally's life now became very much easier. She still worked for the new master, but lived at home enjoying being mistress of her own small domain. Always an avid reader, she now had more time to indulge in this pleasure, and often took a book in one hand and her candle in the other and made her way to bed before nine o'clock, there to read until St Patrick's great clock struck midnight and the candle must be blown out.

She had been given a pile of books from her dead master's library when things were being sorted out, and these were to keep her occupied in her leisure moments for many years to come. Contentment of mind, more rest, and plenty of good country air and food began to show their effect on Sally. Hitherto small and rather skinny, she now began to put on flesh and soon became a little dumpling of a woman, albeit as quick on her feet as ever despite a certain breathlessness. She was now well on in her forties and her neighbours gave her no comfort.

'You be bound to put it on at your age,' said one.

'Better be fat and happy,' said another, 'than a bag o' bones.'

'You won't lose it now, my dear,' said a third smugly. ''Tis on for good when 'tis put on at your time of life.'

Sally was secretly nettled at this embarrassment of flesh. She let out seams, moved buttons and unpicked waistbands hoping, in vain, that one day she might revert to her former size. But the months grew into years and Sally's bulk grew too.

One sunny evening she sat in her back porch with a very

strange book in her hand. It was one of those bequeathed to her by her late master, a leather-covered exercise book which she had not troubled to open before. In it she found a number of recipes written out in a crabbed angular hand, in ink which had faded to a dull brown. They were not particularly interesting to Sally. Cooking was not one of her major interests and such household hints as: 'A Useful Polish for Ebonised Mahogany,' or 'A Valuable Amelioration for Children's Croup', which were also included in the book, did not stir her imagination. She yawned widely, and was about to put the book away and prepare her simple supper, when a heading caught her eye. It said: 'An Infallible Receipt for Losing Weight'.

Tilting the book to get the maximum light from the setting sun, Sally read with growing excitement.

To be sure, some of the ingredients sounded perfectly horrid. A basinful of pig's blood beaten with a pound of honey, some goose grease and a plover's egg was bad enough, thought Sally, but when an impressive list of ground herbs, moistened with cuckoo-spit, was to be added to it, then the concoction would surely be nauseating.

'Seal Top of Paste with Pig's Lard to Exclude Air,' said the recipe, and added in capital letters: 'PARTAKE SPARINGLY.'

Sally considered the page. Revolting it might be, but it was supposed to be infallible. The title said so. Would it be worth trying? She read the list of ingredients over again with close attention. The herbs would be easy to obtain, either from her own garden or the Parrs'. Cuckoo-spit glistened in all the meadows of Fairacre, honey stood ready in its comb on her pantry shelf, pig's blood and goose-grease could be obtained fairly readily. The plover's egg would be the most difficult article to procure, but somewhere on the flanks of the downs which sheltered Fairacre a boy's sharp eyes would be able to find a plover's nest, she felt sure.

The biggest problem was the assembling of all these ingredients without arousing suspicion. There are no secrets capable of being hidden in a village, as Sally well knew. It was not that she feared ridicule alone. Within her time she had seen old women ducked in the horse pond because their neighbours had suspected them of dabbling in witchcraft, and although the exercise book purported to be a straightforward recipe book there was something suspiciously sinister about the weight-reducing recipe. Sally decided to go about her task with the greatest circumspection. Who knows, in a few months' time she might have the trim slim figure of her youth? It was worth the trouble.

All went well. Even the plover's egg was obtained with comparative ease from a shepherd boy who, carrying six eggs to her cottage in his cap, was glad to earn a silver sixpence. One evening, after work, Sally prudently drew the curtain in her kitchen against prying eyes, and set about making the paste.

It smelt terrible and looked worse. It was yellowish-grey in colour, and speckled abominably with the ground herbs. Sally felt that she could not bring herself to taste it that evening, but would hope for strength in the morning. She retired to bed, with the reek of the concoction still in her nostrils.

It looked singularly unattractive by morning light, but after breakfast Sally put the tip of a spoon into the jar and bravely swallowed a morsel.

'I must do as it says and partake sparingly,' she told herself as she washed the spoon.

All that week she continued with the treatment. There seemed to be no result, but Sally was patient, and in any case expected to wait some weeks before her bulk began to diminish. Sometimes she felt a slight giddiness a few minutes after swallowing the stuff, but when one considered the nature of the ingredients this was hardly surprising.

One morning she decided to take a slightly larger dose. The clock on the mantel shelf told her it was later than usual, so that she flung the spoon in the washing-up bowl and set off at a brisk trot to the big house at the end of the village. She was perturbed to find that her gait was impaired. It seemed almost impossible to keep her heels on the ground, and Sally found herself tripping along on her toes, scarcely touching the ground at all. At the same time the giddiness occurred with some strength.

'Very strong stuff,' thought Sally to herself. 'Small wonder one's bid to partake sparingly!'

She took care to reduce the dose during the next week or two. By now it was high summer. Plumes of scented meadow-sweet tossed by the roadside, and the bright small birds kept up a gay clamour as they flashed from hedge to meadow and meadow to garden. Sally tried on her summer print gowns with growing despair. They were as tight as ever. Buttons burst from the strained bodices and waistbands gaped as Sally strove in vain to ram her bulk into the protesting garments.

'Dratted stuff!' panted Sally. 'Never done me a' aporth of good!' She surveyed herself in the small mirror which she had tilted forward in order to get a better view of her figure. Exasperation flooded her bulky frame. It was no good. She would simply have to make new dresses. These had been let out to their furthest limit.

She struggled out of the useless frocks, dressed in her former gown, and went sadly downstairs. The offending pot stood on the kitchen shelf.

'For two pins,' exclaimed Sally aloud, 'I'd throw you where you belongs – out on the rubbish heap!'

She was about to bustle about her household chores, when a thought struck her.

'Maybe I ain't been taking quite enough,' thought Sally. 'It's worth trying.'

Today was the perfect day to make an experiment. It was Sunday, and she need not go out anywhere. If a giddy attack followed the taking of too much medicine, then she could simply lie down until she recovered.

'And if it do make me giddy, but it works, then 'twill be worth it,' said Sally aloud. 'I can always take it at nights afore going to bed and sleep the giddiness off afore morning.'

She took a large spoon, dipped it deeply into the reeking mixture, and bravely downed it.

For a moment, nothing happened, apart from a slight feeling of nausea which taking the stuff habitually gave her. And then, to Sally's horror and alarm, her feet left the ground and she began to rise steadily to the ceiling. She bumped her head against the central rafter with some violence, and was about to scream loudly with combined pain and terror when prudence checked her.

'A fine thing if the neighbours saw you now,' she told herself severely. 'Look a proper fool, you would.' She tried to quieten her panicky heart, and the fear of ridicule, as well as being suspected of witchcraft, helped to keep her tongue silent.

It was uncomfortable and strange bobbing loosely about the ceiling trying to dodge the iron-hard rafter and the hanging oil lamp suspended from it, but Sally had always been of a philosophic strain and decided to make the best of a bad job.

' "What can't be cured must be endured," ' quoted Sally, running a finger along the top of the white china lamp shade. It was thick with dust, and Sally clucked disapprovingly at such filth in her house.

'No doubt about it: "Out of sight is out of mind." I must take this lot down and give it a real good wash in some suds.' A pang seized her. 'If I ever do get down,' she added despairingly. She propelled herself by pushing her hands against the ceiling until she was level with the high shelf where she stored bottling jars and preserving pans. To her horror she saw a large black beetle, dead and on its back, in the pan she kept for making pickles and chutney.

''Tis really shameful,' Sally scolded herself. 'If it hadn't been for this misfortune I'd never have realized what a slut I am.'

Below her the potatoes waited in a bowl of water to be

'Be you upstairs?' went on the voice. Sally heard the clang of the metal door scraper. Lawks a mercy, what if she came in? Sally's throat dried at the very thought. She clung to the pan shelf with trembling fingers, praying with all her might. The kettle began to bubble steadily, and the cat jumped noisily on to the table among the dishes.

'You home, Sal?' said the voice, a little louder. The door scraper clanged again, then silence fell. At last, there was the sound of muttering and the slow fading of footsteps along the brick path to Sally's gate. Sally covered her face with her grimy hands and wept with relief. Ten minutes later, her body began to feel more solid and manageable. She found she could control the direction of her legs and arms with growing accuracy, and slowly she sank groundwards.

The first thing she did was to make a good strong pot of tea and carry it into the living-room to recover. A fine cabbage, obviously brought by her neighbour, waited on the threshold. She must go and thank her, when her legs stopped trembling, and explain that she must have been 'down the garden' when she called.

Meanwhile, sipping and thinking, Sally regained her composure and turned over in her mind the best way of making use of the secret and surprising accomplishment with which she was now endowed.

There now began, for Sally, a period of engrossing interest and pleasure. After her duties at the big house, she hurried home to experiment with her essays in levitation. She found that by taking a small amount of the concoction she could hover about a foot above the ground for a period of roughly ten minutes. This gave her ample time to tidy shelves, wash out high cupboards, dust the picture rail and so on, tasks which had always been irksome to one of her low stature.

She found it wholly delightful to be without weight, and became skilled at balancing herself, with one hand touching a wall, whilst the other performed its task. Naturally, she did not indulge in this secret practice every day. For one thing, she still feared that it might be discovered by her neighbours in Fair-acre, and she had no intention of giving them cause for gossip. She found it prudent to keep her 'floating periods' for Thurs-days. Market day in Caxley was on a Thursday, and usually the other inhabitants of Tyler's Row spent their Thursdays hunting for bargains, meeting their friends and catching up with their news amidst the market-day bustle. Alone in her cottage, Sally felt safe from unexpected visitors, and experi-mented with the mixture.

One day she noticed that both the plum tree and the ancient Bramley Seedling apple tree were heavy with fruit. She had wondered for some time if she might dare to practise floating out of doors, and this seemed the time to experiment. There was much to consider before she began.

Of course she must remain unseen by the neighbours. That was the first consideration. It would be wise, therefore, to wait until nightfall to make her first attempt. Then she must be careful to leave a considerable amount of fruit to be picked in the normal way or her neighbours would wonder why she had not borrowed a ladder as was her usual practice.

Then, of course, there was the question of staying in her own garden. She shuddered at the thought of floating out into the blue, as well she might, if she did not take care. It was not so much the *danger* that worried Sally as the *impropriety* of such a mode of travelling. After considerable thought she decided to tie a stout length of clothes line round her waist and to tie a brick to the other end. She would carry the brick, already tied, up in the basket with her. On attaining the correct height she would throw the brick to the ground, remain safely tethered level with the fruit, pick it and place it in the basket, and so get the job done.

Of course, there was more to it than the general plan. For one thing Sally had to calculate the height of the fruit from the ground, how much the brick would weigh and how much of her mixture she needed to take to balance all these factors. But she was determined to try her luck, and one moonless night she crept from the cottage to embark on this adventure.

It was very still and quiet. The windows in the row of cottages were dark. Not a soul stirred. St Patrick's clock had struck one as Sally tip-toed down her stairs, and all Fairacre slept the dreamless sleep of those who live and work in the bracing air of the downs.

A spoonful and a half of the revolting brew was doing its best to settle in Sally's affronted stomach as she approached the plum tree. Already her feet were skimming the grass and she had hardly reached the gnarled old trunk before she began to rise swiftly. For a moment Sally was torn with panic. She felt horribly vulnerable out here in the open and would have welcomed the painful crack of the kitchen rafter on her head, at that moment. She clawed frantically at a substantial branch, as she floated by, and paused to get her breath. Taking a tight grip with one hand, she groped inside the basket on her arm, found the brick and cast it downward.

It seemed to make the most appalling shindy and also jerked Sally cruelly round the waist. Breathless, she listened. Supposing the neighbours were disturbed and looked out of their windows? Supposing the rope broke? Sally gripped the tree even more desperately in her agitation. But the silence engulfed her, and only the distant yelping of a stoat stirred the blackness, as a falling leaf might ruffle the satin smoothness of a still pool.

Emboldened, Sally turned to her task. It was not easy, but it was wonderfully exhilarating to be at large in the tree tops and her basket was soon full. Weight returned to her in roughly half an hour, and Sally crept back to the cottage, basket in one hand, brick in the other, and went, highly elated, to bed.

*

Time passed. A pot of the mixture stood permanently on Sally's larder shelf and she began to take her ability to levitate almost for granted. She was wonderfully lucky in preserving her secret, although over the years she had one or two dangerous moments. One day, for example, she was cleaning her bedroom window inside, floating about eight inches above the rush matting, when her neighbour appeared on the garden path below her and asked if she might borrow some sugar.

'I'll be down in a minute,' Sally replied, doing her best to keep her feet hidden from sight below the window sill.

'Shall I take a cupful myself?' suggested the woman. 'Save you leaving the windows, like?'

'No, no,' answered Sally, trying to sound airy, as indeed she felt. 'I'll bring it round the minute I've finished.'

If she gets in here, thought Sally frantically, she'll be upstairs in double-quick time and I'm aloft here for a good five minutes yet. The woman watched her closely, as she undulated from one pane to the next.

'What you standin' on, gal?' she asked suspiciously.

'My little old stool,' responded Sally, tightening her hold on the curtain and concentrating her attention on one pane. 'Don't you trouble to wait,' she added hastily. 'I'll be round in two shakes.'

To her infinite relief the woman departed, but the incident left Sally severely shaken. It was several weeks before she dared to take another dose.

Under cover of darkness she often repeated her first outdoor experiment and picked fruit for pies and puddings, jamming and bottling. On one occasion the landlord of The Beetle and Wedge had asked her curiously how she had picked her apple tree so clean, and she had said quickly that she had 'given it a good old shake' and the wind had done the rest. He seemed to believe her.

One late October day, when Sally was almost sixty years of age, she gazed with a speculative eye upon her walnut tree.

This was a lofty beauty, of great age, and heavy this year with magnificent nuts. Sally decided to lengthen her rope and to make an assault upon it.

''Tis Thursday,' said Sally aloud, 'and they all be safely at market. By teatime it'll be dark enough to try.'

She made her preparations and made her way to the tree as dusk began to fall. The neighbours' cottages were empty and would remain so for a full hour, as well she knew. What she had not reckoned with was a freshening wind and the enormous collie puppy which came from the farm.

The brick lay at the foot of the tree, half hidden in wet grass. Higher than she had ever been before Sally plucked swiftly at the green walnuts, staining her fingers brown as the basket filled. The wind made things difficult, tugging at her skirts and lifting the boughs from her reach. It grew more boisterous each minute and Sally began to feel alarmed.

'I'll be downright thankful when this lightness wears off,' she said to herself, clinging to a sturdy branch. At that moment she became conscious of a rhythmic tremor running up the rope. There, busily gnawing at it, just above the brick, was the collie puppy. Caution thrown to the winds, Sally screamed at him.

'Be off, sir! Get away, you rascal!'

The puppy wagged a delighted tail and continued his gnawing. His strong white teeth, busy at their task, seemed to grin at her. Sally began to pelt him with walnuts, but he was unperturbed. Slowly but surely the strands were severed, until a particularly fierce gust of wind caught Sally unawares, broke the rope completely, and jerked her violently from the walnut tree. Still screaming, Sally rose abruptly another twenty or thirty feet, and began to twirl this way and that as the wind blew her on an erratic course clean across the village.

Over and over Sally rolled, like an escaped balloon, and soon she felt sick as well as frightened. But her innate common sense began to assert itself, and just as she had accepted the first ridiculous position against her own kitchen ceiling so, in this present predicament, she did her best to come to terms with the situation.

First, she stopped screaming. On no account would she draw attention to herself. She'd got herself in this pickle, and she'd get herself out of it. Dusk was falling fast and with luck her progress through the sky would pass unnoticed. The roaring of the wind would distract people's attention from unusual sounds above them. Heads down against the onslaught, they would probably be intent on getting home, Sally comforted herself.

Her own travelling arrangements next occupied her thoughts. The rope trailed behind her like an unwieldy tail. She hauled it painfully in towards her, rolling the end loosely round one arm. This steadied her a little, and by gripping it between her feet, a few inches below her billowing skirts, she was more likely to stay upright, she discovered. True, she still twirled and bobbed in a highly distracting fashion, but at least she was travelling with a little more decorum and her skirts were hanging in approximately the right direction. Her bun had come down and her locks streamed in the wind, but Sally found this remarkably refreshing. It was years since she had felt the wind blowing through her loose hair.

She floated dangerously close to the spire of St Patrick's and noticed how remarkably dirty the weather cock was at its tip. Below her she could see the new village school and the little playground, now mercifully empty. The village street wound its way beneath her, and she was thankful that it too appeared to be empty. Her pace was brisk, for the wind was now a gale and the noise from the topmost branches of the elms beyond the school almost deafened her. She looked down upon the untidy rooks' nests swaying dizzily at the top of the trees, and then swirled onwards towards the open fields between Fairacre and Springbourne.

At last, she began to lose height. Her weight began to return and she braced herself for the descent to earth. Alas, by this time she was in the great park of Springbourne Manor and heading at incredible speed towards the avenue of lime trees which bordered the drive to the house. Closing her eyes and gripping the rope tightly, Sally awaited the crash. It came with a vast rending of boughs and garments. Dazed and bruised, Sally came to rest a good thirty feet above ground, securely enmeshed in lime branches and the remains of a squirrel's drey.

She was discovered by a cowman, who was making his way home after milking. By that time she had thrown the rope off and descended carefully as low as she could. The last twelve feet, unfortunately, consisted of trunk alone and it was while she was trying to brace herself to jump that the man arrived.

To Sally's relief he was a man of few words.

''Old on,' he said. 'I'll get a ladder.'

He returned in a few minutes and helped her down. They walked part of the way to Fairacre together in silence. At length he turned in to his cottage gate.

'Good night,' he bade her and then added: 'How d'yer get up there?'

Sally began the tale she had already manufactured. It involved being chased by a bull, and was the best she could manage under the trying circumstances. She was aware, as she came to a faltering halt, that her rescuer was not impressed.

'Must be a damn good leaper,' he observed drily, and went indoors.

Sally, bruised and weary, dragged herself homeward, took the pot from the larder shelf and threw it resolutely on to the rubbish heap.

Later that evening she thrust the exercise book into her fire and, holding it firmly down with the poker, she watched it burn to ashes.

She had flown for the last time.

'Well, there it is, Miss Read,' said Mr Willet, rising from his chair. 'Take it or leave it. That's what Sally told my mother a year or two later, just afore she died.'

'I don't disbelieve you,' I said slowly. 'It's a wonderful story. It's just that – somehow –'

'Well, what?' asked Mr Willet, blowing out his moustache fiercely. 'Proper doubting Thomases, some people be!'

'It's just that it seems extraordinary that no one ever saw her. Particularly on the last journey, I mean.'

'Ah, but they did! There was two little boys, brothers they were, as had been sent down to the pub. They saw Sally, and rope and all, skidding along over The Beetle and Wedge, and tore 'ome to tell their mum and dad. 'Course, all they got was a clump on the ear-'ole for being such a pair of liars, so they never said no more. And years later, when the poor ol' girl had gone, the landlord at the pub said he'd seen her picking plums two or three times, but never liked to say so.'

'I wonder why not?' I exclaimed.

Mr Willet sighed patiently. 'You a school teacher and you don't know 'uman nature yet!' he commented. 'Why, people don't mind being thought downright evil and wicked, but they fair hates to seem fools. Ain't you learned that yet, Miss Read?'

He opened the kitchen door and looked out into the windy darkness.

'That coke'll have to wait till morning now. Good-bye, miss, and thanks for the tea. See you bright and early.'

And he vanished into the night.

3. JINGLE BELLS

Mr Willet was as good as his word, and next morning, 'bright and early', I had my breakfast to the accompaniment of the brushing up of coke in the distance. He was still at it when I crossed to the school, wielding the broom vigorously in his capable hands, his breath wreathing his head in silvery clouds.

'Nasty cold morning,' I called to him, scurrying towards shelter.

'This keeps me warm,' he replied, pausing for a moment to rest on his broom. 'But I s'pose I shan't be doing this much longer.'

'Only three days,' I agreed. 'And then it's the lovely Christmas holidays!'

'You should be ashamed!' said Mr Willet reproachfully. 'Young woman like you, wishing your life away.'

But it was too cold to argue, and I only had time to wave to him before whisking into the shelter of the lobby.

The last day of term, particularly the Christmas term, has a splendour of its own. There is an air of excitement at the thought of pleasures and freedom to come, but there is also a feeling of relaxation from daily routine made much more acute by the deliciously empty desks. Books have been collected and stacked in neat piles in the cupboard. Papers and exercise books have been tidied away. All that remains to employ young hands in this last glorious day is a pencil and loose sheets of paper which have been saved for just such an occasion.

Of course, work will be done. There will be mental arithmetic, and some writing; perhaps some spelling lists and paper games, and stories told to each other. And today, the children knew, there would be Christmas carols, and a visit to the old grey church next door to see the crib recently set up by the vicar's wife and other ladies of the village. The very thought of it all created a glow which warmed the children despite the winter's cold.

They entered more exuberantly than ever, cherry-nosed, hair curling damply from the December air and wellingtons plastered with Fairacre mud. I began to shoo them back into the lobby before our virago of a caretaker discovered them, but I was too late.

Mrs Pringle, emerging from the infants' room where she had just deposited a scuttle of coke on an outspread sheet of *The Times Educational Supplement*, looked at them with marked dislike.

'Anyone 'ere seen fit to use the door scraper?' she asked sourly. 'Don't look like it to me. What you kids wants is an hour or two scrubbing this 'ere floor like I 'ave to. That'd make you think twice about dirtying my clean floorboards.'

She cast a malevolent glance in my direction and stumped out to the lobby. The children retreated before her, observing her marked limp, a sure sign of trouble.

The clatter of the door scraper and the bang of the heavy Gothic door announced Mrs Pringle's departure to her cottage, until midday, when she was due to return to wash up the school dinner things. The children's spirits rose again and they sang 'Away in a Manger' with rather more gusto than perhaps was necessary at prayer time.

The infants departed to their own side of the partition and my class prepared to give part of its mind to some light scholastic task. Multiplication tables are always in sore need of attention, as every teacher knows, so that a test on the scrap paper already provided seemed a useful way of passing the arithmetic lesson. It was small wonder that excitement throbbed throughout the classroom. The paper chains still rustled overhead in all their multi-coloured glory and in the corner, on the now depleted nature table, the Christmas tree glittered with tinsel and bright baubles.

But this year it carried no parcels. Usually, Fairacre school has a party on the last afternoon of the Christmas term when mothers and fathers, and friends of the school, come and eat a hearty tea and watch the children receive their presents from the tree. But this year the party was to be held in the village hall after Christmas and a conjurer had been engaged to entertain us afterwards.

However, the children guessed that they would not go home empty-handed today, I felt sure, and this touching faith, which I had no intention of destroying, gave them added happiness throughout the morning.

The weather grew steadily worse. Sleet swept across the playground and a wicked draught from the skylight buffeted the paper chains. I put the milk saucepan on the tortoise stove and the children looked pleased. Although a few hardy youngsters gulp their milk down stone-cold, even on the iciest day, most of them prefer to be cosseted a little and to see their bottles being tipped into the battered saucepan. The slow heating of the milk affords them exquisite pleasure, and it usually gets more attention than I do on cold days.

'It's steaming, miss,' one calls anxiously.

'Shall I make sure the milk's all right?' queries another.

'Can I get the cups ready?' asks a third.

One never-to-be-forgotten day we left the milk on whilst we had a rousing session in the playground as aeroplanes, galloping horses, trains and other violently moving articles. On our return, breathless and much invigorated, we had discovered a sizzling seething mess on the top, and cascading down the sides, of the stove. Mrs Pringle did not let any of us forget this mishap, and the children like to pretend that they only keep reminding me to save me from incurring that lady's wrath yet again.

In between sips of their steaming milk they kept up an excited chatter.

'What d'you want for Christmas?' asked Patrick of Ernest, his desk mate.

'Boxing gloves,' replied Ernest, lifting his head briefly and speaking through a white moustache.

'Well, I'm havin' a football, and a space helmet, and some new crayons, and a signal box for my train set,' announced Patrick proudly.

Linda Moffat, neat as a new pin from glossy hair to equally glossy patent leather slippers, informed me that she was hoping for a new work-box with a pink lining. I thought of the small embroidery scissors, shaped like a stork, which I had wrapped up for her the night before, and congratulated myself.

45

'What do you want?' I asked Joseph Coggs, staring monkey-like at me over the rim of his mug.

'Football,' croaked Joseph, in his hoarse gipsy voice. 'Might get it too.'

It occurred to me that this would make an excellent exercise in writing and spelling. Milk finished, I set them to work on long strips of paper.

'Ernest wants some boxing gloves for Christmas,' was the first entry.

'Patrick hopes to get –' began the second. The children joined in this list-making with great enthusiasm.

When Mrs Crossley, who brings the dinners, arrived, she was cross-questioned about her hopes.

'Well now, I don't really know,' she confessed, balancing the tins against her wet mackintosh and peering perplexedly over the top. 'A kitchen set, I think. You know, a potato masher and fish slice and all that, in a nice little rack.'

The children obviously thought this a pretty poor present but began to write down: 'Mrs Crossley wants a kitchen set,' below the last entry, looking faintly disbelieving as they did so.

'And what do you want?' asked Linda, when Mrs Crossley had vanished.

'Let me see,' I said slowly. 'Some extra nice soap, perhaps, and bath cubes; and a book or two, and a new rose bush to plant by my back door.'

'Is that all?'

'No sweets?'

'No, no sweets,' I said. 'But I should like a very pretty little ring I saw in Caxley last Saturday.'

'You'll have to get married for that,' said Ernest soberly. 'And you're too old now.' The others nodded in agreement.

'You're probably right,' I told them, keeping a straight face. 'Put your papers away and let's set the tables for dinner.'

*

The sleet was cruelly painful on our faces as we scuttled across the churchyard to St Patrick's. Inside it was cold and shadowy. The marble memorial tablets on the wall glimmered faintly in the gloom, and the air struck chill. But the crib was aglow with rosy light, a spot of warmth and hope in the darkness. The children tip-toed towards it, awed by their surroundings.

They spent a long time gazing, whispering their admiration and pointing out particular details to each other. They were loth to leave it, and the shelter of the great church, which had defied worse weather than this for many centuries.

We pelted back to the school, for I had a secret plan to put into action, and three o'clock was the time appointed for it. St Patrick's clock chimed a quarter to, above our heads, as we hurried across the churchyard.

I had arranged with the infants' teacher to go privately into the lobby promptly at three and there shake some bells abstracted earlier from the percussion band box. We hoped that the infants would believe that an invisible Father

Christmas had driven on his sleigh and delivered the two sacks of parcels which would be found in the lobby. At the moment, these were in the hall of my house. I proposed to leave my class for a minute, shake the bells, hide them from inquisitive eyes and return again to the children.

This innocent deception could not hope to take in many of my own children, I felt sure, but the babies would enjoy it, and so too would the younger ones in my classroom. I was always surprised at the remarkable reticence which the older children showed when the subject of Father Christmas cropped up. Those that knew seemed more than willing to keep up the pretence for the sake of the younger ones, and perhaps because they feared that the presents would not be forthcoming if they let the cat out of the bag or boasted of their knowledge.

I settled the class with more paper. They could draw a picture of the crib or St Patrick's church, or a winter scene of any kind, I told them. Someone wanted to go on with his list of presents and was readily given permission. The main thing was to have a very quiet classroom at three o'clock. Our Gothic doors are of sturdy oak and the sleigh bells would have to be shaken to a frenzy in order to make themselves heard.

At two minutes to three by the wall clock Patrick looked up from drawing a church with all four sides showing at once, and surmounted by what looked like a mammoth ostrich.

'I've got muck on my hand,' he said. 'Can I go out the lobby and wash?'

Maddening child! What a moment to choose!

'Not now,' I said, as calmly as I could. 'Just wipe it on your hanky.'

He produced a dark grey rag from his pocket and rubbed the offending hand, sighing in a martyred way. He was one of the younger children and I wondered if he might possibly half-believe in the sleigh bells.

'I'm just going across to the house,' I told them, squaring my conscience. 'Be very quiet while I'm away. The infants are listening to a story.'

All went according to plan. I struggled back through the sleet with the two sacks, deposited one outside the infants' door into the lobby, and the other outside our own.

The lobby was as quiet as the grave. I withdrew the bells from behind a stack of bars of yellow soap which Mrs Pringle stores on a lofty shelf, and crept to the outside door to begin shaking. Santa Claus in the distance, and fast approaching, I told myself. Would they be heard, I wondered, waggling frantically in the open doorway?

I closed the door gently against the driving sleet and now shook with all my might by the two inner doors. Heaven help me if one of my children burst out to see what was happening!

There was an uncanny silence from inside both rooms. I gave a last magnificent agitation and then crept along the lobby to the bars of soap and tucked the bells securely out of sight. Then I returned briskly to the classroom. You could have heard a pin drop.

'There was bells outside,' said Joseph huskily.

'The clock's just struck three,' I pointed out, busying myself at the blackboard.

'No. *Little* bells!' said someone.

At this point the dividing door between the infants' room and ours burst open to reveal a bright-eyed mob lugging a sack.

'Father Christmas has been!'

'We heard him!'

'We heard bells, didn't we?'

'That's right. Sleigh bells.'

Ernest, by this time, had opened our door into the lobby and was returning with the sack. A cheer went up and the whole class converged upon him.

'Into your desks,' I bellowed, 'and Ernest can give them out.'

Ernest upended the sack and spilt the contents into a glorious heap of pink and blue parcels, as the children scampered to their desks and hung over them squeaking with excitement.

The babies sat on the floor receiving their presents with

awed delight. There was no doubt about it, for them Father Christmas was as real as ever.

I became conscious of Patrick's gaze upon me.

'Did you see him?' he asked.

'Not a sign,' I said truthfully.

Patrick's brow was furrowed with perplexity.

'If you'd let me wash my hand I reckon I'd just about've seen him,' he said at length.

I made no reply. Patrick's gaze remained fixed on my face, and then a slow lovely smile curved his countenance. Together, amidst the hubbub of parcel-opening around us, we shared the unspoken, immortal secret of Christmas.

Later with the presents unwrapped, and the floor a sea of paper, Mrs Pringle arrived to start clearing up. Her face expressed considerable disapproval and her limp was very severe.

The children thronged around her showing her their toys.

'Ain't mine lovely?'

'Look, it's a dust cart!'

'This is a *magic* painting book! It says so!'

Mrs Pringle unbent a little among so much happiness, and gave a cramped smile.

Ernest raised his voice as she limped her way slowly across the room. 'Mrs Pringle, Mrs Pringle!'

The lady turned, a massive figure ankle deep in pink and blue wrappings.

'What do you want in your stocking, Mrs Pringle?' called Ernest. There was a sudden hush.

Mrs Pringle became herself again. 'In my stocking?' she asked tartly. 'A new leg! That's what I want!'

She moved majestically into the lobby, pretending to ignore the laughter of the children at this sally.

As usual, I thought wryly, Mrs Pringle had had the last word.

4. MRS NEXT-DOOR

One of the most exhilarating things about the holidays is the freedom to wander about the village at those hours which are, in term time, spent incarcerated in the class room. There is nothing I relish more than calling at the Post Office, or the village shop, in the mid-morning, or afternoon, like all my lucky neighbours who are not confined by school hours.

A few days before term began I set off to buy stamps from Mr Lamb, our postmaster. It was a sharp, sunny January morning, with thin ice cracking on the puddles, and distant sounds could be heard exceptionally clearly. A winter robin piped from a high bare elm. Cows lowed three fields away, and somewhere, high above, an airliner whined its way to a warmer land than ours.

Nearer at hand I could hear a rhythmic chugging sound. As I turned the bend towards the Post Office I saw that it came from a cement mixer, hard at work, in front of a pair of cottages which were being made into one attractive house.

A group of my school children hovered nearby, gazing at the operations. Some trailed shopping bags, and I could only hope that their mothers were not in urgent need of anything, for it was obvious that the fascination of men at work was overpowering. Patrick was among them, gyrating like a dervish, as an enormous scruffy dog on a lead tagged him round and round.

''Ello, miss,' he managed to puff on his giddy journey, and the others smiled and said 'Hullo' in an abstracted fashion. The workmen seemed to be getting far more concentrated attention than is my usual lot, I noticed.

As I waited my turn to be served, I looked through the window at the scene. I had ample time to watch, for this was Thursday, pensions day, and several elderly Fairacre worthies were collecting their money. Mr Lamb had a leisurely chat with each one, and as we all had a word with each other as well, it was a very pleasant and sociable twenty minutes, and we all felt the better for it.

The cottages had been stripped of their old rotting thatch, and the men were busy making a roof of cedar shingles. Watching them run up and down ladders I suddenly remembered that it was in one of these cottages that Mrs Next-Door had lived. Miss Clare had told me her story soon after I arrived as school mistress at Fairacre School.

It happened to be the first time I had visited Miss Clare's cottage at the neighbouring village of Beech Green. She had lived there since she was six years old. When I first met her she was in charge of the infants' class at Fairacre, a wise, patient, white-haired teacher who had taught there for half a century.

It was a gloriously hot August afternoon when I set out to walk to Miss Clare's, and I very soon found that it was much further than I realized. I toiled up a short steep hill, and leant thankfully upon a field gate near the summit. Cornfields spread before me, shimmering in the heat. Scarlet poppies dropped a petal or two, and high in the blue a hawk hovered motionless for a while, and then painted invisible circles with its wing-tip, slipping languidly and elegantly round the sky.

I resumed my travels, but determined to catch the bus home. Luckily it was market day, and a bus would leave Caxley just before six o'clock, passing Miss Clare's cottage about half past.

After one of Miss Clare's sumptuous teas, and a great deal of chatter, we walked together to her white gate. Two hawthorn trees flank it, and have met above to form a thick archway. In its welcome shade we waited, she on her side of the gate, and I on the other, ready to dart to the edge of the road when the bus came in sight.

An old lady, very upright on an ancient bicycle, pedalled slowly past, and wished us 'Good evening'.

When she was out of earshot, Miss Clare said, 'That's Mrs Next-Door. At least, she's really Mrs Wood, and my nearest neighbour, but I think of her as Mrs Next-Door.' She began to laugh, and then noticed my puzzled air. 'Of course, I forgot. You don't know the story of Polly, who was the original Mrs Next-Door. It happened years ago in Fairacre and was as good as any serial story to us in the village.'

She leant comfortably upon her gate in the shade of the leafy archway and embarked on a gay snippet of Fairacre's history.

A few years after the Great War of 1914–1918, when Fairacre was doing its best to settle down again to peaceful village affairs, two young couples moved into the pair of thatched cottages opposite the Post Office, within a few weeks of each other.

The first pair were named Leslie and Bertha Foster. They were both big, fair and rather slow, with one boy, Billy, who was almost five years old. When they arrived, soon after Michaelmas Day, Bertha was again in an interesting condition; or, it might be more correct to say, in a condition interesting to the village. Fairacre speculated upon the possible date of the unknown's arrival, its sex, and the many vicissitudes it would cause its mother before, and during, birth.

Leslie Foster was the newly appointed cowman to Walnut Tree Farm, and as he had an aunt in Fairacre his history was fairly well known. But his wife was a Caxley girl and the village watched closely to see how she would settle down.

On the whole she was approved. She was friendly and hard-working. By the evening of the first day her house was clean and tidy, and new curtains hung at the windows. To be sure, Fairacre was not at all certain about the curtains. Most people had lace ones, a few others had flowered cretonne, and the gentry seemed to go in for damask or velvet as they had done for years. But Bertha's curtains were of plain cream cotton, and she had stitched five rows of coloured braid along the bottom. The braid was a deep blue, exactly the same colour as the one cushion in the room, which was placed squarely upon the seat of Leslie's wooden armchair. Some thought the curtains were 'a bit far-fetched and arty-crafty', but one or two younger people thought them 'real pretty and up-to-date'.

A few weeks later, the second cottage became occupied. Mike Norton was also going to work for the same employer as his neighbour, for these were tied cottages. They had not moved in earlier because a faulty chimney had needed attention. His wife Polly was thin and dark. It was noticed, by keen eyes around them, that their house was not put in order as quickly as the Fosters' had been, and that Polly's curtains were extremely shabby and obviously make-shift.

There were no children, but many a wife told another that Polly Norton looked a bit peaky and as they had been married now for six months (so they had heard) perhaps she had good cause.

The two families became friends. The men did not have the same opportunity to exchange confidences, obstetric and otherwise, which their wives had, for they only saw each other briefly on the farm and were both glad to rest indoors when they reached home in the evening. But the two women spent a great deal of time in each other's houses and often took Billy for a walk in the afternoon together.

Within a fortnight Bertha had told Polly that her second was due in January and that she wanted a girl, and Polly had coyly mentioned her hopes for the following June. She had set her heart on a boy and was already trying to decide between the names Mervyn and Clifford. Bertha's girl was to be called

Maria, after Leslie's mother, and Polly secretly thought it a very common name indeed.

Thus began a halcyon period of exchanging knitting patterns, comparing the discomforts of early and advanced pregnancy, and shopping frugally in Caxley for all those things incidental to a new baby's arrival. Despite Bertha's slowness, her greater experience and her upbringing made her the leader of the two. She had been brought up in a respectable home in Caxley, had been taught well at one of the town schools and enjoyed the advantage of a mother who was an excellent cook and dressmaker. Bertha's few shillings went a good deal further than Polly's.

Polly was one of a large and somewhat feckless family from Beech Green. This was her first home and she was anxious to make it as splendid as she could without taking too much time and trouble in doing so. As soon as Mike brought home his first week's wages she clamoured for money for new curtains.

'Can't be done this week,' said her husband ruefully. 'You'll 'ave to put a bit by regular.'

Polly saw the sense in this and reckoned that she should have enough to buy the material before Christmas. She discussed the matter eagerly with Bertha, and this was her neighbour's first shock.

'If you don't mind,' said Polly brightly, 'I'd like 'em just exactly like yourn.'

Bertha was seriously taken aback. 'Well,' she began doubtfully, in her slow voice, 'I don't truthfully know as –'

Polly cut in swiftly. 'I reckons they're the prettiest curtains as I've ever seen. And another thing, the two houses'd look much nicer with matching curtains in the front. Dales had some real nice cream material in their sale last week, and I can get the braid there too.'

It was quite apparent to Bertha that the matter was as good as settled. Nettled though she was, she did not protest. After all, there was really nothing to stop Polly from having similar curtains, she told herself, and for the sake of the coming baby she tried not to feel upset.

But for the rest of the day, resentment smouldered in Bertha's breast. When Leslie came home she poured the tale into his ears.

Leslie, cold, tired and busy with his rabbit stew, did his best to smooth things over.

'I shouldn't fret about it. Don't hurt you if the curtains are the same. My ma says: "Imitation is the best form of flattery." Come to think of it, Bertha, it's a compliment, really. Shows she likes your choice.'

Bertha was somewhat mollified by this aspect of the matter. In any case, she did not want to fall out with her neighbour, and nothing more was said. Nevertheless, the incident rankled, and when the curtains were hung at last, she felt crosser than ever when she saw that the braid was the identical width and colour, and arranged in exactly the same five rows.

'Should have thought she could've had red or green, or summat different,' exclaimed Bertha to her husband. 'I should be ashamed to be such a copycat.'

Bertha's placid countenance was quite pink with wrath and Leslie again had to act as a soothing agent. The baby was now due, and whether the curtains next door had anything to do with the arrival of a fine daughter that night, no one could tell. The birth was easy, and Leslie was able to set off to work at his usual time, leaving Bertha and Maria in the capable hands of the local midwife.

'Ain't she just lovely?' breathed Polly admiringly, when she came round to see the baby. Her sharp eyes fell upon the cradle. It had been dressed in yard upon yard of spotted muslin, by Bertha's mother, and caught at the top with a splendid pint satin bow.

'You never showed me the cradle,' she said reproachfully.

Bertha, sleepy and content, smiled upon her. 'It was at my ma's. She only brought it over yesterday. What's more, she

57

made two bows, one pink and one blue, so's we'd have the right one.'

Polly was full of admiration. United in baby-worship, the two neighbours were in happy accord.

But this blissful state of affairs was not to last long. Spring arrived, and a double row of purple crocuses bordered Bertha's path. Behind them stood a fine row of polyanthuses heavy with buds. In Polly's identical border, there were also purple crocuses, and behind hers grew an equally fine collection of polyanthus plants.

'Tis too bad!' exclaimed Bertha to Leslie, thoroughly vexed. 'She knew I'd put them in. And I wouldn't mind betting her spring flowers come out yellow, same as ourn!'

They did, and Bertha's wrath grew. The tart comments which hovered on her tongue she managed to restrain, however, although she wondered at times if a bit of plain speaking would be a good thing.

Her baby was now a few months old, a big, fair, placid child like her parents. Billy had started school and Bertha was free to attend to her neighbour when she felt the onset of birth pangs. Polly was unduly fearful, clinging to Bertha in much agitation.

'Don't 'ee leave me till Mrs Drew comes!' she begged, naming the local midwife.

'Don't fret,' answered Bertha soothingly. 'I'll stay with you, but I think you'd be better upstairs.'

'No, no,' responded Polly. 'I'll walk about down here and get Mike's dinner ready atween whiles. Keeps my mind off it a bit, to have summat to do.'

Bertha saw the sense in this and did not press the matter. She was greatly relieved, though, when the midwife came and hustled her patient upstairs.

The baby was a long time arriving. Bertha and Leslie could hear muffled activity in the bedroom next door to their own.

'I do feel downright sorry for Polly,' murmured Bertha, the memory of her own experiences still fresh in her mind. 'It must be over soon, that's one comfort.'

But the baby had not arrived when the Fosters rose next morning. Mike came round, haggard and unshaven, to ask Leslie to take a message to the farm.

'She's about all in,' he said. 'Dammit all, that's the last baby we're having. Never thought it'd be such a set-to.'

Bertha and Leslie made light of it, teasing him, but he was too tired to appreciate badinage, and returned moodily to his home.

At midday the child was born. The midwife called in to tell Bertha it was a girl.

'They're both asleep, and can do with it,' declared the old woman who had brought half Fairacre into the world.

'I'll look in tomorrow,' promised Bertha, 'when she's feeling better.'

The next morning, a posy in her hand for Polly and a freshly-made pie for Mike's supper in her basket, Bertha went next door. She called, but there was no reply. She mounted the stairs and gently pushed open the bedroom door.

What Bertha saw, before the opening had widened enough to include a view of mother and child, made her grip the posy in a furiously clenched fist. For there, beside the bed, stood a cradle which was the replica of her own, even to a splendid pink satin bow.

Bertha swallowed her rage and tip-toed into the bedroom. The creaking of the old boards awakened Polly.

'Oh, Bertha!' she said, with such affection and relief that Bertha's anger melted. ''Tis lovely to see you. Take a peep at the baby. Fancy me having a girl, just like you!'

Bertha could have said that it caused her no surprise, but this was hardly the time to be so uncharitable. In any case, the new-born infant quite won her heart with its red puckered face, cobwebby black hair and skinny fingers.

'Ain't she a real beauty!' she exclaimed with sincerity. A thought struck her. 'What are you going to call her?'

'Mildred,' replied the mother. 'It begins with M, just like yourn.'

Bertha was thankful that the child was not to be another Maria, and turning her eyes from the ribbons and flounces of the hated cradle, she settled the posy in water, made Polly some tea, reiterated her congratulations and returned next door.

Billy arrived home from school and was told the news. He took it stolidly. Babies did not mean much to Billy. If anything, he disapproved of them. They drew attention to themselves, he knew, to the detriment of their older brothers' welfare. But he brightened at the thought of telling Miss Clare, his teacher, all about it when he went to school next morning.

Miss Clare was as impressed with the news as he had hoped she would be, but Billy's eyes did not miss the flicker of amusement which crossed her kind face when he said:

'And it's a girl! Just like ourn!'

At playtime Miss Clare told the news to Mr Benson, the headmaster. In common with the rest of Fairacre, he had watched the doings of the pair of cottages with amusement and considerable sympathy for the much-tried Bertha Foster.

'Isn't that typical?' he commented. 'Poor Mrs Foster! I wonder what Polly will call it. Maria, no doubt, and it will have an identical pram.'

The village hummed with the news.

'Give Polly her due,' said one fair-minded neighbour, 'she couldn't help it being a girl. Now, could she?'

'She could help her curtains and the flowers in the front and this 'ere new cradle she's got,' answered a less charitable listener. 'Bertha must be a proper angel to stay friends with a copycat like Polly.'

Time passed. It was a long hot summer and both babies flourished. Bertha's polyanthuses were succeeded by sweet williams and then asters. So were Polly's. Bertha whitewashed two large stones and set them one each side of her doorstep as ornaments. So did Polly. Leslie bought Bertha a canary in a cage for her birthday. Mike, under pressure, did the same for Polly.

By now, relations were decidedly strained between the two women, although they maintained a surface civility. Billy, overhearing many a tart comment at home, often told a tale to Miss Clare who did her best to discourage him. She found this comparatively easy. It was not so easy to stem the flow of confidences which Bertha began to pour into her unwilling ear when she came to meet Billy from school. It was at this stage that the name 'Mrs Next-Door' began to be used in a fruitless attempt to veil Polly's identity from the young listeners milling round them.

'That Mrs Next-Door,' Bertha would whisper, 'has done it again. Pink asters, same as mine. It do fairly make my blood boil at times!'

'Ignore it,' Miss Clare used to answer. 'It really doesn't matter, you know.' But secretly she had every sympathy with poor provoked Bertha. How long, she wondered, would her patience last?

The children added fuel to the fire by teasing Billy.

'Your Mrs Next-Door's got a hat with daisies on, just like your mum's!'

'I see Mrs Next-Door's got a canary now!'

'Mrs Next-Door's got a pink bedspread on the line this morning. Looked like the one your mum had out last week!'

At last the storm broke. The immediate cause, as Fairacre had foretold, involved the two babies. Christmas was now at hand, and as usual, a teaparty for the whole village was to be held in the school. Anyone was welcome to this festivity, whether a parent or not, and it was usual for all the women, and one or two old retired men, to foregather on this village occasion. The school children, dressed in their best, looked upon themselves as hosts.

Bertha took considerable trouble with her own appearance and even more with Maria's. The child was dressed in a white silk frock, embroidered with forget-me-nots on the bodice, and over this creation wore a blue coat edged with swansdown and a bonnet to match. Bertha had seen this delicious set in a Caxley shop window and had been unable to resist it. This was the first time that Maria had put it on, and very beautiful she looked.

Bertha pushed her daughter proudly towards the school. The afternoon was cold and foggy, but Maria's face glowed from inside the becoming blue bonnet. She was much admired by the throng at the school.

About twenty minutes later Polly arrived, carrying Mildred. To the amusement of some, the resentment of others, and the speechless fury and astonishment of poor Bertha, the child had on exactly similar garments to Maria's. Bertha pointedly turned her back towards the newcomers and did her best to appear unconcerned, knowing that she was the centre of all eyes.

The party appeared to be as gay as it always was, but for Bertha it was sheer misery. She was one of the first to leave, pushing Maria in her finery, with Billy clinging to the pram, at a pace which taxed the strength of all three.

It was now dark. Maria was strapped into her high chair and Billy was told to look after her. Before Leslie came home, Bertha intended to confront her infuriating neighbour. She returned to the gate to await Polly's homecoming.

'Now she's going to have it!' Bertha told herself fiercely. 'I been too meek all along, sitting down under her impudence. I'll settle her!'

The sound of footsteps and the familiar squeak of Polly's pram wheels heralded her approach. Bertha advanced like some avenging fury.

'I'll thank you,' she began ominously, 'to step inside here a minute, Mrs Norton.'

This was the first time that Polly had been so called by her neighbour, and she was at once on her guard.

'What's up?' she inquired, trying to sound at ease, but her voice trembled.

'You knows as well as I do what's up!' breathed Bertha menacingly. 'You dare to dress up that kid of yours just like my Maria and parade it in front of all Fairacre! Trying to make me a laughing-stock! I've had enough of you and your copying ways!'

Polly tried to laugh, but she was very frightened. There is nothing more terrifying than a calm woman suddenly aroused. She had no idea that placid Bertha could feel such venom, or express it with such menace.

'No law against buying a coat and bonnet for my baby, I suppose?' queried Polly.

'No, nor curtains, nor flowers, nor hats, nor bedspreads, same as mine,' burst out Bertha, 'but you're not going to do it any longer, my girl, or you'll be in trouble! Take it from me, Polly Norton, if I ever sees any more copying from you I'll be round at your place and black your eye for you! I've just about had enough, see?'

She thrust a red furious face close to Polly's startled one and slammed the gate between them. Polly, much shaken, moved slowly towards her own.

'I'll tell –' she began truculently.

'You'll tell no one,' Bertha cut in. 'All the village is on my side. You've branded yourself as a plain copycat. I ain't saying no more to you. *Not ever*. But just you mark what I've said to you!'

Still pulsing with righteous indignation, Bertha returned indoors to attend to the children and Leslie's tea.

'I feels all the better for that,' she told herself. 'It's cleared the air. Come to think of it, I should've done it months ago.'

Now that battle was joined, Bertha found life much more straightforward. She simply ignored her neighbour. If she met her in the garden, or in the village street, she had the exquisite pleasure of looking clean through her. Polly retaliated with a toss of the head or a muttered aside. The village watched with avid interest. There were a few who maintained that Polly was not as bad as she was painted, but the majority felt she had got off lightly in the affair and that Bertha had every justification for cutting off relations with her neighbour.

The two husbands found the whole thing very trying. At work, they talked normally to each other, each being careful to leave his wife's name out of the conversation. At home, they did their best to soothe their wives and keep out of trouble's way. It was not easy. Both women were expecting again, Bertha in October and Polly a month later, and tempers were frayed all round.

However, Polly had seen reason in Bertha's tirade that dark evening, and although she would not admit that she was in the wrong, she took care not to rouse her fire again by any obvious copying. Unfortunately, much remained that had been done before the split occurred. The canaries still sang and fluttered in the two front windows. The white stones flanked the two doorsteps, the curtains, the bedspreads and the babies' coats still remained identical, for neither would give way.

Even worse was the simultaneous ripening of the two rowan trees in the front gardens. Bertha's had been planted soon after their arrival. Polly's a month or two later. This year Polly's was covered in bright red clusters of berries. Bertha's was decidedly inferior. Bertha, now near her time, a massive unwieldy figure venturing no further than the garden, watched her neighbour picking sprays to take indoors. It gave her no comfort to see that Polly was wearing a blue flowered smock over her bulk exactly like the one she had on. They had been worn during their earlier pregnancies and one could hardly expect Polly to throw hers away. Nevertheless, Bertha found the sight annoying. Would she never be free from Polly shadowing her?

A week later Bertha was brought to bed. Mrs Drew arrived in the morning confidently expecting to be back in her own cottage in time to cook her midday dinner. But the day wore on, Bertha continued her labours, Leslie ate bread and cheese for his dinner, the same for his tea, and went post-haste for the doctor at six o'clock when Mrs Drew clattered down the stairs in a state of urgent alarm.

Fairacre watched with some agitation. What could be happening to Bertha? Always had her babies as easy as shelling peas! Could Mrs Drew have bungled things? Not like her to send for the doctor! Mind you, she was getting on a bit; perhaps she was a shade past it!

So the tongues wagged. Doctor Martin was seen to enter the cottage at a quarter to seven. No one saw him leave. Of course it was dark, but the doctor's old Ford car made enough noise to rouse the dead. What could be going on?

As St Patrick's church clock struck eleven Dr Martin was drying his hands in Bertha's crowded bedroom. He was smiling broadly, but his eyes were on his patient. Her eyes were closed, her hair, damp and dishevelled, clung to her forehead. Mrs Drew was busy with baby clothes. Leslie Foster, summoned from his vigil below, had just approached the bed. He looked thunderstruck, as well he might. Beside his exhausted wife lay three tightly-wrapped snuffling bundles.

He stroked the hair back from his wife's hot forehead.

'Bertha?' he whispered questioningly.

Her eyes opened slowly. She gazed at Leslie and then at the three small faces beside her. A look of intense joy lit her face.

'Let Mrs Next-Door copy *that*!' cried Bertha triumphantly.

5. A Tale of Love

The alterations to the pair of cottages where Polly and Bertha had once lived took many weeks. The children's interest in all that went on continued unabated. The four workmen who were engaged on the job became their friends and heroes, and I became more and more annoyed as the children arrived late for school.

'You can miss your playtime,' I announced to a little knot of malefactors who entered noisily, bursting with good spirits, at a quarter past nine. 'I'm tired of telling you to be punctual.'

They looked at each other with dismay.

'But we was only givin' the workmen a hand, like,' said Richard, assuming an air of injured innocence. 'They had an ol' bucket they was pulling up to the top windows, see, on a bit of rope –'

'On a little wheel, sort of –' broke in Ernest, his eyes alight at the happy memory.

'A *pulley*, he means, miss,' said John, sniffing appallingly. 'They has cement in this 'ere bucket and it's heavy to lug up the ladders, so they has this wheel thing called a *pulley*, miss, as pulls it up. That's why it's called a *pulley*,' explained John patiently, as though to a particularly backward child.

'I daresay,' I said shortly. 'And nine o'clock is not the time to stand and watch it. Get to your desks at once, and for pity's sake blow your nose, John.'

There followed a great fuss of pocket-searching, feeling under his jersey, exploring sleeves, looking in his desk and so on, accompanied throughout by sniffs and exclamations of surprise and dismay.

'Don't seem to have one, miss,' said John at length.

'Get a Kleenex from the cupboard,' I said ominously, 'and don't let me hear another squeak, or sniff, from you for the rest of the morning!'

This sort of thing went on intermittently throughout the early part of the spring term and I should be heartily glad, I told myself, when the workmen had vanished and the new house was occupied. Mrs Pringle agreed with me.

'Bad enough sweeping up honest Fairacre mud,' boomed the lady, after school one afternoon, 'without bits of cement off their boots, and shavings and nails and that out of their pockets. And when it comes to *this*,' added Mrs Pringle opening a massive fist and thrusting it before my nose, 'it's time to *speak*!'

In her palm lay some glutinous grey matter which I recognized as putty.

'Stuck on the lobby wall, if you please,' said Mrs Pringle, disengaging the stuff with a squelch and putting it, unasked, on my desk. 'I thought it might be that chewing gum again when I first saw it, and then I thought, "Not likely. Not that sized lump. No one could get a lump that big in his mouth. Not even Eric Williams, and dear knows his mouth's big enough, on account of his poor foolish mother feeding him with a dessert-spoon at six months." So I looked closer and saw it was this 'orrible putty. Them workmen want sorting out, Miss Read, letting the children have such stuff.'

'I believe they've nearly finished,' I answered, trying to soothe the savage breast. I glanced at the clock. Amy was coming to tea and it was already past four.

Mrs Pringle grunted disbelievingly. 'I knows workmen,' she said darkly. 'Got no sense of time. I feel downright sorry for that couple waiting to move in. They'll be lucky to close their own door behind them before Easter at this rate.'

This was the first I had heard of the future occupiers and though, as any normal villager, I should dearly have loved to hear more, I did not intend to probe Mrs Pringle for details, and, in any case, it was time I put on the kettle for Amy. I made my way to the door. Mrs Pringle, who can read my thoughts much too easily for my comfort, sent a parting shot after me.

'Name of Blundell,' trumpeted Mrs Pringle. 'Could tell you more, but I can see you're not interested.'

I caught the glimpse of smug triumph on her unlovely face as I closed the door.

Amy and I were at college together many years ago. We lost touch with each other and only met again when I came to Fairacre. She had moved to Bent, a village a few miles south of Caxley, when she married, and so knew more about the Caxley neighbourhood than I did.

Amy is a dynamic person, full of good works and good ideas. I only wish I had half her energy. It is always exhilarating to have a visit from her and I looked forward to an hour or two of her company on this particular afternoon.

The car arrived as I set tea. Amy, elegant as ever in a new suit, emerged with a bunch of daffodils and a new hair style. We greeted each other warmly and I complimented her on her looks.

'Do you like it?' she asked, patting her variegated locks and preening herself.

'Very much,' I answered truthfully. 'I like all those stripes, like a humbug.'

Amy looked at me with distaste. 'Like a humbug!' she echoed disgustedly. 'What a dreadful way of putting it!'

'What's wrong with it?' I asked. 'I'm very fond of humbugs, and those auburn streaks remind me of the treacly ones.'

Amy bit delicately into a sandwich.

'It cost a fortune,' she said sadly. 'And took hours to do,

with all the strands sprouting through a bathing-cap affair. I thought James would like it, but he hasn't noticed yet.'

I inquired after James, her husband, and learnt that he was away for the night at a conference in the north. To my mind, James has a suspiciously large number of overnight engagements, but it is no affair of mine, and Amy is wise enough not to discuss the matter with me.

'You know,' said Amy, looking at me closely, 'I think you could take this high-lighting effect. It would do something for you.'

'Now, Amy,' I begged, seriously alarmed, for I have had many a battle with my old friend about my mousy appearance, 'please don't start on me again! I am a plain, shabby, middle-aged woman with no pretensions to glamour. I like being like this, so leave me alone.'

Amy waved aside my pleading and took another sandwich.

'A few glints in your hair, some decent make-up, and a good strong pair of corsets would work wonders for you,' said Amy. 'Which reminds me – I want you to come to the Charity Ball at the Corn Exchange next month!'

'Never!' I cried, with spirit. 'You know I can't keep awake after eleven o'clock. And I don't like dancing. And I haven't got a frock to wear anyway.'

Amy sighed.

'Then it's time you bought one. You simply can't waste the whole of your life in this one-eyed village. You never meet a soul –'

'I do,' I protested. 'Every day. I meet far too many souls. There are thirty-odd to be faced every morning.'

'I mean *men*,' snapped Amy with exasperation. 'There's no reason why you shouldn't get married, even at your age, and it's time someone took you in hand and made you see reason.'

'But I don't *want* to get married!' I wailed. 'I should have done it years ago if I'd intended to do.'

'And who,' said Amy coldly, 'ever asked you?'

I began to laugh.

'Well there was that neighbour of yours who was in a constant state of inebriation and wanted someone to keep him from drinking –'

'You can't count him,' said Amy firmly. 'He asked everyone.'

'I can't think of anyone else at the moment,' I said.

'I can tell you one thing,' said Amy, 'if you take up this attitude, and refuse to make the Best of Yourself, then you are doomed to be an old maid.'

'Suits me,' I said comfortably. 'Have some more tea.'

Amy stirred her second cup thoughtfully. 'There's still time,' she assured me. 'Look at Elsie Parker. Blundell, I mean. She's managed it.'

'Blundell?' I queried. 'Not the Blundells who are moving to Fairacre?'

Amy looked interested, and ceased stirring. 'It's quite likely,' she said slowly. 'They are having a pair of cottages knocked into one house somewhere or other.'

'It's here,' I assured her feelingly, 'I should know. The children spend most of their time watching the workmen. It was Mrs Pringle who mentioned the name Blundell only this afternoon.'

'That must be Elsie,' said Amy, 'and her newly-caught husband. Well, well, well! So they're settling in Fairacre!'

Amy produced a beautiful gold cigarette case, a present from James after a week away, lit a cigarette, and settled back in a cloud of blue smoke.

'Well, go on,' I urged. 'Tell me about my neighbours to be!'

And, smiling indulgently, Amy began.

It was generally agreed, in the little village of Bent, that Elsie Parker was an uncommonly pretty girl. She was the only child born to Roger and Lily Parker a year or two after the First World War. Her father returned from his arduous, if undistinguished, duties as an army baker to start afresh as part-owner of a small general store on the southern outskirts of Caxley.

At first, he cycled the few miles to work on a venerable bicycle, but as the business prospered he changed to a small second-hand van with which he began to build up a modest delivery round. People liked Roger Parker. He was hard-working, honest and utterly reliable. If he said that he would bring the pickles in time for Monday's cold lunch, then you could be quite sure that the jar would be with you before the potatoes had come to the boil! He deserved to prosper, and he did.

By the time Elsie was six, the shabby delivery van had been changed for two larger new ones which spent the day touring the district and the night safely locked up in the new shed at the rear of the general stores. Roger now owned a bull-nosed Morris tourer which he drove to work each morning. At the week-ends he polished it lovingly and then took his wife and pretty little daughter for a drive.

Elsie was the apple of her parents' eyes. She had a mop of yellow curls, lively blue eyes with exquisitely long curling lashes, and a smile that disarmed even the most curmudgeonly. Needless to say, she was the belle of the infants' class at Bent village school and was accompanied to and from that establishment by a bevy of small admirers.

Her first proposal of marriage came when she was seven. It came from the shabbiest of her escorts, whose nose was constantly wet, despite a rag pinned to his dirty jersey, and whose attentions had long been deplored by Mrs Parker. Elsie turned him down promptly, but gave him one of her heart-turning smiles as she did so, for she was a kind child.

It was an experience which was to occur many times in the future, and as time went on Elsie was to learn many refinements in the art of rejecting a suitor. But, as a first attempt and for one of such tender years, the present rejection was commendable – a blend of firmness and gentleness, lit by a certain light-hearted awareness of an honour received, which many an older maiden could not have bettered. The young man ran ahead to school, and after shedding a few hot tears in the blessed privacy of the boys' lavatory, recovered his good spirits and continued to accompany his goddess as before – without hope, certainly, but also without rancour.

Hard on the heels of this proposal came another, from an urchin almost as disreputable as the first. He too was turned down, and in an unguarded moment Elsie mentioned both incidents to her mother. She was much distressed.

'I can't think why such *dirty* boys like you!' exclaimed poor genteel Mrs Parker. 'You mustn't encourage them, Elsie. It won't do! It really won't do at all!'

If Mrs Parker had been capable of giving the situation a moment's clear thought she would have realized that it was the very difference in her daughter's appearance and nature which acted as a magnet to the rough rumbustious boys. Those glossy curls, the freshly-starched voiles and the enchanting scent of Erasmic soap created a being of such sweet cleanliness that she was well-nigh irresistible to the lesser washed.

'Why don't you play with some of the other boys?' asked Mrs Parker. 'There's Jimmy Bassett and Stanley Roberts,' she went on, naming the firstborn at the flourishing new garage on the main road to Caxley, and the vicar's son who would be going on to his preparatory school next term. Mrs Parker had a nice regard for the social ladder.

'Jimmy lisps,' said Miss Parker, speaking truly. 'And Stanley Roberts dropped a dead rat in old Mrs Turner's well last week.'

'*Stanley* did?' exclaimed Mrs Parker, much shocked. 'The vicar's son? A dead rat?'

'Mrs Turner's chapel,' explained Elsie succinctly.

The matter was dropped.

At the age of ten Elsie was taken from the village school and travelled daily into Caxley to attend a larger establishment run by some charming and hard-working nuns. She wore a corn-flower blue uniform which enhanced the beauty of her colouring and very soon the schoolboys who travelled on the bus with her were jostling for the place beside her. Elsie treated them with happy impartiality, bestowing conversation, smiles and sympathy upon whichever escort had been lucky enough – or rough enough – to gain the seat next to her.

On more than one occasion during her time at the convent school Elsie was drawn quietly aside by one of the sisters and given a few words of mild reproof. It was not fitting, she was told, to be seen at the centre of a crowd of the opposite sex day after day. It gave the school a bad name. She was advised to be polite but distant, kind but not too kind. Dreadful dangers, it was hinted, could attend too great an interest in the male sex.

It was all rather hard on Elsie. She did not encourage the young men, they simply gravitated towards her as wasps to a sun-ripe pear. Her father, made aware of his daughter's attractions by a dulcet word or two from Sister Teresa, decided to take Elsie to school with him in the car and collect her again in the afternoon. But this state of affairs did not last long. It was most inconvenient for Roger to leave the business. Sometimes lacrosse or tennis kept Elsie late, sometimes a half-holiday meant that she was out early. Gradually the arrangement fell through, and Elsie returned to the bus and the adoration of her swains.

At seventeen, still unscathed by love, Elsie left school and began training to be a nurse. She was at a hospital in London but spent as many weekends as possible at Bent. By now Roger was what is known in the north as 'a warm man'. A wing had been built on to the small four-square house where Elsie had been born, and a field next door had been acquired to ensure future privacy. Roger, who as a young man had voted Liberal, bought his ready-made suits from a Caxley outfitters, and enjoyed mustard with mutton, now helped himself to mint sauce instead, had his suits made in London, and voted

Conservative. He worked, if anything, harder than ever, was much respected in Caxley, and continued to give the same never-failing service which had built up the business.

Mrs Parker, too, rose with her husband. Her hopes were centred on Elsie with more concentration than ever before. In London, she felt sure, there must be many eligible bachelors. Elsie could have whomsoever she wanted, of that she was positive, for she was now at her most beautiful and the stimulation of work and life in London had given her added gaiety and poise. At weekends Mrs Parker combed the neighbourhood for likely young men, and the field next door was transformed into a tennis court, set about with the very latest garden chairs and a dashing swing seat with a canopy and cushions covered in wisteria-entwined cretonne. Delicious snacks were eaten in the gnat-humming twilight, laughter set the tall lemonade glasses tinkling and the young men feasted their eyes on Elsie Parker, cool, adorable and completely untouched by love.

Of course, it was inevitable that when Elsie fell in love the affair would be disastrous. As might be expected, Elsie's heart was first touched by a married man. He was a doctor who visited the hospital, an unremarkable man, running to fat, and so swarthy that he needed to shave twice a day. He had occasion to speak to Elsie now and again, and had no idea of the emotion which he unwittingly aroused. His presence alone affected Elsie. Her legs trembled, her hands shook, her throat grew dry and her head grew dizzy. She found it almost impossible to take in his orders.

'That Nurse Parker,' the doctor commented to one of his colleagues, 'is practically an imbecile. Talk about a dumb blonde!'

'It's love,' said the other laconically. He was sharper-eyed than most.

'Rubbish!' snorted Elsie's hero, and dismissed the whole conversation from his mind. He had a perfectly good wife, four children, a house with a mortgage, and no intention of getting entangled with a silly chit of a nurse, even if she was as handsome as Nurse Parker.

Elsie's love grew as the months went by, although it was given no encouragement. At weekends her mother noted the abstracted air, the paler cheek, the slight, but becoming, loss of weight. She longed to be taken into her daughter's confidence, relishing her role as understanding mother, but Elsie said nothing. In an earnest desire to cheer the girl Mrs Parker began to plan a small party for her nineteenth birthday.

'Oh, mum!' protested Elsie, when the project was broached. 'Let's skip my birthday this year. Honestly, I just don't feel like a lot of fuss.'

'You'll thoroughly enjoy it,' said Mrs Parker firmly. 'You've been moping long enough – about what I can't say, though I can guess – and it's time you pulled yourself together. I'll make all the arrangements.'

'I'd much rather you did nothing,' replied Elsie shortly. She had no energy or time for anything else but her preoccupation with the adored. Her mother, however, was undeterred. Invitations went out, food and drink were ordered, the local dressmaker was summoned to take Mrs Parker's ever-increasing measurements, and a Saturday night in June was appointed as the time of celebration. Scarcely aware of what was happening, Elsie acquiesced listlessly in the plans.

Work at the hospital seemed doubly hard in the warm weather. There was too, an air of profound disquiet hanging over the whole nation, for this was 1939 and the threat of world war came closer daily.

On the day before Elsie's birthday party the weather was close and thundery. Patients complained in their hot crumpled beds, nurses' tempers were short and the doctors' were even shorter. Shortest of all, it seemed, was the temper of Elsie's beloved. He was a sorely tried man. One of his children had mumps, his wife was prostrated with a migraine which could well last a week, his mother-in-law, whom he detested, was advancing plans to make her permanent home with theirs, the cat had been sick in full and revolting view of the breakfast table, and he had had considerable difficulty in starting his car that morning.

On arrival at the hospital he found that one of his cases in the men's surgical ward had developed alarming complications, and it was this that Elsie overheard him discussing with the sister on duty. Elsie was busy sluicing rubber sheets but could hear the beloved voice above the splashing of the water.

'Keep a nurse by him for the next hour,' he was saying, his words clipped with anxiety. Sister's reply was inaudible.

'Anyone you like,' responded the doctor. 'Anyone but Nurse Parker. She gets worse as she goes on.'

Elsie dropped the sheet she was washing and ducked her head as though she had received a physical blow. She felt stunned with shock. As from a great distance, she surveyed her submerged hands resting on the bottom of the deep sink. The clear cold water acted as a magnifying glass, and every hair and pore looked gigantic. Elsie observed the tiny bubbles on the fleshy part of her thumb, uncannily like the seed pearls her father had given her on her confirmation day.

Her mind seemed to dwell, with unusual clarity, on many things long forgotten. The terrible words, uttered a second before, and all that they implied, had as yet no real meaning for her. She remembered the beads of sweat on the hairy upper lip of one of her sixth-form admirers whom she had not met, or thought of, for years. She remembered bright hundreds and thousands, scattered on plates of junket, which she used to love as a child. She dwelt with compulsive intensity on the visual memory of a spider's web spangled with drops of dew. And all the time her gaze was fixed upon the tiny bubbles clustering on her thumb.

She was roused from her trance by the sound of sister

returning. All that day she went automatically about her duties, oblivious of the world about her. Late that night, lying straight and cold in her bed at the nurses' hostel, the tears began to flow, running down the side of her temple and dripping silently into the pillow. She wept noiselessly at first, and then, as the treachery and cruelty of those dreadful words began to burn into her, the paroxysm increased in intensity until she was choking with tears, her head throbbing and her chest aching with pain.

When dawn came she was red-eyed, swollen-faced and in a state of complete exhaustion.

'A cold,' she told her fellow nurses. 'I'm going home this afternoon anyway. I'll get over it during the weekend.' She was reported sick, took the two aspirins handed to her, and fell to weeping again. In the early afternoon she rose, dressed, packed her case and went to the station. She felt like a very frail old lady just recovering from a serious illness.

The sight that met her eyes on her return home brought her almost to a state of collapse. In the long room of the new wing she found her mother. The blonde parquet floor, the pride of Mrs Parker's heart, was stripped of its rugs and shone with much polishing. Against the wall stood tables already dressed in virgin-white cloths. Flowers were banked on window sills, lamps were wreathed with garlands. The room awaited young company, music, laughter and, above all, the gay presence of the daughter of the house.

Elsie put down her case very carefully. She felt that she might overbalance or even faint dead away. Her mother looked at her with a smile. She seemed not to notice anything amiss. Her mind was too occupied with ices, cherry sticks, blanched almonds and wine glasses to register much else.

'I'm ill,' announced Elsie. Her voice seemed to sound a long way off. She tried again, intent on making herself understood. 'I'm not well,' she said a little louder. 'I can't be at the party.'

'Elsie!' breathed Mrs Parker incredulously. She advanced

towards her, her poor face creased with worry. 'Can't come to the party? But, Elsie, you must – you simply must!'

She gave a small despairing gesture with one hand indicating the preparations. Elsie leant against the wall and closed her eyes. Inside her eyelids was imprinted the face of the man she loved. She studied it intently. Her mother was speaking again. Now her voice was firmer, her resolution returning.

'A nice lay-down,' she was saying. 'Slip under the eiderdown for an hour or two. I'll bring you up your tea and an Aspro. You'll soon be as right as ninepence.'

As if in a dream, Elsie found herself being propelled upstairs, her clothes removed, and her unprotesting body thrust into her bed. Still concentrating on her beloved's swarthy face she dropped instantly into a heavy sleep.

Her mother roused her at seven. The anxiety in Mrs Parker's face brought all Elsie's misery flooding back. She longed to turn away and abandon herself again to grief, but her mother, she knew, could not be disappointed. She rose and dressed, automatically making-up that lovely face which seemed recovered from its earlier ravages, and going at last to take her place in the hall to welcome her guests. She felt as though some part of her had died, and that she dragged it with her, a cold heavy weight, draining strength from her.

To outward appearances she seemed much as usual, lovely, smiling and as desirable as ever. Halfway through the evening, the vicar's son engineered a trip into the garden with his hostess, and there poured out his heart whilst offering his dank hand. With all her habitual skill Elsie extricated herself and contrived to leave the young man tolerably resigned. During the last waltz, she received her second proposal of the evening, but was cool-headed enough to realize that claret-cup had enflamed this suitor as much as her own looks. He was thanked, refused and mollified, all within the time it took to dance from the French windows to the dining table. Grief, it seemed, had not dulled either Elsie's wits or her attractions.

She returned to work, her passion still raging. Elsie thought bitterly that those who say that unrequited love soon dies know very little of the matter. In the face of her beloved's impatience, and even dislike, despite the torturing memory of those chance-heard words, Elsie adored him more as the weeks went by. It was enough to walk the same corridors, to touch the same door handles, to read the same hospital notices. When, on September the third, war was declared and a week later she heard that he had gone into the RAF and was to be posted almost immediately as medical officer to a windswept station in Scotland, she felt that she could not live without his presence.

But work, with all its blessed urgency, drove complete despair away. There were patients to be evacuated, wards to reorganize and a hundred and one matters to attend to. Only at night, before she fell asleep, did Elsie have any time to mourn her beloved, and then the pain was almost more than she could bear.

On Christmas Eve she heard terrible news. The doctor and two other officers had been killed in a car accident as they returned to the station late one foggy night. After the first few days of shock and grief, an extraordinary change came over Elsie. It was as though released, at last, from the bondage of her infatuation, she found freedom. It was over. Nothing could hurt him now, and nothing could hurt Elsie for that reason. She could look around, begin to live again, welcome kindness, affection and admiration and, perhaps, one day, return it.

During the years of war Elsie Parker was the cause of much head-shaking in Bent.

'A fast hussy!' declared one righteous matron, with three plain unmarried daughters. 'A proper flibbertigibbet, always running after the men!'

'No better than she should be, I don't doubt, up there in London where her parents can't see her!' quoth another.

There was certainly a hard gaiety about Elsie these days.

She was now Sister Parker, conscientious and hard-working in the hospital. But off duty Elsie craved excitement. The admirers were more numerous than ever. Americans, Poles and Norwegians joined Elsie's village wooers, and she parried their advances with the same skill, if not perhaps quite the same endurance, as before.

When the war ended Elsie was twenty-five. There was a spate of weddings as the young men returned home. The villagers of Bent smiled kindly upon the newly-married couples and welcomed with genuine joy the offspring who were born into a world full of shortages, inordinately tired, but at least at peace.

And still Elsie remained unattached. The years slipped by. Roger Parker died one winter. His wife followed him two years later. Elsie, as sole heir, found herself in control of the house, a flourishing business and a comfortable sum of money in the bank. She was now thirty-eight. Her hair was untouched by greyness; in fact, its golden hue was rather brighter than it had been. Her teeth, though much-stopped, were her own. Her figure was as trim as ever, her blue eyes as devastating. Level-headedly, Elsie took stock of her position.

The business could carry on, as it was doing, under its reliable manager. She would give up nursing, return to her home at Bent, and get married. Without her parents she might well be lonely. A husband was the thing and, with luck, there might still be time for children. Elsie set about putting these practical plans into action.

Within three months she was ensconced in the house, had joined the Caxley Golf Club and the Caxley Drama Group. She gave a handsome contribution to Caxley Cottage Hospital in gratitude for the kindness extended to her parents and was made a member of the hospital board. Her garden was lent for various local functions, she visited and was visited, and generally took her place in the gentle whirligig of Caxley's social life. People were genuinely glad to see her so engaged. The

Parkers had always been liked, and Elsie deserved a break after those years of nursing, they told each other.

Unfortunately, Elsie's aims were only too apparent and soon became the object of derision by the less charitable. She had never been a very subtle person. One of her charms was her openness. Now that time was running short for Elsie, she became alarmingly direct in her hunt for a husband. Naturally, eligible men were scarce. In Caxley society, at that time, there were half a dozen elderly bachelors, about the same number of widowers, and a few middle-aged men separated from their wives for an interesting variety of reasons.

They were not a very inspiring collection, but Elsie was a realist, and did not expect to find anyone who could compare, even remotely, with her first and only love. She looked now for kindness, companionship and protection. If humour and some physical attraction were added, she would count herself lucky, she decided. Financial stability was not essential, for her own position could comfortably support a husband, if need be.

Her first choice fell upon one of the widowers, a childless man in his forties, who was a partner in one of Caxley's firms of solicitors. She had known him slightly during her years of nursing and knew him to be liked by the little town. He played golf and took leading parts in Caxley plays. Elsie pursued him resolutely and charmingly, to the surprise of the flattered man and the intense interest of the neighbourhood. But, before long, the hunt was off. Elsie, to her dismay, found that her intended had one small, but unforgivable, fault. He did not wash – at least, not enough.

After this set-back, Elsie began to wonder if *cleanliness* perhaps should take precedence over *kindness* on her list of desirable qualities. She had not reckoned to be troubled by such elementals, and was not impressed by excuses put forward by well-meaning friends who seemed to have guessed the cause of her withdrawal.

'Poor dear Oswald,' they said. 'So terribly cut up by Mary's death, you know. Seemed to go all to pieces. You can see that he really needs a woman to look after him.'

Maybe, thought Elsie privately, but not to the extent of washing his ears for him or cleaning his teeth. Personal fastidiousness, heightened by a nurse's training, did not condone greasy collars, black fingernails and the same filthy handkerchief for a week. Oswald, in his expensive, well-cut and smelly suits, was rejected.

Others, observing Elsie's aims and aware of her comfortable circumstances, made themselves pleasant. Elsie earnestly did her best to see them in the role of husband, never blinding herself to the true aim of their attentions but willing to ignore it if other less ignoble qualities were present. Too often there were none.

Time passed. Elsie continued her search, an object of pity to some and derision to others. She was still lovely, though now in her forties, and her energy seemed unimpaired. But at heart she was beginning to despair. Was marriage never to be her lot?

One bleak December afternoon she made her way to the churchyard at Bent bearing a bright-berried cross of holly for her parents' grave. She walked slowly between the mounds, reading the well-known inscriptions yet again.

'*Loved and Loving wife of John Smith*,' said one. '*A beloved wife and mother*,' said a second. '*This stone was erected by a sorrowing husband to the memory of his much beloved wife*,' said a third.

All wives, all loved, all missed, all mourned, thought Elsie bitterly. Of what use was beauty, health, a loving heart and worldly possessions, if marriage never came? What would be written on her own tombstone for others to read?

Elsie Parker, Spinster? What a hateful word that was! She hastened her steps at the very thought, and reached her parents' resting-place.

'*And Lily, his dearly-loved wife*,' read Roger's daughter. '*In death they are united*.'

Controlling an impulse to rush away from the spot, Elsie set the cross gently against the headstone, stood motionless in the biting cold and offered up a small prayer for her parents, and for their only child.

She made her way quickly to the gate, carefully averting her eyes from the inscriptions around her. There was only one other person in the churchyard, and he too was setting a holly wreath upon a grassy mound. As she came near him he stepped forward into her path. He was a big dark man, much about her own age, and unknown to Elsie.

'Elsie Parker?' said the man gently. She nodded.

'I'm John Blundell,' said the man. 'I'd have known you anywhere. But you've forgotten me.'

Elsie felt a warm surge of recognition.

'John!' she exclaimed. 'My goodness, how many years is it since we saw each other?'

'I left Bent to join up in 1939,' he said. 'I don't think we've met since then, though I've heard about you.'

Elsie looked at him. John Blundell, the little dirty boy who had been her very first suitor! Undoubtedly he had prospered. His air was quiet and authoritative, his appearance immaculate. He had come a long way from the ragged child with the handkerchief pinned to his jersey who had been such a faithful admirer all those years ago.

She remembered, in a flash, that she had heard of his marriage during the war, but no further details. Lily Parker had risen above the station of the Blundells and had not passed on news of this family to Elsie.

'I'm still living at the old house,' said Elsie. 'Where are you now?'

'Near Southampton,' said John Blundell, falling into step beside her. 'I've a small shipping business there.'

'Alone?' asked Elsie, probing gently.

'No, I've got two sons, both married now. They help me to run it. They're good boys.'

They emerged from the yew-flanked gateway into the village square. A beautiful glossy car was waiting near the railings of the village school which they had both attended so long before.

'I'll run you back, if I may,' said the man. They drove at a sedate pace to Elsie's home.

'Do have some tea with me,' said Elsie. 'You don't have to hurry back, do you?'

He must not be too late, but he would love some tea, he said. They talked until it was half past six, and during that time Elsie learnt that he had married an Italian girl whose father was in an Italian shipping line and was a man of some substance. Their two sons were born in Italy. They had come back to England for the boys' schooling. The climate had not suited his wife but she refused to leave him during the winters to run the business alone, and had contracted Asian 'flu, five years before, which had proved fatal.

It was apparent that he had loved her dearly. His voice shook as he told the tale in the shadowy firelit room and Elsie was reminded of his early tears when she had so light-heartedly turned him down at the tender age of seven.

This was the first of many meetings. Elsie knew, before a month had gone by, that this would end happily. Despite local tales to the contrary, Elsie did not pursue John Blundell. There was no necessity. There was mutual attraction, affection and need. Before the end of February they were engaged, and the marriage was arranged to take place after Easter. To Elsie it seemed wonderfully fitting that her first suitor should also be her last.

'And so, you see,' said Amy, lighting another cigarette, 'it all ended happily. Elsie adores the boys and the first one is going to live at the old house at Bent with his wife and children. Elsie and John want something smaller, and I think they both want to be at a little distance from Bent. Everyone says they're tremendously happy, even though they are, well – somewhat *mature*.'

Amy eyed me speculatively. I returned her gaze blandly.

'Funnily enough,' I said, 'I had my first proposal at the age of seven. I was fishing for frogs' spawn at the time. Not a very glamorous pursuit, when you come to think of it.'

Amy leant forward with growing interest. 'What happened to him? Do you ever hear?' Clearly, she was hoping that history would repeat itself.

'I heard only the other day,' I told her. 'He's doing time for bigamy.'

6. BLACK WEEK

I suppose everyone encounters periods when absolutely everything goes wrong. The week after my friend Amy's visit was just such a one, and it left Fairacre village school and its suffering headmistress sorely scarred.

On Monday morning I awoke to find that there was no electricity in the house. I am not a great breakfast-eater and can face a plate of cornflakes with cold milk as bravely as any other woman on a bleak March morning. But it is very hard to go without a cheering pot of tea, and this I saw I should have to do, for the clock stood at twenty to nine – inevitably, I had overslept – and the oil stove would not boil water in time.

A wicked north-easter cut across the playground. A few wilting children huddled in the stone porch.

'Go inside!' I shouted to them, as I bore down upon them.

'Can't get in!' they shouted back. I joined the mob. Sure enough, the great iron ring which lifts the latch failed to admit us.

'Mrs Pringle's inside, miss,' said Ernest.

'Well, why didn't you knock?' I asked, mystified.

'She don't want us mucking up her floor, she says.'

'What nonsense!' I was about to exclaim, but managed to bite it back. Instead I hammered loudly with the iron ring. After some considerable time, during which icy blasts played round our legs and blew our hair all over our faces, there was the sound of shuffling footsteps, the grating of a key, and Mrs Pringle's malevolent countenance appeared in the chink of the door. I widened the crack rapidly with a furious shove and had the satisfaction of hearing a sharp bang occasioned by the door meeting Mrs Pringle's kneecap.

'Can I have a word with you?' I said with some asperity, ignoring her closed eyes and martyred expression. The children surged past us to their pegs in the lobby, and I went through to my room followed by Mrs Pringle. As I guessed, her limp was much in evidence. I hoped that this time the affliction was genuine. Judging by that crack on the kneecap, it might well be.

'I have asked you before, Mrs Pringle,' I began in my best schoolteacher manner, 'to leave the door open when you arrive so that the children can come inside. It isn't fit for them to be out in this weather.'

Mrs Pringle arranged a massive hand across her mauve cardigan and gasped slightly. She replied with an air of aggrieved dignity.

'Seeing as the lobby floor was wet I didn't want the children to catch their deaths in the damp atmosphere,' began the lady, with such brazen mendacity that I felt my ire rising.

'Mrs Pringle,' I expostulated, 'you know quite well that you locked the door because you wanted to keep the floor clean.'

Mrs Pringle's martyred expression changed suddenly to one of fury. 'And what if I did? Mighty little thanks I gets in this place for my everlasting slaving day in and day out. What's the good of me washing the floor simply to have them kids mucking it up the minute it's done, eh?' Fists on hips she thrust her face forward belligerently. 'And what's more,' she continued, in a sonorous boom audible to all Fairacre, 'you've no call to give me a vicious hit like you done with the door. My knee's almost broke! I could have you up for assault and battery, if I was so minded!'

'I'm sorry about your knee,' I said handsomely. 'Of course, if you'd left the door unlocked there would have been no need to push our way in.'

'H'm!' grunted Mrs Pringle, far from mollified. 'No doubt I'll have to lay up with this injury, and with the stoves drawing so bad as they are with the wind in this quarter *someone's* going to find a bit of trouble!'

She limped heavily from the room, wincing ostentatiously.

For the rest of the day she maintained an ominous silence. I can't say I let it worry me. Mrs Pringle and I have sparred for many a long year and I know every move by heart. Now I confidently awaited her notice, and was rather surprised when it was not forthcoming.

The wind was fiendish all day. Every time the door opened, papers whirled to the floor. The partition developed a steady squeak as the strong draught shook it, and the door to the infants' lobby made the whole building shudder every time an infant burst forth to cross to the lavatory.

During afternoon playtime, when my back was turned for three minutes, Patrick, trying to shut the windows with the window pole lost his balance and broke an upper pane, bringing down a shower of glass upon the floor and a shower of invective upon himself. Now we had an even fiercer draught among us, accompanied by banshee wailing among the pitch pine rafters. We were all glad when it was time to go home.

Mrs Pringle, black oilcloth bag swinging on her arm, stumped into the lobby as I went out. She stared stonily before her and did not deign to answer my greeting. Past caring, I fled through the wind to the haven of my little house, craving only peace and tea.

On Tuesday I woke to hear the hiss of sleet on my bedroom window. The playground was white, and the branches of the elms swayed in the same wicked north-easter. Luckily, the electricity was functioning again, and after breakfast I made my way over to the school to see if the stoves were doing well.

They were not going at all. Mrs Pringle, with devilish timing, was going to give in her notice this morning, I could see. Meanwhile, sleet and snow blew energetically through the broken pane, and the usual cross-draughts stirred the papers on the walls.

Mr Willet arrived as I was lighting the stove in the infants' room. His face was red with the wind's buffeting, and his moustache spangled with snowflakes.

'Here, I'll do that,' he said cheerfully. 'They tell me her ladyship's gone on strike again.'

'I'm not surprised,' I said, and told him about yesterday's fracas.

'She's a Tartar,' commented Mr Willet. 'But never you fear, we'll manage without her. Soon as these 'ere stoves is drawing, I'll paste a bit of brown paper over that there broken window. Best tell the Caxley folk to come and do a bit of glazing, I suppose. That's too high for me to manage this time.'

The children arrived. Ernest handed me a note. The handwriting was Mrs Pringle's.

'Am laid up with my damaged knee,' it said. 'Doctor is coming today and may say give in my notice. Will let you know. Matches is short.

Mrs Pringle.'

Matches were not short, they were non-existent, as I had discovered, but by now the stoves were going, in a sullen black mood, and little puffs of smoke occasionally escaped from them. Mrs Pringle had been correct about their dislike of a north-east wind. The stoves resented it as much as we did. As the fuel grew warm the smoke increased, and we worked throughout the morning among lightly-floating smuts and eye-watering fumes.

Mr Willet, working perilously on an inadequate ladder as he blocked up the hole in the window pane, left his lofty perch now and again to survey the stoves.

'Beats me,' he said, scratching his head. 'I'll bet Mrs P. put the evil eye on 'em before she left!'

It seemed more than likely.

In the afternoon Eileen Burton complained of a stiff neck. I was about to dismiss this as a result of the draughts, but observing her flushed appearance I took her temperature. It was over a hundred, her neck glands were painful and she had not had mumps. I surveyed her anxiously.

'My cousin's just had them,' she told me. 'And we often plays together.'

There was nothing for it but to wrap her up warmly, put her in my car and run her home at playtime. How many more, I wondered, peering through the gloom of the smoke-filled room on my return, would succumb in the next few days?

The sleet had changed to heavy snow by Wednesday morning, but mercifully the wind had dropped and the stoves behaved themselves.

The relief was tremendous, and I began to enjoy school without Mrs Pringle's presence. But the snow brought its own problems. The children were excited and fussy, quite incapable of working for more than three consecutive minutes, and standing up to look out of the windows whenever it was possible to see 'if it was laying'.

'Eggs or bricks?' I asked them tartly but, quite rightly, they did not rise to this badinage and I was forced to give an elementary grammar lesson in the middle of a spirited account of Moses in the bulrushes, knowing full well that neither would bear much fruit.

The snow was certainly 'laying'. It was coming down thick and fast, large snowflakes whirling dizzily and blotting out the landscape as effectively as a fog. It was nearly six inches deep by midday, and the dinner van was remarkably late. Surely there were no drifts yet, I thought to myself, to hold up Mrs Crossley on her travels? She was usually at Fairacre between half past eleven and twelve, then having Beech Green's dinner to deliver before returning to her depot.

At twelve the children who go home to dinner departed. There was still no sign of the van and I was beginning to wonder if I should telephone the depot when Patrick came running back to school, followed by the rest of the home-dinner children, all in a state of much agitation.

'Mrs Crossley's slipped over,' shouted Patrick.

'And spilt all the gravy,' shouted another. He seemed to think that the loss of gravy was more important than Mrs Crossley's accident.

'She's hurt her leg,' volunteered a third.

By this time all my pupils, clad and unclad, were out in the snowy waste of playground. I made a valiant attempt to restore order, banishing the unclad indoors and telling the others to accompany me to the scene.

The dinner van had pulled up just out of sight of the school, and Mrs Crossley had started to walk bearing a pile of large tins propped against her chest. When we reached her she had struggled back to the van and was sitting sideways in the driving seat, massaging an ankle. I could see by the look of pain on her face and the swelling of the joint that she had a severe sprain.

A pool of brown gravy stained the snow, but that was the only culinary casualty. Two of the bigger boys carried Fair-acre's food into school while poor Mrs Crossley hobbled to my house supported by half a dozen anxious children and me. She lay on my sofa looking very woebegone.

'So silly of me,' she said, near to tears. 'I must have stepped awkwardly on a hard lump of snow. I couldn't see over the tins.'

'You stay there,' I said, 'and I'll give you first aid in two shakes. In the meantime, drink this.'

I poured out a tot of brandy. Mrs Crossley shuddered.

'Knock it back!' I said firmly, tucking a rug over her. 'I'll just see that the children aren't throwing the dinner all over each other and I'll be back.'

As is so often the case in a crisis, the children were behaving in an exemplary manner. They had served themselves, said grace, and were eating with the utmost decorum when I called in. I gave them much well-deserved praise, begged them to keep it up, and left them smug with self-righteousness.

'I simply must get Beech Green's dinner to them,' was Mrs Crossley's greeting on my return.

'I'll ring Mr Annett,' I assured her, 'and he can come and collect it. But let me see to this ankle.'

'Oh please,' begged Mrs Crossley, 'do ring Mr Annett and the depot! I shan't have an easy moment till it's done!'

You won't have an easy moment for some time with that ankle, I thought, watching it turn from red to mauve as I listened to Beech Green school's telephone bell.

Mr Annett answered promptly. Yes, he would come at once. Could he take Mrs Crossley to her doctor or her home or fetch her husband? I was full of admiration for Mr Annett's rapid grasp of the situation and practical help. But Mrs Crossley, from the sofa, preferred to rest for a little and to stay where she was.

I then rang the depot who promised to send someone to collect the van, and only when that was done would Mrs Crossley put her poor swollen ankle into my amateurish hands. By the time I had strapped it firmly, made her some tea, and promised to run her back after school, it was time to go back to school.

The classroom was beautifully quiet. The dinner things had been cleared away; but on the tortoise stove stood a dinner plate, carefully covered by another.

Ernest lifted it from the stove with the folded duster and placed it reverently before me on my desk.

'Bin keepin' it hot for you, miss,' he said. And it was only then that I realized that I had missed my meal.

I lifted the lid. The gravy had dried to a papery skin, and the slices of meat were curling with the heat. It all looked horribly daunting, but touched by the children's kindness I bravely took up fork and knife. Watched by their solicitous eyes I ate my dinner thankfully.

The snow did not cease all day, and I drove Mrs Crossley home after tea through a positive blizzard. Luckily the roads were passable and I was soon home again. There was still no word from Mrs Pringle and I could hear Mr Willet manfully filling the coke buckets as I put the car away. What would Thursday hold, I wondered, as I ploughed through the snow to my front door?

It held, I discovered next morning, three more cases of mumps and no word from Mrs Pringle. It was still bitterly cold but the snow had stopped during the night. I crunched it underfoot as I crossed the playground and could imagine the snowballing that would delight the children at playtime.

The stoves had resumed their sulky behaviour and filled the two classrooms with smoke. We tried the damper open, shut, and halfway open with exactly the same result. At length we resigned ourselves to the inevitable and resumed our interrupted work on fractions in the midst of an acrid blue haze.

The vicar called during the morning. The Reverend Gerald Partridge is as near a saint as it would be possible to find in any village. His mild sweet face usually wears a vague benign smile, but today he appeared much agitated. At the sight of the smoke, his alarm grew.

'Good heavens!' he cried aghast. 'Are you on fire?'

'I wish we were,' I replied. 'We're only smouldering. The stoves object to a north-east wind.'

'It all looks very uncomfortable,' said the vicar, approaching the tortoise stove warily, as though expecting it to explode. 'I gather that Mrs Pringle is not with you at the moment,' he added delicately. I told him why.

'Yes, yes. I heard that there had been a little upset,' nodded the vicar understandingly. He is much too wise and diplomatic to take sides and, in any case, I suspect that he thinks 'our little upsets' are six of Mrs Pringle's making and half a dozen of mine. And he is probably right.

The vicar now began to twist his leopard-skin gloves together unhappily.

'I have a really dreadful confession to make, Miss Read,' he began. 'I simply cannot put my hand on that pamphlet you lent me about religious books for the young from the Oxford University Press.'

'It doesn't matter in the least,' I assured him. 'I had quite finished with it.' But he seemed too sunk in self-mortification to hear.

'You see, I put it most carefully on the hall table, and this morning my wife and the two girls began spring-cleaning.' The two girls, incidentally, are two buxom Fairacre matrons of sixty-two and sixty-five.

'And not only had the pamphlet gone,' continued the poor man, 'but the hall table and the rugs and chairs – and to tell you the truth, every room in the house is completely upside down.'

Knowing his wife's vigour and the matching energy of 'the two girls' I could imagine the state of the vicarage only too clearly. This visit, I suspected, might be in the nature of a brief escape.

I did my best to calm his fears and accompanied him out to his car.

'Just look at that splendid bullfinch!' exclaimed Mr Partridge, his face lighting up.

'Splendidly picking off my plum buds,' I responded grimly, though I had to admit that the vivid little creature was a cheerful sight on that bleak day.

The vicar climbed into his car, and looked at me anxiously through the window. 'Don't hesitate to close the school, my dear, if the stoves prove too intractable. It can't be good for your lungs, or the dear children's, to inhale those fumes. What a pity Mrs Pringle is away! She is the *tiniest* bit difficult, I realize, but she has a wonderful way with stoves.'

Before I could reply, he gave me a disarming smile, let in the clutch and shot erratically away down the lane.

During the dinner hour I consulted Mr Willet about my little cat.

For several days he had been off his food, and I had supposed that a diet of local mice had been preferred to the delicacies offered by me. But this morning he looked wretched, sitting four-square with paws tucked under him, and his eyes half-closed.

'Fur balls,' pronounced Mr Willet.

'I'll get the vet,' I said at once.

'Ain't no need to get him out from Caxley,' said Mr Willet. 'You give ol' Tib a spoonful of liquid paraffin to oil the works. He'll be as right as rain tomorrow.'

'Are you sure?' I asked doubtfully.

'Positive!' Mr Willet assured me. 'This time of year they loses their winter coats, see, and keep all on a-licking themselves tidy, and swallering great 'anks of 'air. It all gets twizzled up inside 'em. Liquid paraffin's the stuff.'

I thanked him and watched him return to his daily coke-sweeping. What a tower of strength and information Mr Willet was!

I poured out a dessertspoonful of liquid paraffin and approached the unsuspecting cat. It is not easy to open a cat's mouth in order to administer medicine, as everyone knows. It is harder still when you are attempting it alone, and particularly when you have been foolish enough to pour out the dose beforehand and are trying not to spill it. Somehow or other I got most of it into the side of Tibby's mouth, and was just beginning to congratulate myself, when he gave his head a violent shake and ejected at least half the oil over my beautiful new suede shoes.

I returned, growling, to afternoon school, recounting my luck to Mr Willet en route.

'I'll give you a hand after school,' he said cheerfully. 'You allus wants two to cope with a cat, and then the cat nearly allus wins.'

He looked at my stained shoes sadly.

'It do seem to be one of those weeks, don't it?' he observed. And I agreed, with feeling.

There was still no word from Mrs Pringle on Friday morning. Although it was delightful to be without her presence, the school was beginning to look a little worse for wear despite my own efforts and Mr Willet's.

The snow, luckily, was melting fast, but plenty managed to find its way into the building. With it were the usual flotsam and jetsam of school life, and plentiful sprinkling of additional matter from the workmen at the Blundells' new home.

'If anyone brings any more nails, putty or shavings into this school,' I said threateningly, 'I shall ring up the builders and tell them what is happening.'

The putty in particular was a sore trial. It seemed to be the thing to have a small lump under one's desk, or about one's person, and the children's hands had never been so filthy. By dint of constant nagging I was beginning to make a little headway against this infiltration.

We were all glad that it was Friday. It had been a trying week for everyone. By the afternoon I was beginning to feel a little more hopeful. The stoves were emitting only half as much smoke as before, only one more case of mumps had occurred overnight, Tibby appeared to be on the mend, a new pane of glass had replaced the broken one, and I had decided to find a substitute for Mrs Pringle if I did not hear from the lady during the weekend.

But Fate still had one more blow in store for us. Jimmy Waites, on returning from play, set up a wail.

'I bin and lost my half crown!'

'Where was it?' I inquired.

'Under my desk. Someone's pinched it!'

Now, if anything makes me cross, it is this kind of glib accusation. I spoke sharply.

'Rubbish! And in any case, you know you should have given it to me to mind. What was it for?'

'Half of cheddar, two boxes of matches and a pricker for the Primus,' gabbled Jimmy. Obviously he had been repeating this to himself all the afternoon.

Then began the search. We turned the whole place upside down. We shifted desks, turned out likely cupboards, and completely wrecked the room. It was not to be found.

Our Friday afternoon story had to go by the board. By now I was beginning to wonder if someone perhaps had succumbed to temptation. The half crown had been seen by Jimmy's neighbours. It was there at playtime. Jimmy had been in and out of the room himself during that time.

It was a mystery that must be solved.

'We'd better look in our clothes,' I said. It is a job that I hate doing, but things looked suspicious. Pockets were turned out, socks rolled down, children jumped up and down to see if any coins would emerge from jerseys and trousers. But nothing was forthcoming.

By now it was time to say prayers and go home. In the middle of the hubbub the door opened and in stumped Mrs Pringle, complete with black bag. She surveyed the chaos grimly. 'Seems this place wants a bit of doing-up,' she boomed, but made no move to discard her coat and hat.

'Sit down for a moment, Mrs Pringle,' I said. 'We're in rather a pickle.'

'*That*,' said the lady with emphasis, 'is plain for all to see!' She folded her arms across her capacious bosom and watched the scene majestically.

'We'll have one last look,' I said desperately to the children. 'It must be somewhere in this room. If it doesn't turn up now I shall have to think about keeping you all here until it is found.'

There was something in my tone that made them realize the seriousness of the occasion and they began to look frenziedly about them, bending under desks, running their hands along the high window sills and scrabbling in the dusty corners of the classroom. Quite rightly, they resented being suspected, and I hated, just as much, the feeling that I was suspecting them.

It was Mrs Pringle who discovered the half crown. The only calm person in the room, she had perhaps a clearer eye than the rest of us. 'If it's a *coin* you're looking for,' she shouted above the din, 'it's there!'

She pointed at the back view of Jimmy Waites himself. The child was kneeling under his desk, and cleaving to the instep of his wellington boot was a glutinous lump of the ubiquitous putty. There, embedded in it, was the missing half crown.

After we had congratulated Mrs Pringle and each other, I improved the shining hour by pointing out the absolute necessity of leaving putty severely alone, and then dismissed them.

There was genuine relief in their farewells. The dark shadow of distrust was lifted, the half crown was restored and Fairacre school could relax again.

'The vicar told me you was in trouble,' said Mrs Pringle austerely, when the children had gone. 'And though I doubt if my knee will ever be the same again, I knows where my duty lies.' She advanced, limping, towards the stove. 'Been letting it smoke, have you?' she said.

I felt that this was hardly the correct expression, but was not given time to reply. To my amazement, Mrs Pringle lifted a mighty hand and smote the pipe about a foot above the stove itself. The smoke, which had been dribbling gently from the crack in the lid, ceased emerging immediately.

'Gets a bit out of true sometimes,' observed Mrs Pringle with satisfaction. 'Well, I'll get the place to rights while I'm here, so's we can be straight for next week.'

'Thank you, Mrs Pringle,' I said meekly, bowing my head, with secret relief, to the inevitable.

7. THE FAIRACRE GHOST

The Easter holidays are probably more welcome than any other, for they mark the passing of the darkest and most dismal of the three school terms and they herald the arrival of flowers, sunshine and all the pleasures of the summer.

At this time, in Fairacre, we set about our gardens with zeal. Potatoes are put in, on Good Friday if possible, and rows of peas and carrots, and those who have been far-sighted enough to put in their broad beans in the autumn, go carefully along the rows, congratulating themselves, and hoping that the black fly will not devastate the young hopefuls in the next few months.

We admire each other's daffodils, walk down each other's garden paths observing the new growth in herbaceous borders, and gloat over the buds on plum and peach trees. We also observe the strong upthrust of nettles, couch grass and dande-lions among the choicer growth, but are too besotted by the thought of summer ahead to let such things worry us unduly.

It is now that the vicar gets out his garden funiture – a motley collection ranging from Victorian ironwork to pre-war Lloyd-loom – and arranges it hopefully on the vicarage ver-andah. Now Mr Mawne, our local ornithologist, erects a hide at the end of his lovely garden in order to watch the birds. He weaves a bower of pea-sticks, ivy-trails and twigs upon the wood and sacking framework, as intricate as the nests of those he watches.

Now the cottage doors are propped open with a chair, or a

large stone, and striped cats wash their ears or survey the sunshine blandly through half-closed eyes. Tortoises emerge, shaky and slower than ever, from their hibernation, and sometimes a grass snake can be seen sunning itself in the dry grass.

This is the time for visiting and being visited. For months we have been confined. Bad weather, dirty roads, dark nights and winter illnesses have kept us all apart. Now we set about refurbishing our friendships, and one of my first pleasures during this Easter holiday was a visit from my godson Malcolm Annett, and his father and mother.

It was a perfect day for a tea party. The table bore a bowl of freshly-picked primroses, some lemon curd made that morning, and a plentiful supply of egg sandwiches. Mr Roberts, the farmer, has a new batch of Rhode Island Red hens who supply me with a dozen dark brown eggs weekly. These are lucky hens, let me say, garrulous and energetic, running at large in the farmyard behind the house, scratching busily in the loose straw at the foot of the ricks, and advancing briskly to the back door whenever anyone emerges holding a plate. No wonder that their eggs are luscious compared with the product of their poor imprisoned sisters.

After tea we ambled through the village, greeting many old friends who were out enjoying the air. Mrs Annett used to teach at Fairacre before she married the headmaster at our neighbouring village Beech Green so that she knows a great many families here. Mr Annett is choirmaster at St Patrick's church at Fairacre, so that he too knows us all well.

We walked by the church and took a fork to the left. It is a lane used little these days, except by young lovers and Mr Roberts' tractors making their way to one of his larger fields. A dilapidated cottage stands alone some hundred yards from the entrance to the lane.

We stopped at its rickety gate and surveyed the outline of its ancient garden. A damson tree, its trunk riven with age, leant towards the remaining patch of roof thatch. Rough grass covered what once had been garden beds and paths, and nettles and brambles grew waist high against the walls of the ruin.

The doors and windows gaped open. Inside, on the ground floor, in what had once been the living room of the cottage, we could see hundredweight paper bags of fertilizer propped against the stained and ragged wallpaper. They belonged to Mr Roberts and were waiting to be spread upon his meadows any day now. Upstairs, the two small bedrooms lay open to the sky. The thatch had retreated before the onslaught of wind and weather, and only the frame of the roof stood, gaunt and rotting, against the evening sky.

'It must have been pretty once,' I said, looking at the triangle of garden and the rose-red of the old bricks.

'The vicar told me it was lived in during the war,' said Mr Annett. 'It housed a family of eight evacuees then. They didn't mind it being haunted, they told Mr Roberts.'

'Haunted?' we cried. I looked at Mr Annett to see if he was joking, but his face was unusually thoughtful.

'It is, you know,' he said with conviction. 'I've seen the ghost myself. That's how I came to hear the history of the place from the vicar.'

'Is that why it stays empty?' I asked. It was strange that I had never heard this tale throughout my time at Fairacre.

Mr Annett laughed. 'No, indeed! I told you people lived in it for years. The evacuees said they'd sooner be haunted than bombed, and spent all the war years here. I think Roberts found it just wasn't worth doing up after the war, and so it is now in this state.'

We looked again at the crumbling cottage. It was too small and homely to be sinister, despite this tale of a ghost. It had the pathetic look of a wild animal, tired to death, crouching in the familiar shelter of grass and neglected vegetation for whatever Fate might have in store.

'When did you see the ghost?' I asked.

Mr Annett sighed with mock impatience. 'Persistent woman! I see I shall have no peace until I have put the whole uncomfortable proceedings before you. It was a very frightening experience indeed and, if you don't mind, I'll tell you the story as we walk. Even now my blood grows a little chilly at the memory. Brisk exercise is the right accompaniment for a ghost story.'

We continued up the lane, with young Malcolm now before and now behind us, scrambling up the banks and shouting with the sheer joy of living. With the scents of spring around us, and the soft wind lifting our hair, we listened to the tale of one strange winter night.

Every Friday night, with the exception of Good Friday, Mr Annett left the school house at Beech Green and travelled the three miles to St Patrick's church for choir practice.

Some men would have found it irksome to leave the comfort of their homes at seven in the evening and to face the windy darkness of a downland lane. Mr Annett was glad to do so. His love of music was strong enough to make this duty a positive pleasure, and although his impatient spirit chafed at times at the slow progress made by Fairacre's choir, he counted Friday evening as a highlight of the week.

At this time he had much need of comfort. He was a young widower, living alone in the school house, and ministered to by a middle-aged Scotswoman who came in daily. The death of his wife, six months after their marriage, was still too painful for him to dwell upon. She had been killed in an air raid during the early part of the war, and for Mr Annett life would never be the same again.

One moonlit Friday evening in December, some years after the war had ended, he set out as usual for Fairacre. It was so bright that he could have driven his little car without head-lights. The road glimmered palely before him, barred with black shadows where trees lined the road.

He was early, for he had arranged to pick up some music from Miss Parr's house and knew that the old lady would want him to stop for a little time. However, when a maid opened the door, he was told Miss Parr had been invited to her nephew's, but the music had been looked out for him.

He drove to St Patrick's, and went inside. It was cold and gloomy. No one had yet arrived, and Mr Annett decided to use his time in taking a stroll in the brilliant moonlight. There was an unearthly beauty about the night that chimed with the young man's melancholy. He made his way slowly along a little used lane near the church, and let sad memory carry him on its flood. It was not often that he so indulged himself. After his wife's death, he had moved to Beech Green and thrown himself, almost savagely, into school life. He had filled his time with work and music, so that he fell asleep with exhaustion rather than the numbing despair which had first governed every waking hour.

He passed a broken down cottage on his left, its remnants of thatch silvered with moonlight. Just beyond it a five-barred gate afforded a view of the distant downs. Mr Annett leant upon its topmost bar and surveyed the scene.

Before him lay the freshly ploughed fields, the furrows gleaming in the rays of the moon. Further away, a dusky copse made a black patch on the lower flanks of the downs. Against the clear sky their mighty bulk looked more majestic than ever. There was something infinitely reassuring and comforting about their solidity, and the young man, gazing at them, let the tranquillity about him do its healing work.

It was very quiet. Far away, he heard a train hoot impatiently as it waited for a signal to allow its passage westward. Nearer, he was dimly conscious of the rustling of dead leaves at the foot of an old crab apple tree which stood hard by the gate. Some small nocturnal animal was foraging stealthily, wary of the silent man nearby.

Sunk in his thoughts, he was oblivious of the passage of time, and hardly surprised to notice that a strange man had appeared in the lane without any noise of approach.

He came close to Mr Annett, nodded civilly, and leant beside him on the gate. For a moment the two men rested silently side by side, elbows touching, and gazed at the silvered landscape before them. Despite the stranger's unexpected advent, Mr Annett felt little surprise. There was something gentle and companionable about the newcomer. The schoolmaster had the odd feeling that they were very much akin.

Vaguely, he wondered if they had met before somewhere. He shifted along the gate – the stranger seemed excessively cold – and turned slightly to look at him.

He was a loosely-built fellow, of about Mr Annett's age, dressed in dark country clothes which seemed a pretty poor fit. He wore an open-necked shirt and a spotted neckerchief, tied gipsy fashion, round his throat. He had a small beard, light in colour, which gleamed silver in the moonlight, and his fair hair was thick and wiry.

'Full moon tomorrow,' commented the stranger. For such a big man he had a remarkably small voice, Mr Annett noticed. It was almost falsetto, slightly husky and strained, as though he were suffering from laryngitis.

'So it is,' agreed Mr Annett.

They relapsed again into contemplation of the view. After some time, Mr Annett stirred himself long enough to find some cigarettes. He offered the packet to his companion.

'Thank 'ee,' said the man. 'Thank 'ee kindly, but I don't smoke these days.'

The schoolmaster lit his cigarette and surveyed the man. 'Haven't I seen you before somewhere?' he asked.

'Most likely. I've lived in Fairacre all my life,' answered the man huskily.

'I'm at Beech Green,' said Mr Annett.

The man drew in his breath sharply, as though in pain. 'My wife came from Beech Green,' he said. He bent his head forward suddenly. By the light of the moon Mr Annett saw that his eyes were closed. The use of the past tense was not lost upon the schoolmaster, himself still smarting with grief, and he led the conversation from the dangerous ground he had unwittingly encountered.

'Whereabouts in Fairacre do you live?' he asked.

The man raised his head and nodded briefly in the direction of the ruined cottage nearby. Mr Annett was puzzled by this, but thought that perhaps he was nodding generally in the direction of the village. Not wishing to distress him any further, and realizing that his choir must be soon arriving at St Patrick's, Mr Annett began to stir himself for departure. It was time he moved, in any case, for he had grown colder and colder since the arrival of the stranger, despite his warm overcoat. The stranger only had on a long jacket, but he seemed oblivious of the frost.

'Well, I must be off,' said Mr Annett. 'I'm due to take choir practice at seven thirty. Are you walking back to the village?'

The man straightened up and turned to face the schoolmaster. The moonlight shone full upon his face. It was a fine face, with high cheekbones and pale blue eyes set very wide apart. There was something Nordic in his aspect, with his great height and wide shoulders.

'I'll stop here a little longer,' he said slowly. 'This is the right place for me. I come most nights, particularly around full moon.'

'I can understand It,' said Mr Annett gently, scanning the sad grave face. 'There is comfort in a lovely place like this.'

A burst of laughter broke from the stranger's lips, all the more uncanny for its cracked wheeziness. His wide-open eyes glittered in the moonlight.

'Comfort?' he echoed. 'There's no comfort for the likes of me – ever!' He began to tear savagely at the neckerchief about his throat. 'You can't expect comfort,' he gasped painfully, 'when you've done this to yourself!'

He pulled the cloth away with a jerk and tore his shirt opening away from the neck with both hands. By the light of the moon, Mr Annett saw the livid scar which encircled his neck, the mark of a strangling rope which eternity itself could never remove.

He raised his horror-filled eyes to those of the stranger. They were still wide open, but they glittered no longer. They seemed to be dark gaping holes, full of mist, through which Mr

Annett could dimly discern the outline of the crab apple tree behind him.

He tried to speak, but could not. And as he watched, still struggling for speech, the figure slowly dissolved, melting into thin air, until the schoolmaster found himself gazing at nothing at all but the old gnarled tree, and the still beauty of the night around it.

The vicar was alone in the vestry when Mr Annett arrived at St Patrick's.

'Good evening, good evening,' said the vicar boisterously, and then caught sight of his choirmaster's face.

'My dear boy, you look as though you've seen a ghost,' he said.'

'You speak more truly than you realize,' Mr Annett answered soberly. He began to walk through to the chancel and his organ, but the vicar barred his way. His kind old face was puckered with concern.

'Was it poor old Job?' he asked gently.

'I don't know who it was,' replied the schoolmaster. He explained briefly what had happened. He was more shaken by this encounter than he cared to admit. Somehow, the affinity between the stranger and himself had seemed so strong. It made the man's dreadful disclosure, and then his withdrawal, even more shocking.

The vicar put both hands on the young man's shoulders. 'Poor Job,' he said, 'is nothing to be frightened of. It is a sad tale, and it happened long ago. After choir practice, I hope you will come back to the vicarage for a drink, and I will do my best to tell you Job's story.'

The younger man managed a wan smile.

'Thank you, vicar,' he said. 'I should be glad to hear more of him. I had a strange feeling while we were together –' He faltered to a stop.

'What kind of feeling?' asked the vicar gently.

Mr Annett moved restlessly. His brow was furrowed with perplexity. 'As though – it sounds absurd – but as though we were brothers. It was as if we were akin – as if we shared something.'

The vicar nodded slowly, and sighed, dropping his hands from the young man's shoulders. 'You shared sorrow, my son,' he said as he turned away. But his tone was so low that the words were lost in a burst of country voices from the chancel.

Together the two men made their way from the vestry to the duties before them.

The vicarage drawing room was empty when the vicar and his guest entered an hour or so later. A bright fire blazed on the hearth and Mr Annett gratefully pulled up an armchair. He felt as though he would never be warm again.

He sipped the whisky and water which the vicar gave him and was glad of its comfort. He was deathly tired, and recognized this as a symptom of shock. Part of his mind longed for sleep, but part craved to hear the story which the vicar had promised.

Before long, the older man put aside his glass, lodged three stout logs upon the fire and settled back in his chair to recount his tale.

* * *

Job Carpenter, said the vicar, was a shepherd. He was born in Victoria's reign in the year of the Great Exhibition of 1851, and was the tenth child in a long family. His parents lived in a small cottage at the Beech Green end of Fairacre, and all their children were born there. They were desperately poor, for Job's father was a farm labourer and times were hard.

At ten years old Job was out at work on the downs, stone-picking, bird-scaring and helping his father to clear ditches and lay hedges, but by the time he was fifteen he had decided that it was sheep he wanted to tend.

The shepherd at that point was a surly old fellow, twisted with rheumatism and foul of tongue. Job served a cruel apprenticeship under him and in the last year or two of the old man's life virtually looked after the flock himself. This fact did not go unnoticed by the farmer.

One morning during lambing time, Job entered the little hut carrying twin lambs which were weakly. There, stretched upon the sacks stuffed with straw which made the old man's bed, lay his master, open-eyed and cold.

Within two days Job had been told that he was now shepherd, and he continued in this post for the rest of his life. He grew into a handsome fellow, tall and broad, with blond wiry hair and a curling beard. The girls of Fairacre and Beech Green found him attractive, and made the fact quite plain, but Job was shy and did not respond as readily as his fellows.

One day, however, he met a girl whom he had never seen before. Her family lived in Beech Green, but she was in service in London. Job's sister worked with her and the two girls were given a week's holiday at the same time. She walked over to see Job's sister one warm spring evening and the two girls wandered across the downs to see the lambs at play.

Job watched them approach. His sister Jane was tall and fair, as he was. Her companion was a complete contrast. She was little more than five feet in height, with long silky black hair coiled in a thick plait round her head, like a coronet. She had a small heart-shaped face, sloe-dark eyes which slanted upwards at the corners, and narrow crescents of eyebrows. Job thought her the prettiest thing he had ever seen.

Her name was Mary. To Job, who had a deep religious faith, this seemed wholly fitting. She was a queen among women. Job had no doubts this time and no shyness. Before Mary's week of holiday had ended the two young people came to an understanding.

It was Christmas time before they saw each other again, and only a few letters, written for them by better-schooled friends, passed between Mary and Job during the long months of separation. They planned to get married in the autumn of the following year. Mary would return to London and save every penny possible from her pitiful earnings, and Job would ask for a cottage of his own at Michaelmas.

He was fortunate. The farmer offered him a little thatched house not far from the church at Fairacre. It had two rooms up and two down, and a sizeable triangle of garden where a man could grow plenty of vegetables, keep a pig and a few hens, and so go more than half way towards being self-supporting. A few fruit trees shaded the garden, and a lusty young crab apple tree grew in the hedge nearby.

The couple married at Michaelmas and were as happy as larks in their new home. Mary took work at the vicarage and found it less arduous than the living-in job in London. She was a quick quiet worker in the house and the vicar's wife approved of her. She was delighted to discover that her new daily was also an excellent needlewoman, and Mary found herself carrying home bundles of shirts whose collars needed turning, sheets that needed sides to middling, and damask table linen in need of fine darning. She was particularly glad of this extra money for, by the end of the first year of their married life, a child was due, and Mary knew she would have to give up the scrubbing and heavy lifting for a few weeks at least.

The coming of the child was of intense joy to Job. He adored his wife and made no secret of it. The fact that he cleaned her shoes and took her tea in bed in the mornings was known in Fairacre and looked upon as a crying scandal, particularly by the men. What was a woman for but to wait upon her menfolk? Job Carpenter was proper daft to pander to a wife in that namby-pamby way. Only laying up a store of trouble for himself in the future, said the village wiseacres in The Beetle and Wedge. Job, more in love than ever, let such gossip flow by him.

The baby took its time in coming and as soon as Job saw it he realized that it could not possibly survive. His experience with hundreds of lambs gave him a pretty shrewd idea of 'a good do-er' or a weakling. Mary, cradling it in her arms, smiling with happiness, suspected nothing. It was all the more tragic for her when, on the third day, her little son quietly expired.

She lay in a raging fever for a fortnight, and it was months before she was herself again. Throughout the time Job nursed her with loving constancy, comforting her when she wept, encouraging any spark of recovery.

In the two years that followed, two miscarriages occurred and the young couple began to wonder if they would ever have a family. The cottage gave them great joy, and the garden was one of the prettiest in the village, but it was a child that they really wanted. Everyone liked the Carpenters and Job's demonstrative affection for his wife was looked upon with more indulgence by the villagers as time passed.

At last Mary found that she was pregnant yet again. The vicar's wife, for whom she still worked, was determined that this baby should arrive safely, and insisted on Mary being examined regularly by her own doctor. She engaged, too, a reputable midwife from Caxley to attend the birth, for the local midwife at that time, in Fairacre and Beech Green, was a slatternly creature, reeking of gin and unwashed garments, whose very presence caused revulsion rather than reassurance to her unfortunate patients.

All went well. The baby was a lusty boy, who throve from the time he entered the world. Job and Mary could hardly believe their good fortune and peered into his cot a hundred times a day to admire his fair beauty.

One early October day, when the child was a few months old, Mary was sitting at the table with a pile of mending before her. The boy lay asleep in his cradle beside her.

It was a wild windy day. The autumn equinox had stirred the weather to tempestuous conditions, and the trees in the little garden flailed their branches in the uproar. Leaves whirled by the cottage window and every now and again a spatter of hail hit the glass like scattered shot. The doors rattled, the thin curtains stirred in the draught, and the whole cottage shuddered in the force of the gale. Mary was nervous, and wondered how poor Job was faring outside in the full force of the unkind elements.

As the afternoon wore on, the gale increased. Mary had never known such violence. There was a roaring noise in the chimney which was terrifying and a banshee howling of wind round the house which woke the baby and made him cry. Mary lifted him from his cradle to comfort him, and walked back and forth with him against her shoulder.

There was a sudden increase in the noise outside – a curious drumming sound in the heart of the fury. To Mary's horror she saw through the window the small chicken house at the end of the garden swept upward and carried, twisting bizarrely, into the field beyond. At the same time a great mass of straw, clearly torn from a nearby rick, went whirling across the garden and, as it passed, one of the apple trees, laden with golden fruit, snapped off at the base as though it were a flower stem.

Mary could scarcely believe her eyes. She stood rooted to the spot, between the table and the fireplace, her baby clutched to her. The drumming sound grew louder until it was unendurable. Mary was about to scream with panic when a terrifying rumble came near at hand. The chimney stack crashed upon the cottage roof, cracking the rafters like matchwood, and sending ceilings, furniture, bricks and rubble cascading upon the two terror-stricken occupants of the little home.

When Job arrived at the scene of the disaster, soaked to the skin and wild with anxiety, he found the whole of one end of his house had collapsed. No one was there, for the neighbours were all coping with troubles of their own, and there had been no time to see how others were faring in the catastrophe that had befallen Fairacre in the matter of minutes.

He began tearing at the beams and sagging thatch with his bare hands, shouting hoarsely to his wife and son as he struggled. There was no answer to his cries. A ghastly silence seemed to pervade the ruined house, in contrast to the fiendish noises which raged about it.

An hour later, when neighbours arrived to help, they found him there, still screaming and struggling to reach his dead. Sweat and tears poured down his ravaged face, his clothes were torn, his battered hands bleeding. When, finally, the broken bodies of his wife and child were recovered, Job had to be led away, and only the doctor's drugs brought him merciful oblivion at the end of that terrible day.

In the weeks that followed, while his house was being repaired, Job was offered hospitality throughout Fairacre, but he would have none of it. As soon as the pitiful funeral was over, he returned numbly to his work, coming back each night to his broken home and sleeping on a makeshift bed in the one remaining room.

Neighbours did their best for him, cooking him a meal, washing his linen, comforting him with friendly words and advice. He seemed scarcely to see or to hear them, and heads shook over Job's sad plight.

'There's naught can help him, but time,' said one.

''Tis best to let him get over his grief alone,' said another.

'Once he gets his house set to rights, he'll start to pick up,' said a third.

Fairacre watched poor Job anxiously.

The men who had been sent to repair the cottage worked well and quickly. Their sympathy was stirred by the sight of the gaunt young man's lonely existence in the undamaged half of his tiny house.

At length the living room was done. The bricks which had crashed on that fateful afternoon had been built again into the chimney breast. The broken rafters had been replaced, the walls plastered and whitewashed afresh.

Job met the men as he trudged home from work. They called to him with rough sympathy.

'It's ready for you now,' they shouted through the twilight. 'We've finished at last.'

A kindly neighbour had gone in to replace his furniture.

'There now,' she said, in a motherly burr, 'you can settle in here tonight.' But Job shook his head, and went into his old room.

Sad at heart, the good old soul returned home, but could not forget the sight of Job's ravaged face. 'I'll go and take a look at him,' she said to her husband later that evening. 'If the lamp's alight in the room then I'll know he's settled in, and I'll go more comfortable to bed.'

But the window was dark. She was about to turn homeward again when she heard movements inside the cottage and saw the living room door open. Job stood upon the threshold, a candle in his hand. Breathless, in the darkness of the garden, the watcher saw him make his way slowly across the room to the chimney breast. He put down the guttering candle, and rested his fair head against the brickwork. Before long, his great shoulders began to heave, and the sound of dreadful sobbing sent the onlooker stealthily homeward.

''Tis best by far to leave him be,' comforted the neighbour's husband, when she told him what she had witnessed. 'We'll go and see him in the morning. It will be all over by then.'

But there was little comfort for the woman that night, for the spectacle of Job's grief drove all hope of sleep away.

Next morning they went together to the house. Her heart was heavy with foreboding as they walked up the little brick path. Inside the silent house they found him, with a noose about his neck, hanging against the chimney breast which had crushed his wife, his child, and every hope of Job himself.

* * *

There was an uncanny silence in the sunny lane as Mr Annett finished speaking.

'And that', he said soberly, 'is the tale of poor Job, as the vicar told it to me.'

Suddenly, a blackbird called from a hazel bush, breaking the spell. Despite the sunshine, I shivered. We were alone, for Malcolm and his mother had gone ahead to pick primroses from the steep banks, and though we were surrounded by the sights and scents of spring I remained chilled by this strange winter's tale.

'You're sure it was a ghost?' I asked shakily.

'Other people have seen Job,' answered Mr Annett, 'and the vicar knew all about him. But I believe I am the only person that Job has spoken to.'

'I wonder why?' I mused aloud.

'Perhaps he felt we had much in common,' said Mr Annett quietly.

I remembered suddenly Mr Annett's own tragedy. He, too, had adored a young wife and had lost her in the face of overwhelming violence. He too had watched a broken body removed to an early grave. There was no misery, no depth of hopelessness which Job had known, which was not known too to young Mr Annett.

We were summoned abruptly from the shadowy past by the sound of young Malcolm's excited voice.

'There's a nest here,' he called, 'with eggs. Come and look!'

'Coming!' shouted Mr Annett, suddenly looking ten years younger. And he ran off, all grief forgotten, to join his wife and child.

8. Mrs Pringle's Christmas Pudding

One of the pleasures of school holidays is the opportunity to join in the village affairs more fully than is possible in term time. When I was asked if I would help the Women's Institute to prepare a party I agreed with alacrity.

Once a year the members of Fairacre WI invite a coach-load of Londoners for the afternoon. Many of the visitors were evacuated to this area from the East End during the last war, and some had their schooling at our village school. Their mothers, now elderly women, lived in our midst, made friends, worshipped at St Patrick's, shared our pains and pleasures, and generally forged bonds which will last a lifetime. It is always a gay afternoon, with much reminiscing about shared memories and much gossip about new babies, marriages, good fortune and bad, which have been experienced since the last meeting.

The visitors were due to arrive at two o'clock. The custom is to greet them at the village hall with the tea urns ready. The main tea – a gargantuan meal – is prepared for five o'clock, but the two o'clock cup is considered the right welcome after their long trip from London and their lunch-time stop on the way.

At one time, we used to prepare our offerings in our own kitchens, converge upon the village hall about two and deposit sandwiches, sausage rolls, cakes and so on upon the dishes provided for the main meal. As anyone who organizes these things knows, the results could be chaotic. Four people who had offered sausage rolls would decide to provide chocolate sponge instead. The six who had promised sandwiches found that the local baker had no sliced bread, and so had opted to provide rock cakes instead, and the carefully prepared lists pinned up in the hall became covered with indescribable scribblings as the two people in charge tried to sort out the muddle.

After a few years of such crises it was decided to leave the matter in the hands of the committee, ably headed by Mrs Partridge, the vicar's wife, who is our President. These noble and efficient ladies ordered the bread, butter and fillings for the sandwiches, and every other necessity, and detailed squads of underlings to prepare the food under their vigilant surveillance in the hall. It worked much better that way, we found.

Consequently, at ten o'clock on the morning of the great day I made my way to the rendezvous, carrying my basket with a knife for buttering, a knife for cutting bread and some tea and sugar as my fool-proof contribution to the festivities.

The hall was buzzing like a beehive when I entered. The card tables which are used for local whist games had been placed at intervals round the hall and covered with bright cloths ready for the visitors. At one end, two long trestle tables were the scene of much activity. Here the noise was at its greatest for about twenty women cut and buttered bread, wielded salt and pepper pots, stacked sandwiches, arranged cakes on plates and generally made as much hubbub as my own schoolchildren.

I joined the throng and found myself between Mrs Mawne and Mrs Willet. Mrs Mawne has lived in Fairacre only a year or two and is the wife of our local ornithologist. His other claim to fame is his wonderful grasp of the church accounts which used to drive the vicar to distraction before Mr Mawne's coming. Mrs Mawne has the happy knack of upsetting everyone in the village by much forthright and tactless comment.

Her remark about the general incompetence, and probable dishonesty of the clergy in money matters, spoken directly to the vicar's wife in the presence of several speechless parishioners, has long been remembered. However, as we all have to live cheek by jowl in the village here, we push such memories to the back of our minds as best we may, and get on with day to day living.

Mrs Willet, the wife of our school caretaker, is a small mouse like creature who looks meek and frail. In fact, she is a dynamic person who gets through more work in twenty-four hours than I do in a week. Her washing line on a Monday morning flies a multiplicity of spotless linen, long before her neighbours have pegged theirs out. Her store cupboards bulge with jams, jellies, pickles and chutneys of her own making. Puddings and pies, batches of scones, roast joints, and a thousand other delicacies stream from her oven to nourish sturdy Mr Willet three times a day. Besides this, she makes her own clothes, sings in St Patrick's choir, enters all the WI competitions, knits, crochets, makes rugs and generally leaves one feeling quite useless and incorrigibly lazy.

Now her hands flew briskly back and forth from potted meat to bread and butter, working at twice the pace and with twice the deftness of my own. Mrs Willet's sandwiches were models of square exactitude. Mine gradually grew more and more rhomboid as the loaf went down. Mrs Willet's crusts sliced away cleanly. Mine broke away raggedly despite my best endeavours. The only comfort was that Mrs Mawne's were, if anything, rather more dilapidated than mine.

We shouted amicably to each other among the din.

'The new people are moving in,' Mrs Willet told me. 'The Blundells. I knew her as a girl. Very pretty, she was then.' I remembered Amy's story, and waited for more.

Mrs Mawne added her usual contribution with her usual tact. 'Looks rather a rackety type now,' was her comment. 'Hair very obviously dyed, and in trade, I hear.'

Mrs Willet began to bridle.

'A very flourishing business in Caxley,' I put in placatingly. If trade is flourishing enough, I notice, there seems to be less antagonism towards it. Mrs Mawne, however, was not particularly moved. She sucked a buttery finger and continued to arrange her sandwiches. It would have made a sanitary inspector's hair curl, but we are tough in Fairacre, and one of our favourite maxims is: 'You have to eat a peck of dirt before you die,' which we quote as we sketchily dust the tomato that has rolled on the floor, or take in the loaf that has been lodged on the outside window sill.

'I shan't bother to call,' said Mrs Mawne, filching my bread knife shamelessly, and making the handle horribly buttery, I observed.

Mrs Willet muttered something which sounded like: 'Fat lot she'll care!' but was unheard by Mrs Mawne. Mrs Willet's neck was growing rosy with suppressed anger and feeling rather nervous with so many knives flashing about, I attempted to be a little peacemaker once again.

'I believe Mrs Blundell used to sing very well,' I began.

'Oh, she sung lovely!' replied Mrs Willet, with enthusiasm. 'Used to come out here with the Operatic during the war, and we had rare old times!'

She gazed round our dingy village hall with affection. The walls are covered with sticky gingery-brown matchboarding and upon its surface hang lop-sided photographs of football teams of long ago, faded brown with age. Stern country countenances, many of them wearing fine moustaches, peer from among the clouds which the damp has drawn over the group. Here and there are pinned such notices as 'Scouts' Rules', 'The Resuscitation of the Drowned' (though we are miles from any water), and 'Suggestions for WI Programme – PLEASE HELP!' By the door there is a dilapidated piece of cardboard on which is printed: PLEASE SWITCH OF THE LIGHT and that missing F has been a thorn in my flesh ever since coming to Fairacre.

Dusty plush curtains, on a sagging wire, screen the minute stage from sight, and the wood is of splintery bare boards with here and there a knot of wood, polished by friction, projecting like a buttered brazil. There is nothing truthfully to gladden the eye in our hall, and yet Mrs Willet looked upon it now with all the doting tenderness of a mother gazing upon her firstborn. Such, I observed, is the power of association.

'A lot went on here during the war,' continued Mrs Willet. 'We used to have canning sessions in here twice each summer – soft fruit time, and then later when the apples and plums were ready. The WI used to bring the canning machine and we spent all day up here. Had some fun, I can tell you!'

'I always bottled mine,' said Mrs Mawne. 'Much more wholesome.'

'Sometimes there'd be as many as thirty of us up here canning,' continued Mrs Willet, ignoring the interruption. 'With the evacuees, and that. Some of 'em will be here this afternoon. You ask 'em, Miss Read, about this hall in the war. Fairly hummed with life it did! We had the clinic here, and First Aid classes, and no end of concerts and whist drives. And when we won the war, we had a proper beanfeast for the Welcome Home!'

'I suppose most of the evacuees had gone home by then,' I said.

'Nearly all,' agreed Mrs Willet sadly. 'We missed 'em, you know. Never really wanted 'em to begin with, as you can guess, but somehow, sharing everything, we got fond of one another – and then, well, they was a larky lot, real mischieful, some of 'em! You couldn't help laughing! There was one – her name was Mrs Jarman – she'll be coming this afternoon, she was a caution. We all reckoned she was the larkiest of the lot. And I'll take my oath,' said Mrs Willet solemnly, turning earnestly towards me, 'that she was at the bottom of that Christmas pudding affair.'

'The Christmas Pudding Affair?' I echoed. 'It sounds like a detective story.'

'Well, it was one what never got explained,' said Mrs Willet. 'I'll tell you what happened – some time.'

And she returned to her sandwich stacking.

When our preparations were completed, we all trooped home to a midday meal and to exchange our pinafores and working attire for more elegant *ensembles* in honour of the visitors.

Efficient and hardworking married women, like Mrs Willet, returned to their kitchens to dish up such succulent dishes as beef casserole or steak and kidney pudding which had been cooking themselves gently since nine or ten o'clock that morning. Scatter-brained spinsters, like me, with no hungry husbands to consider, had a piece of cheese, three biscuits and a cup of coffee, while they propped up their aching feet on a kitchen chair and read the paper. It was a good thing Amy couldn't see me, I thought, as I dusted the crumbs from my lap to the floor. This was Letting Myself Go in the way which caused her such heart-burning. Amy, my censorious college friend, when she lunches alone, sets one place at the dining room table, complete with glass, side plate, table napkin and so on, and eats her meal as decorously as any memsahib.

'And just think of the washing-up!' I said to Tibby, offering him a cheese rind. The disdainful creature took one sniff, flirted his tail and walked away.

'Thousands of poor cats,' I told him severely, retrieving the cheese rind for the birds, 'would give their eye-teeth for a delicious piece of cheese rind like that!' I tossed it through the open window. It was followed immediately by Tibby who devoured it instantly, and I sipped my coffee meditating on the maddening, but absorbing, ways of cats in general.

At ten to two we were all back in the hall awaiting the arrival of the coach. Our hair was freshly brushed, our noses powdered, our handkerchiefs sending out wafts of lavender water or Chanel Number 5 according to taste and income. The sun had come out, the tea urns hissed merrily, rows of blue-banded tea cups covered the trestle tables, and the air was filled with happy expectancy. When the coach drew up in the lane the tea ladies rushed to the urns, and those with less responsibility surged out to meet the visitors.

They were a cheerful crew and dressed much more gaily than we country mice were. Little hats with eye-veils, mauve coats and pink coats, stiletto heels, lots of patent leather, green and blue eyeshadow, flashing earrings and, above all, the high-pitched rapid twang of racy Cockney voices, made us feel that a flock of some exotic birds had suddenly descended upon us, and that we were as drab and unremarkable as our Fairacre hedge sparrows.

There were hugs and kisses, and much bonhomie and badinage as they were ushered into the hall. Over their tea cups the voices rose higher and higher. The noise was deafening. Carrying cups and saucers back and forth to the trestle table I marvelled at the snippets of conversation that came my way.

'Rosie got married last May and they've got a lovely flat at Ruislip, so he's a computer.'

'And our Janice – what was born here, you remember – well, a gentleman's got a very good job for her up the West End, with a flat and all. Makes anything up to sixty pounds a week, she does.'

'Dad's retired now, of course, and all for buying a bungalow at Peacehaven, but I say: "What's wrong with Hackney? Done us all right all these years, and you do see a bit of life!"'

Mrs Willet pointed out Mrs Jarman to me. She was a tiny bird-like woman with sparkling eyes. Her face was as wrinkled as an old apple, but her lips were a vivid orange and her crêpy eyelids were thick with blue eyeshadow. A tiny black velvet hat was lodged jauntily on her yellow hair, and a cigarette dangled between her fingers. She was telling a tale with great animation, her Fairacre audience registering half-shocked delight. She certainly looked 'a larky sort', as Mrs Willet had described. She seemed to epitomize the very spirit of Cockney effervescence and one could guess at her courage and example during the dark days of war.

As I watched her, Mrs Pringle passed bearing a tray. Mrs Jarman's face lit up with devilment and she called out some quip which was drowned in the general hubbub. It was not lost upon Mrs Pringle, however, for that lady's face grew redder than ever and an expression of deep disgust curved her mouth downward. She cast a look of outraged dignity towards the gay party and continued majestically with her tray.

Mrs Willet nudged me. 'No love lost there,' she hissed behind her hand. 'There's no forgiving and forgetting about Mrs P. They fair 'ates each other – she and Mrs Jarman.'

Before long we all set out for a walk round Fairacre in the sunshine, and I had no chance to hear more. But when the massive tea was over, and the coach was packed again with visitors bearing daffodils and farm eggs and hundreds of messages to those left behind in London, and Fairacre WI had cleared up the debris, 'switched of the light,' and locked the hall door, my chance came.

Wearily, Mrs Willet and I walked down the village together and paused by my gate.

'No, I won't come in,' Mrs Willet said, shifting her basket from one arm to the other. 'I've got some flower seeds to put in before it gets dark, but I just wanted to tell you about Mrs Pringle and Mrs Jarman now you've seen 'em together.'

We propped ourselves amicably one on each side of the school house gate. A clump of nearby narcissi sent up wafts of fragrance into the evening air, and Tibby rubbed himself round my tired legs as Mrs Willet unfolded her tale of a wartime feud.

Mrs Jarman and her family arrived in Fairacre in the early summer of 1941. They had endured the air raids which had made their days and nights hideous from September 1940 onwards, sleeping most of the nights in a Tube station and doing their best to carry on a normal life during the day. In May, however, their home was demolished, Mr Jarman was killed, and Mrs Jarman brought her four children to the comparative peace of Fairacre.

The eldest, Clifford, was fifteen, a tousle-headed lad whose rubbery lips seemed constantly glued to a mouth organ. Doreen, known as Dawreen, who was twelve, already ogled the boys, and was affronted when she was made to wash off her lipstick at Fairacre school. Nigel, two years younger, spent his time machine-gunning with outstretched fingers, and Gloria, aged six, was the baby. All four had their mother's blonde hair, but none had quite the vivacity of that irrepressible widow.

The family was billeted in the cottage next door to Mrs Pringle. It was owned by an elderly woman, now dead, called Jane Morgan. Mrs Morgan's husband, like his neighbour, Fred Pringle, was serving overseas. Mrs Morgan looked upon the Jarman family as the price one has to pay in wartime, and was unhappy about their presence, but resigned to it. Mrs Jarman, for her part, thought Jane Morgan 'a stuffy old party, dead from the neck up, but never meaning no harm'. They shook down together fairly well.

It was Mrs Pringle, of course, who really caused the trouble. Her evacuees were an elderly couple who did for themselves in one room of her house. They were a self-effacing pair and were careful to give no cause for annoyance. They crept in and out like mice, giving scared little smiles to their formidable landlady and offering her such small tributes as clothing coupons or morsels of margarine in order to 'keep her sweet', as Mrs Jarman said.

Before long, the Jarman children fell foul of Mrs Pringle. It was their habit to retire to the end of the garden, climb upon the roof of the empty pig sty and there watch the activities of their next door neighbour.

They had a foreign Cockney impudence which Mrs Pringle

abhorred. Fairacre children might have called names or even thrown a clod or two of earth over the hedge. The Jarman children were much more subtle.

'You ever seen anyone what's as broad as she's high?' one would shout to the next. The result would be tempestuous giggles on one side of the hedge and much bridling on the other.

The children watched their neighbour pegging out voluminous nether garments on the line and made rude comments to each other in voices calculated to carry well. 'Never knew Fairacre'd got a barrage balloon, did you?' and so on.

To give Mrs Jarman her due, she corrected the children whenever she found them at fault, administering a brisk cuff or letting fly with a vocabulary as lively as their own. But she needed to work long hours charing at various large houses in the neighbourhood, and the children had a good deal of time on their own.

Mrs Pringle brought matters to a head one day by making a formal call next door to complain. She had donned a hat and gloves to add more dignity to the occasion, and registered majestic disapproval from the cherries nodding on her brim to the steel tips on her war-time heels. Mrs Jarman, just home from work, frying chips on an oil stove and enduring the clamour of four hungry children around her, was not in any mood to be conciliatory.

'What did you say to Mrs Pringle?' she demanded of her innocent-eyed offspring.

'Never said nothin',' said Dawreen glibly.

'Never said a word,' quoth the two younger ones, raising limpid blue eyes to their mother.

Mrs Jarman, brandishing a fish slice, turned to the massive figure in the doorway. 'That's your answer,' she said flatly. 'My kids don't tell lies. Take yourself off!'

Mrs Pringle drew in a long outraged breath. 'They not only tell lies, they're rude, pert little monkeys. And if they was mine they'd get a jolly good hiding for it.'

'Say that again!' yelled Mrs Jarman, advancing menacingly, much to the delight of the juvenile onlookers.

Mrs Pringle took a step or two backward, but did not retreat completely. 'Not that they've had any chance,' boomed the lady, 'as anyone with half an eye can see, looking at you. But if I has any more of their old buck, Mrs Jarman, I shall go to the police – and *the Caxley police*, at that!'

Mrs Jarman, eyes blazing, now rushed upon her neighbour and would have dragged the fruit-laden hat – and the hair beneath it – from her adversary's head, but Mrs Pringle, with a dexterity surprising for one of her bulk, nipped smartly down the garden path and put the gate between them. Mrs Jarman's furious shrieks, punctuated by Mrs Pringle's booms, caused several curtains to twitch in neighbouring windows. Mrs Pringle had just managed to shout something about 'East End scum!' above the din, when the four children, who had been watching the fun from the doorstep, screamed in unison: 'Fat's on fire! Mum, the fat's on fire!' and this diversion brought the ladies' immediate hostilities to a close.

From then on, a state of constant warfare existed between Mrs Pringle and the Jarman family. If the children's ball went over the hedge, Mrs Pringle impounded it with smug satisfaction. When Mrs Pringle's tea towel blew off her line into the next door garden, it ended up flying like a flag from the topmost branch of the Jarman's greengage tree, a position for which the gale was not responsible, despite the assurances of the children.

'We can't reach that, Mrs Pringle,' they said with mock regret, and dancing eyes. 'Ain't it a shame? Must have blowed there in the wind, see?'

And there it fluttered, for several weeks, before being ripped to pieces by the elements and an inquisitive pair of jackdaws who used strips for the adornment of their nest.

The two women never let the opportunity of a verbal brush pass, without making full use of it. In a way, each enjoyed the situation. They were well matched. Mrs Jarman might be quicker and more prolific of vocabulary, but Mrs Pringle had a native malice, and an incalculable capacity for taking umbrage, which stood her in good stead. She moved like a tank into battle, heavy, slow and apparently indestructible. But, now and again, a burst of deadly fire came from that implacable front to score a hit upon Mrs Jarman, the resilient sniper.

One Saturday, a jumble sale was arranged in Fairacre. It was to take place, as always, in the village hall, and on the morning of the day in question a few women went there to set up the tables and sort the jumble into the time-honoured categories of Men's, Women's, Children's, Hats and Shoes, and General Junk.

Mrs Pringle set out laden with a large bundle. All was held together with a faded mackintosh, tied securely round the bulk by the sleeves. Mrs Jarman watched her struggle up the road in a high wind before collecting her own parcel and setting forth.

'Don't want to catch up with that old Tartar,' she said to Dawreen, who was dreamily picking at the flaking paint of the mantel shelf. 'And give over that lark, will you?' she added ferociously, giving the girl a swift box on the ear. 'Don't forget,' she continued, as she whirled about the room for her possessions, 'spuds on at eleven, two large whites from the baker, tell the milkman it's six and fourpence and none of his old buck, keep the cat off the custard and expect me when you see me.'

The door slammed behind her and, despite her desire to let Mrs Pringle arrive first, she found herself entering the narrow doorway with her. Mrs Pringle drew aside with marked distaste.

'Don't mind me breathing the same air, I hope?' commented Mrs Jarman tartly, pushing in first. Mrs Pringle maintained an affronted silence.

About half a dozen women were already at work sorting a

mountain of assorted garments on the floor. Back and forth
hurried another two taking the articles to the right table. Mrs
Pringle, by ancient custom, was in charge of 'General Junk'.
Mrs Jarman had never been forgiven for saying on an earlier
occasion, 'It seemed just right, somehow, to see Mrs P. standing by that label!'

Hers was a comparatively simple task. Saucepans, chipped
vases, lidless casseroles, faded pictures, lop-sided toast racks,
stone hot water bottles, riding boots stuffed with beautiful
boxwood trees, archaic lawn mowers, and many unidentifiable
objects found their way to Mrs Pringle's table. Sometimes large
pieces of furniture flanked her counter: wash stands, fire-
guards, sagging wicker armchairs, and dilapidated bamboo
tables. Once there was the ugliest three-piece suite in Chris-
tendom among 'General Junk'. Competition for this had been
fierce, as well I knew, for on that occasion I had been Mrs
Pringle's feeble assistant and had watched her masterly handling of the sale. It had gone eventually for two pounds to Mrs
Fowler of Tyler's Row. She was going to present it to her
mother in Caxley, and I must say I felt the greatest sympathy
for that unsuspecting old lady.

Now Mrs Pringle deposited her mackintosh bundle with the
other clothes and made her way to her stall. Mrs Jarman fell on
her knees with the other sorters and began to work with spirit.

'Lor'!' she cried, holding up a moth-eaten moleskin waist-
coat. 'Who'd buy this stuff? Talk about "Granny's little old
skin rug"! Gives you the creeps, don't it?'

'My husband's,' said one of the helpers shortly. Mrs Jarman
seemed not a whit abashed. She was rummaging in the bundle
which Mrs Pringle had brought, making disparaging comments
on her discoveries, much to the embarrassment of the Fairacre
women who knew full well how important it was to guard
one's tongue on such occasions.

'Look at this,' cried Mrs Jarman, 'three shirts and never a
button among 'em! Who's pinched the buttons, eh?'

Mrs Pringle, wreathed in sea-grass from the unravelling footstool she was carrying, paused by the group and replied loftily. 'I took the trouble to remove those shirt buttons. They'll do for another day.'

'How's that for meanness!' commented Mrs Jarman, winking at the others. 'The poor chap who buys this will have to go about with his shirt flapping, I s'pose.'

'Some people,' began Mrs Pringle, 'knows their duty to their country in war time, and saves every possible penny, not like some I could mention, not a hundred miles from here, as buys pineapple chunks when there's rhubarb in the garden.'

This side-swipe simply had the effect of bringing Mrs Jarman's usual high spirits to bubbling point. Her blue eyes flashed with the joy of battle joined. The onlookers were half-fearful and half-delighted to see Mrs Pringle in combat with such a worthy adversary.

'Well, I never!' crowed Mrs Jarman. 'Ain't we high and mighty? But I wouldn't stoop to pinching shirt buttons and then giving the rest to the jumble. About as low as you can get, I reckon.'

'It's nothing short of *patriotism*, I tells you,' boomed Mrs Pringle, her neck flushing an ugly red. ' "Save all you can!" they keeps telling us. Well, I'm saving shirt buttons!'

She marched heavily towards her stall somewhat impeded by the strands of sea-grass trailing behind her. Mrs Jarman let out a peal of derisive laughter, and continued with the sorting. But she did not forget Mrs Pringle's last remark.

The jumble sale itself passed off without further incident between the two antagonists. In fact, Mrs Jarman covered herself with glory at the men's stall by her shrewd bargaining with customers. Her clients were kept in spasms of laughter by her barrage of raillery and Cockney patter. At the end of the sale it was discovered that her stall had taken by far the largest amount, and it was generally acknowledged that Mrs Jarman's cheeky approach to the customers was the reason.

'Not much good living near the Caledonian Market all your life, if you can't pick up a few tips!' was Mrs Jarman's reply to those who congratulated her. Needless to say, Mrs Pringle was not among them.

Some months after the sale, at the beginning of November, the good ladies of Fairacre Women's Institute decided to make their Christmas puddings together. They worked out that the whole process would be much cheaper if they made the mixture in one batch and cooked all the puddings in the large electric copper.

The recipe, cut from a daily paper, made grisly reading to those used to the normal ingredients of pre-war puddings. No brandy, stout, fresh eggs or butter appeared in the 1943 recipe. Instead, such dreadful items as grated carrot, margarine, dried-egg powder and – the final touch of horror – 'a tablespoonful of gravy browning to enrich the colour', figured on the depressing list of ingredients. But times were hard, and years of privation had blunted the sensibilities of even the most fastidious. With much cheerfulness, the ladies set about their preparations for making 'An Economical and Nutritious War-Time Christmas Pudding'.

Dozens of pudding basins, each bearing their owner's name on adhesive tape stuck on the base, waited on the long tables. Little paper bags bearing treasured ounces of currants and sultanas, mixed spices, breadcrumbs and two precious fresh lemons, jostled each other near the enormous yellow mixing bowl from the Vicarage. By ten o'clock, the ingredients were being stirred zealously by half a dozen helpers, most of them elderly women, for the majority were doing war work of some sort or other. Mrs Willet busily greased the basins with carefully-hoarded margarine papers, listening to the chatter about her.

'We'll set the copper to *Very Slow*,' said the vicar's wife, 'and then it should be perfectly safe until tea time.

Mrs Willet's staying until eleven-thirty, to make sure it's simmering properly and then the rota begins.'

It had been arranged that one or other of the WI members should look in every hour to see that all was well, and to top up the water in the copper if it was getting too low. Christmas puddings were too precious to be left entirely to themselves for such a length of time.

By eleven, the puddings were ready for immersion. Every household in Fairacre had one, and some had two or three, standing in the water. This was the Women's Institute's practical help towards Christmas, and very well planned the organization had been.

'Here's Mrs Pringle's,' said Mrs Willet, bearing a stout two-pounder to the copper. She peered underneath the basin to read the big black capitals on the tape, before letting it down gently beside the others.

'Then that's the last,' said the vicar's wife thankfully. 'Just time to have a cup of tea before we knock off.'

It was very quiet when they had gone. Mrs Willet took out her knitting and sat by the humming copper. The clock said twenty past eleven and she had promised to stay until half past. As she knitted, she read the list of names pinned on the wall by the copper. During the afternoon she saw that Mrs Pringle and Mrs Jarman were due to call in. Both worked in the mornings and had been unable to stir their own puddings this year.

'2.30 – Mrs Pringle'

'3.30 – Miss Parr' – only that would be her maid, Mrs Willet surmised, and

'4.30 – Mrs Jarman' – who would no doubt rush back to her family in time to fry the inevitable chips on which that ebullient household seemed to exist.

'5.30 – Anyone welcome.' This was when the puddings would be lifted out and handed to their lucky owners. Mrs Willet had promised to help with this chore.

At twenty-five to twelve she lifted the lid, noted with relief that the water was bubbling gently, checked all the switches, wrote a note to the next pudding-minder saying:

'25 to 12. Everything all right.
Alice Willet.'

and made her way back through the village.

At five-thirty a throng of women crowded the steamy hall collecting their basins and lodging them in shopping baskets, string bags or the baskets on the front of their bicycles.

'Got the right one?' called Mrs Jarman to Mrs Pringle, as she watched that lady peering under the basins for her name. 'Bet you've got more fruit in yours than the rest of us!'

Mrs Pringle sniffed and ignored the quip. Depositing her pudding in the black depths of her oilcloth shopping bag, she passed majestically from the hall without deigning to reply.

The fantastic sequel to the pudding-making session might never have been known to Fairacre but for an unusually generous gesture of Mrs Pringle's.

As Christmas Day approached she heard that a large party of the Jarmans' friends were proposing to spend the day next door.

'My heart fair bleeds for poor Jane Morgan,' said Mrs Pringle lugubriously to her son John. 'She'll be crowded out of house and home, as far as I can see, I've a good mind to invite her round here for Christmas dinner.'

Neither Corporal Pringle nor Private Morgan were to be given Christmas leave. Mrs Pringle's sister and a schoolgirl niece, much the same age as John, were coming from Caxley for the day, and as the sister and Jane Morgan knew each other well it seemed a good idea to ask their neighbour to join the party. Jane Morgan was gratefully surprised, and accepted.

The pudding simmered all the morning, and most delightful aromas crept about the kitchen, for there was a duck roasting in the oven as well as the 'nutritious war-time' delicacy on top of the hob. Mrs Pringle and her sister had a good gossip, their children played amicably with their new presents, and except for the ear-splitting racket occasioned by the crowd next door, the benevolent spirit of Christmas hung over all. At twelve-thirty Jane Morgan appeared, thankful to be out of her noisy home, and they all sat down to dinner.

The duck was excellent. The pudding looked wonderful. Mrs Pringle plunged a knife into its gravy-darkened top and cut the first slice.

'Mum!' squeaked John excitedly. 'There's something shining!'

'Sh!' said his aunt. 'Don't give the game away! Perhaps it's a sixpence.'

Mrs Pringle looked puzzled.

'No sixpences in this pudding!' she said. 'In any case, I don't hold with metal objects in food. I always wraps up anything like that in a morsel of greaseproof.'

She put the first slice on a plate for Mrs Morgan. There was certainly a suspicious chinking sound as the pudding met the china surface.

'When I was little,' said Jane Morgan, 'we used to have dear little china dolls in our Christmas pudding. No bigger than an inch, they were! With shiny black heads. We used to put them in the dolls' house, I remember.'

But Jane Morgan's reminiscences were being ignored, for all eyes were on the pudding. There was no doubt about it, there were a great many shiny foreign objects among the other war-time ingredients. Mrs Pringle's breathing became more stertorous as the slices were cut. She sat down heavily in front of the last plate, her own, and then spoke.

'Just pick it over before you take a mouthful. I reckons someone's been playing tricks on us.'

Spoons and forks twitched the glutinous mass back and forth, amongst amazed cries from the assembled company.

When they came to count up the foreign objects they found no fewer than two dozen mother o' pearl shirt buttons.

Mrs Pringle said not a word, but opened a tin of pineapple chunks instead.

Late that night, when the Jarmans' company had roared away and the children had been chased to bed, Mrs Jarman met her landlady in the communal kitchen. Jane Morgan was in her husband's dressing gown, her wispy hair was in a small pigtail, and her teeth had been left upstairs in a glass of water. She was busy filling a hot water bottle.

'Had a good time?' asked Mrs Jarman boisterously. 'We have. Never laughed so much since I came here.'

'That'th nithe!' said Mrs Morgan politely. 'Yeth, I enjoyed it next door, but there wath thomething wrong with the Chrithtmath pudding.'

Mrs Jarman drew in her breath sharply. 'What was up with it?' she inquired.

'It wath abtholutely thruffed with thirt buttonth,' said Mrs Morgan, wide-eyed. 'Mithith Pringle wath dumbfounded.'

'Shirt buttons! echoed Mrs Jarman. She broke into peals of noisy laughter. 'Ah well,' she gasped, through her spasms, 'that should please the old trout! She told me once that she saved shirt buttons!'

Still laughing, she made her way upstairs, followed by her mystified landlady.

Mrs Willet straightened herself and patted my garden gate.

'Well, Miss Read, that's the story. Of course, it was all over Fairacre before Boxing Day sunset. Jane Morgan let it out, in all innocence, and the village was fair humming with the news.'

'Did Mrs Jarman ever admit it?' I asked.

'Never! Swore she never knew a thing about it, but it was her all right. I should know – I remember the pudding list. "2.30 Mrs Pringle". It wouldn't be her, obviously. "3.30 Miss Parr". That was her Annie that popped in then, as law-abiding as they come, and wouldn't dream of doing such a thing. "4.30 *Mrs Jarman*". And "5.30 All welcome." Don't need much working out, when you come to think of it.'

She bent to pick up her basket, and stroked Tibby affectionately. 'I will say though,' she continued, 'that Mrs Pringle minded her manners a bit more after that, when she and Mrs Jarman got together. Ah, she was real mischieful, was Mrs Jarman. You couldn't help liking her.'

Mrs Willet gazed, with unseeing eyes, down the Fairacre lane, her mind on times long past.

'I still miss them, you know, them Londoners. I liked 'em – and always shall. It was good to see them again this afternoon. Took me back to the old days. Say what you like about 'em, Miss Read, Londoners are a larky lot! A real larky lot!'

9. OUTLOOK UNSETTLED

As so often happens when term begins, the weather became idyllic. Great white clouds sailed indolently across pellucid blue skies, and warm winds from the south replaced the sneaky little easterly one which had harassed us throughout most of the Easter holidays.

One warm afternoon, in late April, we propped open the door of the schoolroom with an upturned flowerpot and did our best to turn our attention to learning Robert Bridges' poem 'Spring Goeth All In White'. It seemed an admirable choice in the circumstances, for white narcissi spilt their heady fragrance from the window sill, white daisies, gathered by the children, filled three paste pots on my desk, and an early cabbage white butterfly opened and shut its wings against the south-facing Gothic window.

Nevertheless, it was uphill work. Languor, born of unaccustomed heat, engulfed my class. Shirt necks were opened, sleeves rolled up, jerseys peeled off and stuffed in desks, and the sing-song country voices stumbled heavily through this most tripping of spring lyrics.

Sleepiest of all was young Richard, not yet five, who was spending the day with us while his mother paid a necessary visit to the hospital in our county town. It is not easy to get someone to mind a child in a small village, and I often get urgent requests asking me 'if our youngest can come along with his brother for an hour or two'. If it is possible – and it usually is – we all enjoy the newcomer's company, and it gives him an insight into school routine before he takes the plunge himself later on.

Richard lolled on the desk beside his brother Ernest, who nudged him occasionally and whispered severely to him, with no noticeable result. As we battled on, Richard amused himself by blowing large glassy bubbles from lips as red and puckered as a poppy petal. Ernest, scandalized, bent down to remonstrate.

'Leave him alone, Ernest,' I said mildly. 'He's tired. Perhaps he'll fall asleep.'

'In school?' cried Ernest, deeply shocked.

'Why not?'

Ernest, still looking affronted by my slackness, drew himself up, folded his arms and applied himself sternly to the task before him, ignoring the indolent and shameful child beside him.

Everywhere in the room were emblems of spring. The weather chart for April showed a number of umbrellas, depicting the rainy weather during the holidays, with arrows pointing fairly consistently to the north-east. But a row of triumphant suns, like yellow daisies, blossomed in the last six or seven squares, and the arrows were now happily reversed.

Across the back of the room ran a frieze of spring flowers. Crocuses, daffodils, tulips, and a large number of new species, as yet unknown to Messrs Sutton and Carter, had been cut out of gummed paper and affixed by every hand in the class. Many a fat thumb went home in the afternoon bearing an indented ring round it made by hard-worked school scissors. It was, as the seed catalogues say, 'a riot of bloom' and a very colourful addition to our dull walls.

A new spring poster to encourage savings, showing a bird and its nest, brightened the door between the two classrooms, and the nature table was laden with wood anemones, primroses, violets, sprays of young honeysuckle leaves, a few early coltsfoot and dandelions, and a splendid pot of horse chestnut twigs thrusting out green hands in all directions.

Hard by, the glass fish tank glimmered with shiny frogs' spawn, for all the world like submerged chain-mail. The tiny dots were already beginning to turn into commas, and before long the children's patience would be rewarded by the sight of a myriad thrashing tadpoles. Nothing could be more suitable, I told myself again, than 'Spring Goeth All In White' for such an afternoon.

But, there was no doubt about it, those eight exquisite lines were really more than the children could manage in the circumstances. I felt impatient and cross at their laziness, but was loth to spoil the poem for them by bad-tempered bludgeoning.

In the midst of this impasse, young Richard raised himself, stretched short arms each side of his rumpled head, and said clearly: 'Let's go out!'

There was a shocked silence. The sound of a bee droning up and down the open door could be heard distinctly as the children waited to see what my reaction would be. Sometimes a remark like this will make me fly clean off the handle, and they shivered with apprehension. Ernest's face was scarlet at the effrontery of his young brother.

I looked at the expectant children. 'What about it? Shall we?' I asked.

There was a rapturous roar of agreement, and a general stampede to the lobby.

The air outside was wonderful, heady and honeyed with hundreds of unseen flowers. The elm trees at the corner of the playground were rosy with buds, and noisy with rooks at their building.

We straggled down the village street between the beds of velvety polyanthus and the neat kitchen gardens striped with vegetable seedlings. Birds flashed across our path, dogs panted on cottage doorsteps and a cuckoo's call see-sawed across the afternoon.

All this, of course, was what had held my class in thrall – the compelling imperious spell of spring. Of what use were the frieze, the crayoned sun, the poster, the laden nature table and the captive frogs' spawn? They were but substitutes for the real thing that exploded all around them. It was the babe among us, young Richard, still in touch with the vital stuff of living, who had led us unerringly to reality.

We made our way slowly up the sunny slopes of the downs before throwing ourselves down on the dry springy turf in order to revel to the full in the glory of a warm spring day. Below us spread the village like some pictorial map. The trees were misted with young leaves, and here and there a flurry of white blossom lit up a garden. I thought of our poem left neglected, but felt no regret. Let us savour this now, and then come to Robert Bridges' poem, 'recollecting it in tranquillity', was my feeling.

A row or two of flapping washing caught the eye, and a herd of black and white Friesians, belonging to Mr Roberts, looked like toys as they grazed peacefully in the field next to the school. I gazed at it all with particular interest this afternoon, for I had a problem on my mind. Would it, I wondered, be a good thing to leave Fairacre?

I suppose that most people feel unsettled in the early spring. There must be something in the rising of the sap and the general urgency of the season that makes us long for change and movement. I read the 'Appointments Vacant' at the end of *The Times Educational Supplement* with unusual fervour during March and April, and usually find that this pastime calms the fever in my blood. What about this job in Sicily, I ask myself? Would I really be able to 'TEACH ENGLISH by Direct Method'? Come to think of it, are *any* of my teaching methods direct? Is the teaching of 'Spring Goeth All In White' direct, when one abandons the task to scramble up the springy turf of the downs, for instance?

There is a wonderful post offered in Barbados and another in New Zealand, and several in Dar-Es-Salaam (I only consider those in a warm climate, you notice) but, alas, I am not a communicant member of the Presbyterian Church, nor am I qualified to teach practical brickwork or plumbing. I browse among these delights over my cup of tea, when the children of Fairacre have run home and only the voice of Mrs Pringle, at her after-school cleaning, is heard in the land. After half an hour or so of this mental dallying, I rouse myself, take stock of my nice little school house, the fun I have in Fairacre, and decide I am better off where I am. In any case, the thought of filling up forms and asking people to give references for me, if need be, is enough to dissuade me from any serious application, as a rule. By the end of April my spring fever has usually abated. Fairacre looks more seductive than ever. I find, surprisingly, that I am in love with all the children, and even look upon Mrs Pringle with an indulgent eye. Such is the power of warm weather.

But this year my feelings were stronger. If I really wanted promotion, as headmistress of a larger school, then it was time I stirred myself before I became too decrepit to be considered at all. As Amy, my old college friend, frequently tells me, and reiterated with considerable force the other evening when I mentioned a particular post I had seen advertised, I have been in Fairacre long enough. It might be better for the school, as well as for me, to have a change.

The job which had caught my eye was the headship of a junior and infants' school in south Devon. I knew the little town fairly well from visiting it at holiday times, and because I had friends in the neighbourhood. It was a market town, rather smaller than Caxley, about five miles from the coast, and situated away from the main roads which were so busy in summer time.

I remembered the school particularly. It was a pleasant old building, with a new wing recently added, and an attractive school house adjoining it. A peach tree spread its branches fanwise over its front wall, which faced south, and at the back there was a sheltered walled garden with some fine fruit trees and lawns. One could be very happy indeed there, I had no doubt, and when my friends wrote to tell me of the vacancy and to urge me to apply for it, I fell to thinking seriously of the matter.

The biggest attraction to me was the climate. Fairacre can be bitterly cold in the winter, and the number of gnarled rheumaticky old people in our midst constitutes an awful warning to those with a tendency to rheumatism and its allied diseases. Apart from an occasional bout of influenza I didn't ail at all, but the last winter or two I had been having twinges of rheumatism which I did not like to think of as simply old age. Fairacre School, too, was renowned for its draughts and the inefficiency of its heating system, and latterly I had come to dread the winter months with their fierce blast of winter air from the skylight above my desk, concentrated on the nape of my neck, and the particularly spiteful draught that hit one round the ankles and came from the icy wastes of the outside lobby.

It would be good to work in a snug building tucked into the side of a hill, and with most of its windows facing south. The very thought of that soft mild air made me feel hopeful. I read my friend's advice. I read the advertisement a dozen times. I looked out of my school house window – it was a blustery April evening with a spatter of hail now and again – and I bravely sent for the application forms.

That had been a week ago. The forms awaited my attention still, propped behind the coffee-pot on the dresser, my usual filing place. I must get them off this week if I really intended to apply. I looked again at Fairacre, spread below me, and sighed at the difficulties of making up one's mind.

'You got the belly-ache?' asked Joseph Coggs solicitously, sitting down beside me.

'No, no,' I assured him. 'I was just thinking how pretty the village looked from here.'

A few more children left their pursuits to join us.

'It's the prettiest place in England,' declared Ernest stoutly.

''Sright!' echoed young Richard loyally.

'My auntie,' said John, 'lives at Winchelsea and she says *that's* the prettiest place.'

'Maybe she don't know Fairacre,' suggested someone reasonably. 'What's it like anyway – this ol' Winklesea?'

'*Winchelsea*!' replied John, nettled. 'Well, it's a funny place, because it used to be right by the seaside and now there's a whole lot of flat fields between the town and the sea.'

> 'Below the down the stranded town
> What may betide forlornly waits,'

I quoted, with what I thought was rather a beautiful inflection.

John looked startled. 'I dunno about that, but that's what my auntie told me. She said the sea was right up to the town once.'

'Likely, ain't it?' said Joseph Coggs scornfully. I rose to my feet. I was glad to have some interruption to my thoughts, and it was time we were getting back.

'I'll get the map out when we are in school,' I promised them, 'and you shall see for yourselves. First one to reach the lane has a sweet! Off you go!'

Shrieking and squeaking, they tumbled down the steep slope of the grassy hill leaving me to descend more circumspectly behind them.

In the lane, where the rough track ends and the tarmac begins, Dr Martin's car waited outside Laburnum Villas. As I approached the vociferous mob awaiting me – each claiming that he had arrived first – the doctor came out of one of the ugly pair of houses and watched, with some amusement, as I quelled the riot.

'Playing truant?' he asked.

I said we were.

'Very sensible too. We none of us get enough fresh air these days. When I first came to Fairacre it was lack of decent food which gave me most of my patients. Now it's too much food, and not enough air and exercise.'

He climbed into his car with a grunt of exertion, then leant from the window and laughed. 'I need more myself,' he said. 'How's my old friend Mrs Pringle? Still suffering with her leg?'

'When it suits her,' I replied. There are no secrets to hide from Dr Martin. He has known us all in Fairacre much too long to be hoodwinked. Forty or fifty years, I thought suddenly, Dr Martin has lived and worked in Fairacre! I had a sudden desire to ask him if he had ever felt like moving, but restrained myself.

'Are you feeling quite fit?' he asked, an observant eye cocked quizzically upon me.

'Yes, thank you,' I said hastily. 'Just thinking about something, that's all.'

'You look a trifle pale to me,' said the doctor, twinkling. 'Is it love?'

'No, indeed!' I said, with spirit. 'I'm too old for such capers. More likely to be advancing senility. I'm beginning to suspect that rheumatism's trying to infiltrate my old bones.'

'You aren't the only one in Fairacre,' said the doctor, starting his car. 'Let me know if it gets any worse, that's all. We get such plaguey cold winters here, that's the trouble.'

He waved cheerfully and drove off, hooting to shoo my children to the side of the narrow lane.

The memory of that south-facing Devon school returned to me with overwhelming intensity, as I made my way back to Fairacre School amongst my clamorous pupils.

'Can I get it out now?' asked John as we clanged across the door-scraper.

'Get what out?' I asked bemused.

'Why, the map! You said as you was going to show us Winchelsea, and all that!' He sounded aggrieved. I pulled myself together, and approached the map cupboard.

It is called the map cupboard, and does indeed house the maps, but that is not all. Somehow, everything that has no proper home gets thrown in the map cupboard. There are cricket stumps, old tennis shoes, a pile of china paint palettes which have not been used for years, some dilapidated *Rainbow Annuals* adored by the children during wet dinner hours, part of a train set, a large tin full of assorted pieces of Meccano, and a rusty hurricane lamp which, we tell each other, 'might come in handy'.

The maps jostle together in one corner, and ever since I came to Fairacre I have meant to label them properly and hang them in some sort of order. In practice, I go through *Muscles of the Human Body*, *The Disposition of the Tribes of Israel*, *The Resuscitation of those Suffering from Electrocution*, the tonic sol-fa modulator and a number of maps, ranging from Greenland's icy mountains to India's coral strand, until I find the one I am searching for.

This afternoon was no exception. At length, however, the map of the British Isles was hung over the blackboard and I began my lesson on coastal erosion. Refreshed by their outing the children gave me quite flattering attention.

John bustled out to the map, full of importance, and pointed to Romney Marsh with his yellow ruler, and I did my best to explain the cause of the sea's retreat here. There are times when I wish fervently that I had more geographical knowledge. This was one of them. Mercifully, the children seemed to understand my halting explanations, and I was fired to go further.

'Sometimes,' I said, 'the opposite thing happens. The sea encroaches on the land, and then the bottom of the cliffs gets washed away.' I remembered childhood holidays at Walton-on-Naze, and gave a dramatic account of a garden, and then, finally, the house belonging to it, sliding down the cliffs into the hungry sea. Perhaps I overdid the drama. There was an awed silence when I finished.

John raised his ruler and put it shakily across the Wash. 'It's eaten in there all right,' he commented.

Patrick and Ernest now walked out, unbidden, to take a closer look at the map.

'Look how it's busted its way up here!' exclaimed Patrick, his eyes on the Bristol Channel.

'And here!' echoed Ernest, peering closely at the Thames estuary. 'Looks as though they could meet, real easy, and chop us in half.'

'How quick,' asked Joseph Coggs nervously, 'do the water come?'

'You remember at Barrisford!' queried John. 'It came in as quick as lightning, and terrible strong it was. Fair sucked us off our feet when we was paddlin' and I got my best trousers absolutely soppin'.'

I did my best to calm their fears. If I weren't careful, I could see that I should have some very cross parents coming to see me on the morrow, complaining that their children had been having nightmares.

'Good heavens,' I said robustly, 'it only manages a few inches in a year, at the most. You've nothing to fear here, living in Fairacre. Why, we're safely in the middle,' I assured them, appropriating John's ruler, and pointing out *Caxley* printed in unflatteringly small letters.

These downland children see very little water, and the sea but rarely. There is a very healthy respect for it when they visit the coast, and their apprehension about inundation was understandable. Even today, some of their grandparents have never seen the sea.

St Patrick's chimes began to ring out through the warm limpid afternoon.

'Time to go home,' I said. 'Don't forget, there are miles of dry land between you and the sea, here in Fairacre. Stand for grace!'

Within five minutes the classroom was empty. I returned the

map to the shameful cupboard and made my way across the hot playground. To my surprise, Joseph Coggs was swinging on the school gate. His face was thoughtful, his dark eyes fixed upon the horizon.

'What are you doing?' I asked.

He nodded towards the vast bulk of the downs, quivering in a blue haze of heat. 'I was thinking,' he said huskily, in his hoarse gipsy croak, 'it'd take a tidy long time for the sea to get through all that lot, wouldn't it, miss?'

'It would,' I agreed.

He sighed with relief, clambered down from the gate, and set off along the sunny lane towards his home.

The long envelope, containing the application form, was horribly noticeable, sticking out from behind the coffee pot. I resolved to tackle it later that evening, but first of all I made some tea.

Mr Willet was busy at the bottom of my garden, erecting a fine row of bean poles. He cannot bear to see a few yards of untilled soil, and had insisted on turning a miniature jungle of old gooseberry bushes, draped in dead grass, into a flourishing vegetable patch. The fact that I should never be able to consume a quarter of the crops he was so generously planting did not seem to occur to him, and I was too touched by his kindness to point it out.

I took two hefty blue and white striped mugs of tea down the garden path. Balanced on top of one was a plate bearing a large hunk of fruit cake for my gardener. The heat shimmered everywhere, and some of the polyanthuses were wilting slightly already. My spirits rose at the thought of a possible fine spell.

'Well now, that do be real welcome,' said Mr Willet, grasping the mug in a mud-caked hand. He upturned a wooden box and motioned me politely towards it. I sat down, with a sigh, and let the sunshine soak into my bones. Little rainbows played round my half-shut eyes. This was the weather! They probably had it like this all the time in Devon, I thought.

The sound of steady champing told me that Mr Willet had found the cake.

'You makes a very good fruit cake,' he said indistinctly. 'Moist without being too heavy. And got your cherries well spaced. Takes a bit of doing that. My wife has a rare job with cherries. Flours 'em, or summat, to keep 'em up. You done real well with this, miss.'

I wished I deserved his compliments but truth will out, so I replied dreamily, my eyes still closed, 'Marks and Spencer's!'

'Is that so?' said Mr Willet. 'Well, they does a good job then.'

There was silence except for the sound of mastication and the birds' singing around us.

'You feeling all right?' asked Mr Willet. 'You looks a bit peaky to me, and you ain't drinking your tea!'

I sat up hastily. He was the third person this afternoon to comment on my frail looks. 'I'm fine,' I assured him.

'Don't look yourself to me,' persisted Mr Willet. 'Got a sort of bilious look. You ever had the jaundice?'

'I probably need a change,' I said briskly. 'When we get some sunshine I begin to realize what I've been missing. Perhaps I'd better take a job in France or Italy,' I added lightly.

Mr Willet looked concerned. 'Don't you go flinging off to no foreign parts now!' he warned me. 'Full of mosquitoes and malaria, they tells me, and not a decent drop of water to drink, even if it do come out of a tap. And the food's a proper mess – oily and that – wouldn't do your biliousness any good, you can take my word for it!'

At this moment, Mrs Pringle appeared at the side of the house, and bore down upon us in all her black-clothed majesty. Her oilcloth bag swung upon her arm, and from it poked a corner of the flowered cretonne overall in which she performs her cleaning duties. Obviously, these were now ended and she was on her way homeward.

'Cup of tea?' I asked.

Mrs Pringle shook her head magisterially. 'I never drinks between meals,' she said. 'And I shall be dishing up our high tea in an hour's time.'

Mr Willet whipped a sack from the wheelbarrow and spread it, with a Raleigh-like flourish, on the grass. Mrs Pringle lowered her bulk cautiously upon it, and smiled graciously.

'Ah! Nice to have a set-down! Sometimes I wonder if this cleanin' job's too much for me.'

I wondered what was coming.

'Well, not so much the *cleaning*,' continued Mrs Pringle heavily, 'as the *danger*!'

This was mystifying, but was obviously leading to a grievance.

'Sweeping, I expect. Scrubbing, I expect. A certain amount of back-breaking bending and lifting, I expect,' said Mrs Pringle, rising to heights of rhythmic peroration which made me suspect Welsh blood somewhere among her forebears. 'But *when*,' continued the lady, turning and fixing me with a glittering eye, 'I gets hit over the head through other people's carelessness, then I thinks it's time to *complain*.'

I was about to speak, but was overborne by Mrs Pringle in full spate. Mr Willet and I exchanged martyred looks, and resigned ourselves to more.

'I don't say a word about slatternly goings-on, in the ordinary way. Some are born sluts, no matter how much schooling they've had, and if they cares to muddle along with dust under their beds and the same saucepan for soup as milk, not to mention a bread crock with mildewed crumbs in the cracks, then all I says is: "Well, let them wallow in their muck", and be forbearing. But when those slatternly ways bring damage to *others*, then plain speaking has to be done!'

'Cough it up then,' I said inelegantly. I could recognize the wallower-in-muck all right. 'What hit you?'

'Nelson's Column, by the sound of it,' commented Mr Willet, unimpressed. He dusted some grass from his corduroy trousers, and began to resume his tasks.

'I was sweeping gentle-like by the map cupboard,' said Mrs Pringle with dignity, 'when the broom knocked against the door. It flew open –' here Mrs Pringle flung her arms dramatically apart – 'it flew open, I says, and down crashed a good dozen maps. Gave me a cruel blow on the side of the head – most dangerous place, that is, near the temple!'

'I'm sorry,' I said. 'That catch isn't very reliable.'

'If the maps was hung up properly,' continued Mrs Pringle severely, 'as they always was in Mr Hope's time – and after – we shouldn't get accidents like this. Might have had Concussion. Might have been Disabled. Might have been Laid Out!' intoned Mrs Pringle.

'Pity you weren't,' said Mr Willet shortly. I looked away hastily.

'You're quite right,' I said nobly to the old harridan, 'I really must tidy that cupboard. Do you want something put on your head? Witch hazel, perhaps?'

'Very suitable,' muttered Mr Willet, who was beginning to enjoy himself.

Mrs Pringle gave him a cold glance. 'Nothing, thank you,' replied the lady, with crushing dignity. 'I shall let Nature take its course.'

She began the herculean task of getting to her feet, swaying backwards and forwards and breathing heavily. I put both arms round one of hers and gave a mighty heave. Suddenly, she was erect, red in the face, but triumphant.

'Thank you, Miss Read,' she puffed.

'Here, you don't want to lift great weights like that!' cried Mr Willet, who had only just seen this manoeuvre. 'And you not very well!'

Mrs Pringle looked at me suspiciously. 'Not well?' she echoed truculently.

'I'm perfectly well,' I said.

Mr Willet, no doubt seeing a means of paying out his old enemy, shook his head vehemently. 'She's just been talking about having a change. Can't blame her, either, with folks like you to plague her!'

'A change does us all good,' conceded Mrs Pringle. She looked at me warily as though remembering something. 'As long as it don't last too long. I wouldn't think about a *permanent* change, if I was you. Taking it all in all, you could jump from the frying pan into the fire, and Fairacre ain't a bad place, when all's said and done.' She fished inside her oilcloth bag and produced a brown paper one. 'Six eggs,' said Mrs Pringle, thrusting them upon me. 'I brought 'em up when I come, expecting you'd still be in school, but seems you packed up before time today. Good job the Office don't know what goes on!'

'It's very good of you,' I said, with sincerity. 'Especially after your accident.'

Mrs Pringle grunted and set off up the garden path.

'I'll do my best to put these away tidily,' I promised, patting the paper bag.

'Hm!' commented Mrs Pringle, with one hand on the latch of the gate, 'there's some – no matter how much schooling they've had – what never learns!'

Triumphant as ever, she continued on her way.

Back in the solitude of my house I found myself putting off the task of filling in the application form. I sorted the laundry, cleaned the dining-room windows, shown up in all their squalor by the bright sunshine, and generally fiddled about in a procrastinating mood.

Should I apply or not? Now that the sun shone again, I began to shilly-shally. I remembered the peaceful view from the top of the downs. Mrs Pringle was right when she said that Fairacre took some beating. She seemed to know an astonishing amount about my present proposals, I thought, remembering her advice about making a change. There was little doubt, in my mind, that the lady had been snooping at the contents of the long envelope in the course of her dusting. I had suspected this before. Looking at it in one way, I mused, it was really rather flattering that she advised me to stay. Perhaps she enjoyed my slatternly ways after all!

I paused in my window-cleaning and gazed at Tibby basking on the top of the rainwater butt, one of his favourite spots. How would he react to a move, I wondered?

The chances of getting the job were one in a hundred, I well knew. There would be a host of applicants for such a tempting post, and a house with it meant that there would be double the number, at least. Why not send in my application form, and let the gods decide? After all, if I were lucky enough to be called up for interview, I could make up my mind then.

I groaned in turmoil of spirit. How truly dreadful it is to have to make a decision! No, I was sure that I could not leave this to the gods. This was something I must settle for myself, here and now. Either I applied because I really wanted the post, or I would decide to stay on in Fairacre. Having got thus far, I went over the reasons for and against, all over again. It was a wearing business.

I should simply hate to leave the Fairacre children and all the friends in the village. There would be more children, and friends, in Devon, I answered myself. And this little house is extremely attractive! The Devon one is even better, said my second self. I should be leaving a job which I knew I could manage fairly competently. All the more reason for trying something more ambitious, commented my nagging half.

Perhaps this was the secret. Perhaps I should be more adventurous, stretch myself a little, climb out of my rut. I was too fond of clinging to the present, to the things I knew, the friends about me. Amy was possibly right to urge me to make a change. Fairacre was not the only place in the world. It was time I uprooted myself.

Now or never! I took out the application form from the envelope and spread it on the table. I must say it looked rather daunting. I whipped out my fountain pen before I weakened again, and at that moment the telephone bell rang.

It was Amy. I was glad to hear her voice. Now I should get some much-needed moral support, I felt sure.

'I'm just filling in that application form,' I told her, rather proudly, after the first civilities were over.

'Only just?' asked Amy. She sounded incredulous.

'It doesn't have to be in for a few days yet,' I answered defensively.

'But you've had it there over a week,' answered Amy severely. 'I quite thought it had been sent off long ago.'

I began to feel rather hurt. 'I had to think about it,' I said, in an injured tone.

'Stuff and nonsense!' snorted Amy. 'We worked it all out together last week. In any case, it is your move that I've rung up about.'

'What do you mean – my move?' I asked. 'Aren't you counting my chickens for me rather prematurely?'

Amy brushed my tartness aside. 'I met Lucy Colgate at a party yesterday,' she said, 'and told her about your plans. She's interested in Fairacre School, and I'm pretty sure she'll apply when you leave.'

Lucy Colgate! I was speechless. As if it wasn't bad enough to have Amy busying herself about my affairs, and bullying me into action, without adding the insult of Lucy Colgate. She had been at college with Amy and me, and try as I might – and I must admit I did not try very hard – I could not take to her. I found her domineering, utterly self-centred, and

painfully affected. No doubt she considered me equally unpleasant. In any case, we met as little as possible, but Amy kept
in touch.

The very thought of Lucy teaching in my school and living
in my house was enough to make me bristle.

'Amy,' I said firmly, 'you take too much upon yourself. At
times like this you strain the bonds of friendship to snapping
point.'

'Are you trying to tell me that you are *still* trying to make up your mind?' demanded Amy shrilly.

'No!' I said grimly. 'It's made up now!' And I slammed down the receiver.

Lucy Colgate, I fumed, pacing round the dining-room table. Lucy Colgate living in this house! I could well imagine its transformation, tricked out with the frilly lampshades, Regency stripes and Redouté roses beloved by my old fellow student. As for Mr Willet's vegetable patch, that would be turned into a lawn, sprouting a cretonne garden umbrella with gold fringe, before the first term was over!

The idea of Lucy Colgate queening it in my little school was even more distasteful. Fancy leaving Patrick and Ernest, and Joseph, and Linda – all the adorable and maddening hustle of them, in fact – to the mercies of Lucy! It simply could not be done.

I had a sudden vision of Mrs Pringle's face. How would the two get on?

'The meeting of the dinosaurs,' I told myself, with some relish, my fury beginning to abate. 'What a battle that would be!' I could see Lucy facing Mrs Pringle over the tortoise stoves. Lucy spilling coke, and as yet ignorant of the consequences. Lucy would face many a hazard if she ever found herself in Fairacre School. Why, with any luck, I thought suddenly, the map cupboard door might burst open again and project the contents painfully upon her!

At this uncharitable flight of fancy, I began to laugh. Lucy Colgate and Amy could connive until they were blue in the face! My mind was now made up. I advanced upon the unsullied form.

I hesitated for one moment. This news of Lucy was not the main reason for my decision. It was simply the final straw which weighted the scale in favour of staying. It had made me realize, with devastating clarity, how much Fairacre really meant to me. For that I should be grateful to Lucy always.

With infinite joy, I began to tear the application form into small pieces. Then – slattern to the last – I flung them in the direction of the waste paper basket, unmindful of whether they went in or not. I felt wonderful.

I bounded into the sunlit garden – *my* garden – and positively skipped down the path. As I passed the water butt I let out a joyous shout to the sleeping cat.

'Fairacre for ever!'

For two pins I would have run up the school's Union Jack.

10. The Wayfarer

Strangers are rare birds in the village of Fairacre and cause us as much interest as any hoopoes. We have our annual migrants, of course, and are always eager to see them each year, but they are only half-strangers.

These half-strangers come mainly in the summer. One really can't blame them. Winter comes with a vengeance here, with great roaring winds, cruel frosts and plenty of snow. As most of the visitors are townsfolk, they wisely remain where pavements, buses, indoor entertainment and central heating are available during the worst of the weather. But once spring begins, Mr Lamb, at the Post Office, recognizes the handwriting of friends and relatives of Fairacre natives and looks at the postmarks of London, Birmingham, Bristol and Leeds, and nods his head wisely.

'Asking to come again, no doubt,' he surmises. And, usually, he is right.

As well as these people, we look forward to seeing half a dozen or so regular tradesmen. In May, a small flat cart pulled by an ancient donkey appears in Fairacre. On board are dozens of boxes of seedlings. Alyssum and lobelia for neat border edgings, tagetes and African marigold, snapdragons and stocks, and best of all, velvety pansies already a-blowing in every colour imaginable. Sometimes there is a box or two of rosy double daisies. These I can never resist, and each year they are drawn to my notice by the two dark-eyed gipsies who do the selling.

'Lovely daisies, dear. Better than ever this year. We got new seeds, see. They was more expensive, but we'll let you have 'em the same price as last year, dear, as we knows you so well.' And so I have a dozen or so, as they knew I would, and probably pay more, for I can't possibly remember what I paid the year before. And this they know, too.

While the transaction goes on, the children cluster round the donkey, stroking his plushy nose and murmuring endearments. Somehow, the donkey cart always manages to call on a sunny day, at about one-fifteen, when the school dinner is over and the children are free to enjoy the fun.

'Miss, have you got a lump of sugar?' they plead.

'Miss, the donkey likes carrots, the man says!' cries another.

'Miss, have you got a bit of ol' bread to spare?'

It always ends the same way. Bearing my damp little newspaper parcels, and my much lighter purse, I return to the school house followed by the children and the gipsy woman. I hand over sugar lumps, old apples, the end of a loaf and anything else which, at a cursory glance round my larder, will make acceptable donkey-fodder, and watch the children tearing across the playground with their largesse. But the gipsy woman remains. Her eyes have grown very large and sad, her voice pathetic. She speaks quietly, as one woman to another, on intimate matters.

'I'm not one to beg, miss, as you well know, but the fact is I'm expecting again and hardly a decent rag to fit me. I'm carrying low this time, and not a skirt will go round me.' I wonder, inconsequently, if 'carrying high' would mean that her upper garments would be too tight, but hastily dismiss the idea.

She shuffles a little closer, and looks furtively about her. The whisper becomes a whine. 'Don't matter how old, dear. Or a coat, now. Say you had a coat. Don't matter if it's torn or grubby. Do us a good turn, lady, and see what you can find, if it's only for the sake of the baby.'

I tell her to wait, whisk upstairs, collect a dear faithful old flannel skirt, which I know I shall mourn later, a tartan jacket which Amy unkindly but truthfully told me made me look 'like mutton dressed as lamb', and return.

The skinny dark hands grab them quickly and turn them inside out. The sharp eyes, I notice, are bright with approval.

'Thank you, dearie. God bless you! I've got no money to give you, with all we've got to feed, but I'd like you to have a pot plant off the cart.'

'No, really –' I protest. 'Just take the clothes.'

'You come on!' insists my caller. Meekly, I accompany her to the cart. The donkey, surfeited, is scraping the road with one neat little hoof. The scrunching of sugar lumps can be heard, but not from the donkey.

I choose a handsome pink geranium. We exchange civilities. The couple mount the cart. My skirt and jacket are stuffed under the wooden board that serves as a seat, in company with an assortment of other garments, I notice. We all wave until they are out of sight.

'Ring the bell, Ernest,' I say. 'It's time we were back to work!'

We install the geranium on my desk, as a happy reminder of one of our visitors. It will be a year before we see them again.

Later, the scissor-grinder comes, and we rush out to his Heath Robinson machine with shears and scissors, knives and bill-hooks. Sometime in June, a stocky figure appears pushing a light barrow full of assorted materials and tools. This is the chair-mender and mat-mender. He does rushing, caning and a certain amount of simple carpentry. Doormats are the things be likes mending best, and I remember the pride with which he told me one day that my back-door mat was 'one of the finest ever made in one of Her Majesty's prisons'. I have no way of testing the truth of this statement, but I like to think that I wipe the garden mud from my shoes on a decent bit of British workmanship.

Then, in high summer, more gipsies come, bearing gaudy flowers made of woodshavings and dyed all the colours of the rainbow. Sometimes they bring clothes pegs, clamped together in rows on long twigs, still green and damp from the hazel bushes where the wands were cut and peeled. All these people are known and welcomed. They are as much part of the season as the daffodils or the Canterbury bells.

In addition, we sometimes have a visitor of more exotic caste. Once a tall turbaned stranger, with dusky skin and flashing eyes, called at our cottages. When we appeared, startled, at our doors he chanted: 'You lucky lady! Me, holy man from Pakistan!' And after these opening civilities he displayed the contents of a large suitcase for our delectation. Writing paper, soap, bright ties, hair ribbons, toothpaste – all jostled together to tempt the money from our purses. But I don't think he sold a great deal in Fairacre, for he never came again. Nor did 'the antique dealer' who offered Mrs Pringle ten shillings for her grandfather clock and Mr Willet a pound for the silver teapot left him by a former employer.

But it was another stranger, who called but once, who was perhaps the most haunting of all our visitors. I see his face more clearly than many of my children's, and often wonder what happened to that shabby little figure who visited my house, long ago, and never returned.

It was a still, hot May morning when he arrived. The lilacs, tulips and forget-me-nots shimmered in a blue haze. It was a Saturday, and I had done my weekly washing. It hung motionless upon the line, but was drying rapidly, nevertheless, in the great heat.

I had dragged the wooden garden seat into the shade and was resting there, glorying in the weather, when I heard the click of the gate. A small man, carrying a battered suitcase slung over his shoulder with a leather strap, shuffled up the path. My heart sank. Must I rouse myself to face a jumble of assorted objects, none of which I really wanted, which no doubt awaited my inspection inside the case?

He did not stop at the door, but made his way across the grass towards me, slipped the heavy case from his back, with a sigh of relief, and spoke. 'Mind if I sit down, miss?' he asked. His voice had a Cockney twang and he sounded tired. I nodded and he sat abruptly on the grass, as though his legs would carry him no further.

We sat in silence for a few minutes, he too tired, I suspected, and I too bemused with the sunshine, to make conversation. A bumblebee buzzed busily about the daisies on the grass. It seemed to be the only thing that moved in the garden. At length, I roused myself enough to speak.

'Don't bother to undo your case,' I said.

The man looked faintly surprised. 'I weren't going to. Why should I?'

'I thought, maybe, you were selling things,' I replied apologetically.

'Got nothin' to sell,' he said laconically. He lay back on the grass with his eyes shut, and I studied him.

He was quite old. He was a man in his seventies, I guessed, looking at the grey stubbly hair and his wrinkled forehead. A red band ran round his damp brow, where his cap had been, and a little trickle of sweat crept down his temple. He had a humorous look, and I guessed that he was a cheerful sparrow of a man, in the normal way. At the moment he looked utterly exhausted, and my heart smote me.

'Would you like a drink?' I asked. 'I haven't any beer, but there's cider or lemonade.'

He sat up slowly, his face creasing into a smile. 'I'd like a drop of lemon, miss, thank you,' he replied. He took a red and white spotted handkerchief from his pocket, and I left him wiping his face and neck, as I went towards the kitchen for refreshment.

It was a relief to leave the dazzling garden for the cool shade indoors. I loaded the tray with a jug of lemonade, two glasses and the biscuit tin, and returned.

The stranger struggled up at my approach, and took the tray from me. He poured one glassful of lemonade straight down his throat, sighed, and put it back on the tray.

'I could do with that,' he said, thankfully, watching me refill it. 'I bin on the road since 'arpars six.'

'Have you far to go?' I asked him.

'Making for Weymouth,' he said.

'For a holiday?'

'For good!' he said shortly. He looked away into the distance, turning his glass round and round in his rough hands. There was sadness in his face, but a determination about the set of his mouth that made me wonder what lay behind his journey. I was soon to know.

'I got an ol' friend in Weymouth. We was in the army together. Went all through the war – Ypres, retreat from Mons, the lot. Name of Miller – Dusty Miller, of course.' He gave me a quick sidelong smile. 'We 'ad some good times together. And some narrer squeaks too. "You come down anytime you like," Dusty says to me, whenever we met. "Always a welcome at Weymouth," he says, "for an old comrade!" So I'm going!'

He scrunched a biscuit fiercely. He looked a little defiant, I thought.

''Course, I shouldn't say this,' he said, swallowing noisily, 'but poor ol' Dusty picked the wrong girl when he got wed. Worst day's work he ever done, in my 'umble opinion! Can't think what come over 'im!'

He ruminated for a moment, crossing one leg over the other, and contemplated his battered boots. His spirits were rising with rest and refreshment, and his natural loquacity became apparent.

'Ol' Dusty,' he assured me with emphasis, 'could 'ave 'ad 'is pick of the girls. Fine set-up feller always. Curly hair, good moustache, biceps like footballs. Always ready for a lark. Why, in France –' He stopped suddenly, coughed with some delicacy, and started again. 'After the war 'e 'ad a nice little packet of money saved up. His dad run a little confectioner-tobacco shop down the Mile End Road, and when the old boy conked out in 1920 Dusty sold up and put the money into this caffy at Weymouth. Always bin fond of the sea, 'as Dusty, and I thought that's where 'e'd end up.'

'And so he's been there for a long time,' I observed.

'Ever since. Married a local girl, too. Great pity really.' He sighed, and helped himself to another biscuit. ''Course, you can understand it,' he continued. 'With this 'ere caffy to run, and that, you need a woman to lend a hand. And I must say, she could make two pennies go as far as three. A real 'ead for figures. It's thanks to Edie the place 'as done so well, but she weren't the woman for Dusty. No fun. Never one for a laugh. One of them stringy women, with a sharp nose. A bit white and spiteful, if you know what I mean.'

I said I did. St Patrick's clock began to strike eleven, and my visitor cocked an eye at me.

'Suppose I'd best be getting along,' he said, but with a questioning inflection. 'You must be busy.'

This was the opportunity which I should have seized, but it was so warm that I dallied. I knew that I ought to take my basket and go shopping. There were bedrooms to dust, and a salad to prepare. There were two telephone calls to make and the laundry to sort out. Let all these things wait, I decided.

'I'm not particularly busy,' I replied.

'Well, I'll have another five minutes, if you're sure,' said my visitor, propping himself against a handy tree. 'It's good to 'ave a bit of a chin-wag. I must say I've been a bit lonely since Thursday.' He checked suddenly, and then resumed in a quieter vein.

'Thursday!' he said slowly, as if talking to himself. 'It seems weeks ago! A different life – that's what it seems! Eh, a lot's happened to me since this time last week. Funny, ain't it, the way you go on, year after year, in the same ol' rut, and then, suddenly – phut? Everything's changed. You find yourself starting all over again. Queer, how things 'appen. If you're sure you're not busy, miss, I'll tell you about it.'

I assured him that I had all the time in the world, stretched my legs into the sunshine, and gave him my attention.

The year that Dusty Miller went to Weymouth, it appeared his old brother-in-arms, Alf, got married and set up home near the Elephant and Castle in south London. He and his wife occupied a ground floor flat consisting of a kitchen-living room, a bedroom, and a parlour, known as the front room. The front room was only used on Sundays, or when guests were invited, and housed most of their wedding presents on a large sideboard.

Alf had a steady job as a butcher's roundsman. He was at work at seven-thirty each morning, cutting up the joints for the orders and loading his van. This was his employer's first motor vehicle, and the pride of both men's hearts.

He enjoyed his work. He was quick and friendly, a favourite with his customers who liked his badinage and unfailing cheerfulness. At Christmas time he carried home as much in Christmas boxes from kindly clients as he did in his wage packet.

His wife, Jessie, was a round pink girl with a frizzy fringe and pearl earrings. She liked satin blouses, an evening at the music hall, or a lively sing-song with her friends in the front room. Alf adored her.

They had three children, Frank, Norman and Ursula. The first two were named after relatives, but Ursula derived her name from the pages of a novelette which her mother had been reading a few hours before the baby arrived. The heroine of the novelette had had a particularly affecting experience, at a château somewhere well behind the lines in the First World War, involving a wounded officer of unsurpassed valour and passion, and a great deal of heart-searching on Ursula's part before the final renunciation.

It was all excessively moving, and the baby was to be either Jocelyn – the hero's name – or Ursula. And, eventually, after a prolonged and painful labour, Ursula arrived.

The family thrived, despite cramped conditions. The children ran round the corner to the gaunt Board School as soon as they were old enough. The classes were enormous, the classrooms dark, but the teachers were well-trained and energetic, and the children got on famously.

Occasionally, Alf met Dusty at a British Legion function in London. The families exchanged Christmas cards, and one summer the London family was invited by Dusty to spend a holiday at Weymouth. This was a real treat and the children looked forward to it for weeks. But disappointment was in store. It was quite apparent, when they arrived, that though Dusty was pleased to see them, Edie was not.

'Miserable ol' faggot!' was Jessie's comment, in the privacy of the tiny back bedroom to which they had been shown. 'Some holiday this is going to be, Alf! You should've had more sense than to accept Dusty's invitation. He's properly under her thumb, poor soul!'

It was indeed a most uncomfortable time. The children were scolded if they brought in sand on their shoes, or shells in their pockets. Jessie, bridling, did her utmost to keep silent for the sake of poor shame-faced Dusty, as much as for her own family. But everyone was relieved when Saturday came and they could return home.

The two women pecked at each other's cheeks through their veils. The men shook hands a shade too heartily, and avoided each other's eyes. The children smiled more freely than they had done all the week as they hung out of the train window.

'Never again!' exclaimed Jessie, as the train left Weymouth station. She withdrew two long hatpins from her straw hat, threw it on the rack, fussed up her fringe, and leant back with a sigh.

'That's the last I want to see of Edie Miller!' said Jessie flatly.

It was, in fact, the last that she did see of Edie, or Dusty. For before the year was out, jolly lively Jessie was operated on for cancer, and died under the anaesthetic. Alf was inconsolable.

Ursula was ten at the time of her mother's death. The boys were twelve and thirteen. Jessie's mother, a widow who lived nearby, took over the running of the house and the upbringing of the children. For Alf, it seemed as if the sun had gone for ever. For months he went about, looking like a shadow of his usual jaunty self, but gradually he recovered. His customers were glad to see his return to cheerfulness. He threw himself with renewed fervour into his work and into such activities as the British Legion's affairs. He and Dusty met often, but never spoke of the holiday which had been Jessie's last.

Years passed, and the two boys went out to work in New Zealand, where they married and settled. Ursula took over the housekeeping when their grandmother died, and Alf and his daughter rubbed along fairly well together.

She was nothing like her mother, Alf used to think, watching her at the other side of the hearth. She was thin and angular, with a sharp tongue and a way of tossing her head when crossed, which Alf recognized as a danger signal. He was secretly relieved when she became engaged to a young man from Northampton, and he gave her away without a pang.

Then began for Alf some of the happiest years of his life. He was free to do as he pleased. His work ran smoothly, his health was good, his spirits remarkably gay now that he had the house to himself. A neighbour cleaned the flat once a week, and for the rest of the time the dust gathered gently, the oven remained cold, and only the frying pan and kettle were in general use. Life was very simple.

He began to see more of Dusty Miller. Both men were now in their sixties and had plenty of reminiscences to share. During the Second War Dusty had been to the forefront in Civil Defence at Weymouth. Alf had been in the Fire Service, and both had experienced hair-raising episodes. Somehow, they did not talk of these. It was always the First World War which engrossed their attention. They relived the flight from Mons, the tedium and terror of trench life and the horror of that day when L Battery was wiped out beside them. They reminded each other, too, of lighter moments. Did Alf remember the time when his horse wheeled smartly into the pub yard as was its wont, leaving the colonel, whom he was accompanying, looking thunderstruck on the highway? Did Dusty recall the occasion when he played the piano in the pub, and generous comrades filled his tumbler with Benedictine so that he began to think that he was playing a two-manual organ?

Time passed all too quickly when the old soldiers met. Dusty now ran a small car and frequently took Alf out. Sometimes, Alf stayed a day or two at Weymouth. Edie was civilly welcoming, but it was Dusty who did the real entertaining. The Millers had no family, and all Edie's energy seemed to go into the running of the flourishing business. The two men seemed to see very little of her.

'Don't forget, old boy,' said Dusty on many occasions, 'there's always a home here for you, if you get tired of your own company. Just say the word. Plenty of room for one more.'

Alf was grateful, and failed to notice that on these occasions Edie was either absent, or silent.

When Alf was seventy he had the first real illness of his life. It had been a miserable December, cold and foggy. Mists from the Thames hung over the area where Alf lived and worked, making life doubly difficult at the busy time before Christmas. Handling frozen meat, his hands numb and aching, Alf began to feel his age. The round seemed to take twice as long as usual, hampered as he was with fog and extra orders. Customers were short-tempered, the traffic was frustrating, and Alf looked forward to the Christmas break with more fervour than he had ever felt before.

One night, a few days before Christmas, he returned home late and tired. His chest was unusually painful. To breathe was difficult; to cough was agonizing. Reluctantly, after a night of wakefulness, he dragged himself to the local doctor's surgery.

'Bed for you,' was the verdict. 'Who is there to look after you?'

'No one,' said Alf. 'Well, I've a daughter, but she's in Northampton.'

'See if she can come down,' said the doctor, handing him a prescription. 'I'll be in tomorrow morning.'

Ursula, with a martyred expression, arrived the next evening. She made it quite clear that her duty really lay with her husband and children, that it was most inconvenient to leave home with so much to do, and that only her filial devotion had brought her so swiftly to her father's bedside. Alf thought, yet again, how different she was from her warm-hearted mother. If only his Jessie had still been alive! A tear, born of weakness, crept down his cheek, and Ursula, noticing it, was glad to see how grateful the old fellow was to her.

Two wretchedly uncomfortable days followed, while Ursula grew steadily more dictatorial and her father grew steadily weaker. The doctor, summing up the situation, removed Alf to hospital, warning Ursula that he might not be fit to live alone when he was well enough to be discharged.

'I don't need to be reminded of my duty,' said Ursula, bridling. 'Dad's got a home with us at Northampton whenever he wants it.'

'He'll want it very soon,' the doctor assured her.

It was a sad day for Alf, some weeks later, when he left the flat which had been his home for so long. A few treasured pieces of furniture travelled ahead to Northampton, the rest went to local auction rooms.

One windy March day of blinding rain, Alf took the train to the Midlands, with a very heavy heart.

He knew, as soon as he crossed the threshold, that it would never work. There was something about the angular light wood hat-stand in the hall, and the overpowering aroma of floor polish that met him, which seemed to epitomize the unwelcoming quality of Ursula's abode.

He had been allotted the front room, a bleak, north-facing apartment, sparsely furnished. An iron bedstead, with a thin mattress and frosty white counterpane, took up the space by the window. The lino, printed to look like parquet blocks, shone like a mirror. A skimpy rug slid about the polished surface whenever anyone was rash enough to step on it. A small one-bar electric fire did its best to cast a little warmth into the room, but failed miserably.

Alf's two grandchildren came into the room to greet him. They were an unprepossessing pair. Sandra was a lumpy, sandy-haired eight-year-old, and Roger a skinny, rabbit-toothed boy of eleven. Both had adenoids and breathed habitually through their mouths. As they ate almost without cessation, the spectacle of his grandchildren did not encourage Alf's affection for them.

Their father was a lorry driver, a man of few words, but enormous appetite. It seemed to Alf, in the months that followed, that Ursula spent most of her time peeling great saucepans full of potatoes to assuage his hunger. He did not see much of his son-in-law, as he worked long hours, and Alf regretted this. It would have been nice to have a man to talk to, now and again. With every week that passed, Alf realized, with increasing despair, how bitter it is not to have a home of one's own.

He did his best to remain equable. Indeed, with his unquenchable Cockney spirit, 'cheerfulness kept breaking in', whether he would or no. Ursula resented this. She would have liked to see a proper humility, an appreciation of all her hard work. The gay quip, the sardonic aside, any sort of ironic levity, beloved of Alf, smacked of insurrection to Ursula. It was obvious that the old man would rebel one day and, before long, things came to the boil between Ursula and her father.

The row began, as might be expected, over the children. It was a hot May day, so hot, in fact, that for once Alf was grateful for his cold room. He sat, reading a letter which had come from Weymouth that morning, and looking forward to his tea when the children returned from school.

Dusty wrote as affectionately as ever. He knew, well

enough, that his old friend was unhappy although he had not said so in black and white.

'Don't forget, what I've said before,' wrote Dusty, 'that you are welcome here any time you like to come.'

Alf found great comfort in that sentence. He read it several times before returning the letter to its envelope on the table, and then settled back for a doze.

Before long he awoke. The two children were in the room, the boy gazing out of the window, and Sandra – Alf's anger rose as his senses returned – Sandra was reading Dusty's letter.

He struggled to his feet and made towards the table. 'Don't you dare meddle with my things!' stormed the old man.

The child looked sideways at him and contorted her face, by the lift of one nostril, into a contemptuous sneer. Just so, many years before, Ursula had looked at him, and received a resounding box on the ear.

Without thinking further, Alf repeated the process, and had one moment of unalloyed pleasure as his palm clouted the sandy head. The piercing shrieks that followed brought Ursula hurrying from the kitchen.

''E 'it me, mum! I wasn't doing nothin', mum! 'E just 'it me!'

Ursula's face and neck grew red with wrath. 'You keep your hands to yourself,' she yelled. 'I can remember your bullying ways when I was her age! Don't you think you can knock my kids about the way you knocked us!'

'She was reading my letter –' began Alf, but was brushed aside.

'As though it's not bad enough having you here all the time, burning the firing and the lights, eating us out of house and home –'

'I pay my own way!'

Ursula gave a derisive snort. 'Pay your way?' she echoed. 'And how far do you reckon your bit of pension goes these days?'

Sandra, seeing attention slipping from her, set up a further bout of snivelling. 'Mum, I believe I've got mastoid. I do, really! My ear 'urts somethin' awful where 'e 'it me!'

Ursula threw an arm protectively round her daughter. 'We'll take you down to the hospital after tea.' She rounded again on the old man. 'And if she's got a broken ear drum and is deaf for the rest of her days, she'll have you to thank! The ingratitude! That's what gets me – the ingratitude! Here I am, slaving day in, day out, with never a word of thanks for my trouble, and how am I repaid?'

'Stop play-acting –' began Alf.

'Play-acting!' screamed Ursula. 'Don't you dare insult me after all the harm you've done. I've just about had enough of you and your ways!'

She flung out of the room, dragging Sandra with her. The boy, who had watched the proceedings with sly enjoyment, slid after them. At the door he turned, poked out an impudent tongue, and vanished. Alf was left alone.

He was more shaken than he cared to admit. He shouldn't have hit the girl, he told himself. He was enveloped in a hot wave of guilt and shame. It receded, leaving him shivering with shock. God, what a hole, he thought, looking round the room! To think of spending the rest of his days in this place, with the added misery of Ursula and the children!

His eye fell upon Dusty's letter. In all that bleak room it was the only spot of comfort. Why should he stay? Why should he endure the humiliation of living with Ursula? He had his pension. He had a true old friend – a friend, moreover, who offered him a real home.

With growing purpose he went to his bed, reached beneath it for his battered suitcase, and set it open upon the white counterpane.

Methodically, with the exactitude of an old soldier, he began to pack his possessions. He was off.

*

'That was Thursday,' said the old man, reaching for his glass. He sounded bemused. 'And now it's Saturday. Seems a lifetime ago, miss – a lifetime.'

He gazed into the distance towards the towering downs, but I guessed that he was looking beyond them to the life that he had left behind in Northampton. He looked very old, very vulnerable, to be alone and with no home. I felt uneasy.

'And your daughter?' I inquired. 'You told her where you were going?'

I could imagine the remorse which might well be gnawing at any woman in her position, despite the portrait of flinty-hearted indifference the old man had drawn of her.

'Left a note,' said the stranger perfunctorily. 'Just told her I'd had an invitation from Dusty, and this seemed a good time to go down there.'

'So she'll expect you back some time?' I said. It was a relief to know that he had not burnt his boats completely.

'Never!' he shouted, sitting bolt upright. 'Not if she begged and prayed of me! I've had more'n I can take there. Never again!'

He scrambled to his feet, still looking belligerent. His gaze flickered over the sunny garden as though he saw it for the first time, and he turned to look directly at me. The anger faded into a smile.

'You bin good to me, miss, letting me run on like I have. I must be getting along.'

He fished inside his jacket and brought out a small creased map. He unfolded it carefully, and I noticed that his fingers shook. Across its grubby surface a thick ruled line ran from Northampton to Weymouth.

'There's my route,' he said proudly, holding up the map. 'Always like a bit of map work ever since my Army days. I'm a bit off true here, but no matter. Reckon if I make for Salisbury Plain I shan't be far off.'

He stuffed the map back in his pocket and began to hoist the case across his shoulders again.

'You're not walking all the way?' I asked anxiously.

'Not me!' he said. 'I've hitch-hiked most of it so far, but took a fancy to a walk this morning. Haven't seen the country on a summer day – not to notice it, I mean – ever since Jessie died. Brought her back to me somehow, being alone and peaceful, out in the fresh air.'

'Make for Caxley,' I said. 'But wait here a minute.'

I returned to the house and looked in my purse. As usual it was remarkably light, but there was a pound note. Why, I wondered, was it always the end of the month when such emergencies arose? I hastened out again and pressed it upon him.

'No, miss,' he protested. 'I got a bit by, you know.'

'If you don't get a lift, go by train,' I urged him. 'You don't want to arrive absolutely knocked up.'

He pocketed the note and we walked together to the gate. He was smiling now, as though at some pleasurable secret.

'Can't wait to see ol' Dusty's face when I turn up,' he said, over the gate.

'You haven't told them?' I asked, my heart sinking.

'Why should I?' he replied reasonably. 'I know ol' Dusty means it when he says I can go any time.' His tone was warm and affectionate. His wrinkled old face glowed at the thought of the welcome ahead. He straightened himself up and gave me a smart salute. 'Thanks for everything, miss, bless you! Think of me paddlin' in a day or two!'

Two minutes later, I watched the little figure disappear round the bend of the lane. Despite the sunshine, I shivered, for I could not help thinking of the woman that Dusty should never have married, the stringy one with the sharp nose, who was 'white and spiteful'.

Poor Alf, I mourned, poor Alf!

*

Yes, some of our Fairacre visitors are lively birds. The gipsies, in their clashing colours, look as exotic and gay as any parrot from the East. But I remember Alf as a wren, perky and completely English but somehow infinitely pathetic in his smallness.

I think of him often, the stranger who called but once. Will he ever return?

I can't be certain, but I have a feeling that Alf was on his last flight that summer day.

11. The Old Man of the Sea

'It's my belief,' announced Mrs Pringle, as she baled boiling water from the electric copper into the washing-up bowl, 'that they over-ate themselves.'

'I thought they were rather more abstemious than usual,' I replied. 'Usually they start eating as we reach the end of the lane, and continue until we get to Barrisford.'

'Shameful!' ejaculated Mrs Pringle, flinging a trayful of sticky cutlery into the water. The noise was deafening.

'Then it's a quick dash into the sea, out again, and time for a solid lunch. This time they didn't appear to eat so much on the journey. Unless I'm getting used to it,' I added.

We were trying to probe the mystery of the many absences from school on this particular Monday morning. Almost a third of the desks were empty, and I suspected that general inertia was the common complaint after a long day at the sea on Saturday. Mrs Pringle argued for gluttony alone, but I have never found Fairacre children suffering from delicate digestions. Their appetites, quickened by the winds which sweep the downs, are enormous, and their digestive tracts are quite accustomed to coping with a steady supply of ices, sweets, fruit, fizzy drinks, as well as four hefty meals a day.

'Could be typhoid, of course,' said Mrs Pringle chattily. 'There was a bit on the telly about the sewage going into the sea. Fair gives you the creeps! I said to Pringle: "The way folks live! Thank God we've got a nice wholesome cess-pit!"'

She plunged her hands into the steaming water and

withdrew a fistful of dripping dessert-spoons, lately used for gooseberry pie.

'But can't do you no good, say what you will, to go bathing when that sort of thing's goin' on. As well as dumpin' this atomic rubbish they don't know what to do with. The sea must be proper un'ealthy these days. Me heart bleeds for those poor fish, it do indeed!'

She was now drying the spoons and setting them rapidly in rows. She counted them hissingly, stopped, scrabbled again in the cloudy water, drew blank, and turned to me. Her unlovely face was made even unlovelier by dark suspicion.

''Ere!' said Mrs Pringle truculently. 'You bin featherin' your nest again?'

This charitable remark referred to an unfortunate incident a few weeks earlier when Mrs Pringle had come across a school dessert-spoon in the kitchen drawer at the school house. I had not been allowed to forget this lapse. Mrs Pringle guards the school cutlery – as battered and dingy a collection of plate as one could find anywhere – as if it were the Crown Jewels.

'I find that remark offensive,' I said coldly, moving off to ring the school bell.

'So's stealing!' shouted Mrs Pringle after me, above the clatter. With what dignity I could muster, I pulled the school bell-rope to summon my depleted pupils to afternoon school.

The outing on Saturday had started in brilliant sunshine. By ancient custom, the Fairacre Sunday School and Church Choir Combined Outing takes place on the first Saturday in July. Evidently, many years ago, the schools in this area used to have a fortnight's holiday at the end of June to enable the children to pick the soft fruit crop. At the end of that time, their wages were paid and there was money, as well as the longing, for a jollification. Somehow, the first Saturday in July still remains as the only acceptable day for the annual outing.

Two coachloads set off at eight o'clock, packed with

parents and friends as well as the vociferous children. It was a sparkling morning. Bright drops glittered on the fresh hedges, sunshine glinted on cottage windows, the village pond, and the glossy backs of Mr Roberts' herd of Friesians as they ambled back from being milked. It was most exhilarating.

'Won't last,' said Mr Willet morosely, following his wife into the coach.

He was dressed in his best blue suit, and his boots shone like jet. No gaudy beachwear for Mr Willet when he accompanies us to the sea! He is sexton of St Patrick's, a public figure, and he shows himself to the world as a man worthy of the dignity of his office. He now rammed a small case containing their lunch upon the rack and then bent down to whisper conspiratorially in my ear.

'Where's old misery sitting?'

'Right at the front,' I whispered back, knowing at once to whom this referred.

'Thanks, miss. I'll make for the back,' said Mr Willet, pulling the case from the rack, and departing. I heard him settle with a satisfied sigh, as Mrs Pringle entered, took her place in the front and intimated to the driver that it was now in order for him to proceed.

'Old 'ard, ma,' said the driver irreverently. 'Just gotter check we're all 'ere.'

He hoisted himself from the wheel and turned round to count us.

'All aboard?' he cried at length.

'All aboard!' we echoed cheerfully, and set off for Barrisford.

Mr Willet, as a weather prophet, is usually right, and by the time we had driven through Caxley, the sky was overcast, and remained so for most of the day. Not that this dimmed the spirits of the Fairacre children. They tore along the famous sands, rushed into the waves – but not too deeply, I noticed, for the sea is not really trusted by us landlubbers – and wielded buckets and spades energetically for most of the exciting day.

Their elders enjoyed themselves more sedately, walking along the short pier, scanning the distant horizon through the penny-in-the-slot telescope, and studying the photographs outside the miniature theatre at the very end of the pier. It was a pity, we told each other, that we had to set off for home so early, otherwise we could have seen the variety show. Twelve acts – and all spectacular – it said so!

The air was wonderful, despite the lack of sunshine, tangy and salt upon our faces, and we all had prodigious appetites when we foregathered for high tea at Bunce's, the famous restaurant on the front.

The vicar counted heads earnestly. Were we all assembled? Would someone else check the numbers with him? Thereupon half the company rose to count the other half, and confusion reigned. Order was eventually restored, but we were, it was agreed, one missing.

'Joseph Coggs!' shouted Patrick. 'I saw him mucking about under the pier. Shall I run and fetch him?'

'I think,' said Mr Partridge, the vicar, in his gentle voice, 'we'll wait for five minutes and then send out a search party if he hasn't arrived. No doubt he will be along.'

At that moment, Joseph wandered through the brown and gold swing doors. He was excessively grubby and looked pale and bewildered. No adult from the Coggs' family was present so I took charge of him. He was remarkably quiet during tea, but ate his way steadily through a plate of ham and salad, three iced cakes, a butterscotch sundae and two cups of tea. I was not perturbed by his taciturnity as I watched his eating prowess. He obviously had enough to engross him at the time, and was, in any case, a somewhat uncommunicative child.

Just before six we said a sad farewell to lovely Barrisford for another year, and mounted the coach. Still the skies were sullen. At nine we were back in Fairacre, and at ten o'clock I, for one, was in bed.

Now, on Monday afternoon, it all seemed a very long time ago. Confronting my depleted class I mentally rearranged the timetable. The song, which I had proposed to teach them, must wait until the others returned. A spelling test, and then some revived memories of Barrisford, in words and pictures, should fill our afternoon very usefully and happily.

The spelling test was greeted with groans. Perhaps because they are unbookish children, as a whole, and do not see the printed word as often as I should like, spelling is a weak point at Fairacre. Even their names, when they are first in my class, at the age of seven or so, give some of them trouble, and I silently curse the parents who saddle their poor spellers with 'Penelope', 'Francesca' or 'Reginald'. Perhaps the worst one is 'Ronald'. It has been my lot, for many years, to wrestle with 'Ronlads', 'Rondals' and even 'Ronslads' and very exhausting I have found it.

This afternoon I bullied them through such necessary exercises as the days of the week – 'Wednesday', of course, is the stumbling-block – the months of the year – all, with the possible exception of 'March' and 'June', fearfully hazardous – and a brisk revision of local place names which are invariably written awry. They tottered out to play, quite done up.

Ten minutes in the boisterous air of the school playground soon restored them to their usual vivacity, however, and they settled down to write and draw their impressions of the day at Barrisford. I wandered round the busy classroom, admiring their efforts.

They were much as I expected. Sandcastles topped with flags, sailing boats, rowing boats – even a steamer, though I am positive no steamers come to Barrisford – and unflattering portraits of fellow pupils paddling in zig-zag waves. But Joseph Coggs' picture roused my curiosity.

Beneath a framework of black-crayoned girders stood two figures. One, from the blue striped tee-shirt, I recognized as a self-portrait. The other, about half the size, wore scarlet bathing trunks and a crown on its head. A certain amount of scrawling with a pale blue crayon indicated that water was nearby, and in the distance it looked as though there were a fairytale palace with the conventional spiky towers. I began to wonder if Joseph was remembering the pantomime rather than the trip to the sea.

'Who's this little boy with you?' I asked.

''S'man!' said Joseph.

'But he's only half your size,' I protested. Our art at Fairacre is pretty pedestrian. We make the sun circular, and grown-ups are usually twice the size of children in our pictures.

'So he was!' persisted Joseph. 'But he were a man all the same.'

I was about to pass on and let him enjoy his fantasy, when he pointed out one or two other features.

'This 'ere's the pier, see, I met this man under there. He was only up to my shoulder.'

'Sounds likely, don't it!' scoffed Ernest who had come to see the picture, and was rapidly joined by half a dozen others, who felt like stretching their legs.

'Bet you dreamt it, Joe!' said John.

Joseph's dusky face grew red with anger. His dark eyes smouldered.

'He was a man,' he repeated mulishly. 'He told me. He said he was The Old Man of the Sea and he lived in a palace. That's it there!'

He thrust a black forefinger upon the spiky towers. There was a burst of derisive laughter from the onlookers which I hastily quelled. Joseph was very near to tears and I was not going to see him taunted, inexplicable though his garbled story sounded.

'Ten minutes to finish!' I announced, 'and we'll have a quiet ten minutes, please. I'm looking for someone sensible to help me clear up at home time.'

This, as usual, worked like magic, and peace descended while they finished their scribbling. Partly to keep Joseph from being teased on the way home, and partly because I was intrigued with what lay behind his account of the stranger, I chose him to remain behind after school. The rest of the children ran off, their voices dying away in the distance.

The classroom seemed unnaturally quiet. We could hear the birds cheeping on the guttering, and the whispering of the leaves outside the Gothic window.

Joseph stacked the papers carefully. His own, I noticed, was placed lovingly on top. He brought them to my desk, put them down, and remained gazing at me.

'I ain't lying,' he said abruptly.

'I know you're not,' I answered.

There was silence for a moment, a silence which I did not intend to break first.

'I really did see him under the pier,' said Joseph slowly. 'That's why I was late for tea. That's why –'

He faltered, took a deep breath, and began again. In bits and pieces, fits and starts, the astonishing story came out. To an adult it was both pathetic and comic. To a small boy, it was quite apparent, the encounter had been terrifying and miraculous.

As far as I can gather, Joseph stayed with his younger twin sisters, as he had been bidden to do by his mother, until they had eaten their sandwiches at midday.

The three children had played blissfully with the sand and the shells for which Barrisford is famous, but in the afternoon Joseph began to get restless. The two little girls had started a mammoth earthworks, with which they were entranced. Joseph found the business of digging remarkably boring. After all, he could dig any time in Fairacre. What Joseph wanted to do was to explore.

Mr and Mrs Willet, propped comfortably in the shelter of a breakwater nearby, saw his predicament.

'You go and 'ave a look round, Joe,' said Mr Willet. 'We'll be 'ere for a bit, reading the paper. We'll keep an eye on your sisters.'

Joseph scrambled eagerly to his feet, his dark eyes sparkling, and set off in the direction of the pier.

'Don't forget tea's at half past four,' bellowed Mr Willet, in the voice that carries across the mighty winds of Fairacre. 'Keep your eye on your gold wrist-watch!

Mr Willet gave a mighty chuckle at his own wit. Mrs Willet smiled wanly, and the two little girls looked at him open-mouthed.

''E ain't gotter wrist-watch!' explained one slowly.

'Tch! Tch!' said Mr Willet testily, and shook out the newspaper.

Joseph made his way diagonally across the sand towards the sea. His feet were bare, and he gloried in the feel of the wet ribs of sand under his insteps. The tide was out, leaving pools of every imaginable shape. Here and there were outcrops of slaty black rock. These Joseph found particularly fascinating. Slimy bladder-wrack covered many of them, and he squatted happily on the rubbery mounds popping the salty blisters one after another. There were limpets too, grey, ribbed and conical that he tried in vain to prise from the rock. He was intrigued by the way he could move them a trifle, and then no more, as they put out their defences.

He wandered nearer and nearer to the pier. Here the pools were deeper, and he discovered, for the first time, the brown jelly-like anemones that waved their tentacles and sucked at his finger.

There were a number of people walking along the pier, hanging over the railings, gazing at the sea. Joseph recognized some of the Fairacre party among them. But he was not particularly interested in what went on aloft. It was the great sub-structure of criss-crossed iron girders which Joseph intended to explore.

They were very cold, wet and rusty, he discovered. Brown streaks and green slime coloured their gaunt shapes, and where the water lapped the legs, green fringes swayed to and fro rhythmically.

Joseph made an attempt to climb up one of the girders, but

the iron-work was cruelly hard to hands and feet. Little flakes of metal came off at a touch, and the salty roughness made his finger-tips sore. He abandoned the attempt and stood listening to the strange noises around him.

Above his head came the thudding of people's feet as they walked the planks of the pier. Around him came the constant sound of trickling water as it ran down the girders, or dripped into the rock pools. The wind made a little whistling sound in the iron lattice-work, and always, as a bass accompaniment, there was the rushing and booming of the swirling sea.

It was particularly rocky under the pier. Great flat plateaus of rock overlapped, forming wide irregular steps. At their edge were deep pools, almost black in the dim light beneath the pier. Joseph, stepping into one caught his breath as the water came high above his knees. He scrambled out of the slippery hole, and walked in a more gingerly fashion, peering at this strange and frightening element.

He was now almost at the end of the pier. Above him he could hear people walking round the little theatre. There was a distant sound of tea cups, for a small refreshment room adjoined the theatre. Sometimes a child called. Sometimes a gull wheeled and cried. It was difficult to tell which was the human voice. Joseph found it all wonderful and strange.

At length he came to a large pool. It was overhung by an outcrop of rock and was as dark as ink. Something large, coloured red and white seemed to be floating in it. Cautiously, Joseph approached, knelt upon the slippery rock and peered over.

To his horror he saw that it was the motionless body of a boy. Surely he must be dead! His eyes were closed. His legs and arms floated gently away from the body and his hair moved as rhythmically in the water as the tentacles of the anemones had done.

Fearfully, his throat aching with suppressed screams, Joseph put out a shaking finger and prodded the body.

'Give over!' said the corpse, opening its eyes suddenly.

Joseph flinched away, startled, scraping his knee painfully on the sharp rock. There was a wild thrashing in the pool, the red trunks and legs were submerged and only the top half of the body confronted Joseph.

'Whatcher think you're up to?' demanded the bather. 'Poking people about like that?'

Joseph, never very voluble, found communication more difficult than usual. For one thing, he was in a state of shock. And for another thing, he was extremely puzzled. The stranger was very small. He had believed him to be a boy, possibly two or three years younger than himself, but as soon as he spoke he realized that, despite his small stature, the bather was a grown man.

Somehow it all seemed part of the fantastic world immediately around Joseph. Anything could happen here, among the faintly menacing shapes of the girders and rocks. The cold, salty air was as far removed as it could be from the pollen-laden winds that blew around Joseph's native village. The music of birdsong and rustling trees was exchanged for the queer atonal sound of dripping water and surging sea. He felt as though he had strayed into an unknown world, where colours, shapes, sounds, and now people themselves, were strange and sinister.

Despite his aching throat he managed to swallow and find his voice.

'I'm sorry, sir,' he said tremulously.

Immediately he was glad that he had added that last word to his apology. The little man's face softened. A look of gratification passed over the pudgy countenance, and he wiped the wet hair away from his forehead.

'That's all right, boy,' he said grandly. 'Now you're here you can give me a hand out.'

He presented a cold wet hand to Joseph. It was as small as those of Joseph's little sisters', but on the back were the hairs of a grown man. Joseph tugged with all his strength. There was a good deal of puffing and blowing and then the little man bounced from the pool on to the rocks.

'Get my towel, boy, will you?' asked the stranger, waving towards the direction of a nearby girder at the outside edge of the pier. Joseph saw a bundle propped between the angle of two girders, out of the wet, and made his way carefully across the slimy rocks to do as he was bidden. There was something imperious about the man which awed Joseph. He was glad to be of service to him.

When he came to withdraw the rolled-up towel from its resting place, Joseph was surprised to see that a few yards of rope ladder were tucked in with it. One end was obviously fixed aloft, and Joseph stepped out beyond the pier to see where it went. He could see it lashed securely to the bottom stay of the pier railings. From there it hung down against the girders, flapping gently in the breeze. Joseph guessed that at its full length it would easily reach the sand. Tucked up as it was, a little higher than his head, it was unnoticeable at a cursory glance.

'Come on! I'm damn near freezing!' shouted the man.

Joseph hurried back with the towel. The stranger, jumping up and down with remarkable agility, was covered with goose-pimples. He snatched the towel from Joseph's arms and began to rub himself energetically. Joseph surveyed him with interest.

Now that the water had drained from his hair, Joseph could see that the man was fair. He was thickset and very muscular. His chest and legs were faintly hairy and he had the suspicion of a moustache. His eyes were very blue, his ears very red. Joseph wondered how old he was. It seemed strange to think that he might be as old as his father, and yet he was no bigger than one of his twin sisters!

The man gave his head a final rub, threw the towel round his waist, and turned to look at Joseph.

'Perishin' cold under here,' he said. 'Let's sit outside for a bit.' He indicated the sand beyond the pier. A little faint sunlight was struggling through the clouds, and chasing the shadows across the bay.

The two picked their way across the rocks. At the edge of the pier the man stopped.

'Anyone about?' he asked. Joseph looked up and down the beach. There were a number of people further along, but no one at hand. The most popular beach, where the Willets were already beginning to think of packing up and making their way to Bunce's, lay behind them.

'Can't see anyone,' said Joseph, wondering at the man's sudden desire for privacy. They emerged into the open. It was a relief to feel flat sand again underfoot.

'I'll show you how to warm up after a bathe!' cried the little man, whose spirits seemed to have risen rapidly. He flung off the towel, and did a backward somersault before Joseph could draw breath.

'Cor!' said Joseph, full of admiration. 'Who learnt you that?'

'Never you mind!' answered the man. 'Watch out now!'

He flexed his muscles, stood on his toes, took a deep breath, and then turned three backward somersaults in a row. After the last he stretched his arms above his head, looking this way and that, as though acknowledging applause. Joseph thought he looked just like the acrobat he had seen in the pantomime last Christmas. If anything, he was better, because he was so small and neat. Joseph was entranced.

'That's chicken feed,' said the man. He swaggered slightly, thrusting his thumbs into the top of his red trunks. 'Look at this!'

He stretched his arms again and began to turn cartwheels, with extreme dexterity and rapidity. He wheeled so steadily, that his red trunks and white torso seemed to blur before Joseph's admiring eyes. He must have turned almost twenty times before he ceased and became upright again.

'Ain't you a marvel!' breathed Joseph, awed.

The little man laughed, but was obviously pleased with the boy's admiration. He smote him cheerfully across the shoulders and they sat down together in the shelter of a rock. Joseph compared their outstretched legs. His own were thin and brown, marked with many an ancient scar on the shins, and the fresh scrape across one sore knee. The stranger's were several inches shorter than his own, but twice the thickness, and bulging with muscles.

'D'you live in Barrisford?' asked the stranger.

'No,' said Joseph. 'Do you?'

'Not likely! Not in this one-eyed dump! Do I look as though I live here?'

He cocked a blue eye upon Joseph. Anxious to please this superman, Joseph hastened to apologize, although he himself could see nothing wrong with Barrisford. Indeed, to someone whose home was in the modest confines of Fairacre, Barrisford seemed a splendidly sophisticated place.

'What's your name, sir?' ventured Joseph.

'Ah now! That's telling!' said the little man teasingly. He leant back against the rock, clasping his hands behind his head, and gazed quizzically at the boy with half-closed eyes. 'I think you'd better call me "The Old Man of the Sea",' he said lazily. 'That's where you found me, wasn't it?'

'The Old Man of the Sea,' echoed Joseph, not completely understanding. 'Do you mean you live there?'

The man nodded, grinning at the boy's mystification.

'That's right,' he said. 'I live in the sea. In a palace, in fact. I'm a sort of King, you know, got a crown and that when I'm at home.'

Joseph pondered this. It sounded a bit far-fetched, but why should a grown-up man want to lie? And the whole affair was odd – the queer, dark, under-pier world, the tiny man, the cartwheels! He wanted to know more.

'Where is this palace?' he asked suspiciously.

'If you're not going to believe me,' said the man, suddenly looking sulky, 'I shan't waste my time telling you.'

'Oh, but I do!' cried Joseph, aghast at upsetting this god-like creature yet again.

The stranger appeared mollified. 'Well, if you must know, it's way out beyond the end of the pier, on the sea-bed.'

'What's it made of?' asked Joseph.

'Oh, rocks and stones, and that!' said the man airily. There was a short silence, as though he were thinking heavily, and then he began again. 'Sea shells, too, of course. It's sort of decorated with shells. And we have sea-weed trees in the garden. It's a pretty place. Fish swim in and out the windows. We always keep the windows open. I like a bit of fresh sea-water in the rooms myself.'

Joseph sat contemplating this picture of royal life beneath the waves. He found it wholly enchanting, and only a fragment of his former doubt remained.

'What d'you eat?' he enquired.

'Fish, of course,' replied the little man, opening his blue eyes very wide. 'What fool questions you ask! We've got nets from the garden, straight through the kitchen window, to the larder where we keep 'em.'

'I like fried fish,' said Joseph warmly. This talk of food was beginning to make him hungry.

'Oh, we don't fry ours,' answered the man casually. 'Too wet, you know. Makes it difficult to keep the stove alight.'

'Ah! It would!' agreed Joseph. Somehow, the difficulty of keeping the stove going underwater seemed to make sense of the whole, slightly improbable, situation.

'No, we eat 'em raw,' said the man. 'Very nutritious too.' He suddenly gave a gigantic yawn. 'Ah well, my boy, wish I could stay longer with you, but I'd best be getting along.'

'Back to the palace?' asked Joseph. He half-hoped that he would be invited to accompany him.

The man rose to his feet and began to shake out the sand from his towel.

'Not just yet,' he said, smiling. 'I've got some friends to call on first.' He wrapped the towel round his shoulders.

A distant yelling caused the two to look round. Leaning over the pier railings, just where the rope ladder was fastened, was a small figure. To Joseph it looked like a little girl.

'Come on, Bill!' she shouted. 'It's half past four. Your tea's ready!'

'Coming, Katy!' the little man shouted back, and set off towards the rope ladder with incredible speed. Joseph ran beside him.

He watched him untangle the lower rungs and begin to mount aloft. The strong little arms and legs twinkled over the criss-cross rope, like a monkey in a ship's rigging. Halfway up he stopped and looked down at Joseph's upturned face.

'Hey, boy,' he said, grinning. 'You cut off to your own folk. And don't believe all you hear, son!'

He nipped smartly up the rest of the ladder and through the railings. Joseph watched him untie the rope, his face suddenly solemn and intent. He slung it across his towelled shoulders, with never a backward glance at the boy below, and vanished towards the theatre.

Disconsolately, with the words of his hero echoing in his ears, Joseph obediently retraced his steps, seeking – tardily and reluctantly – his own folk, who were already ensconced amidst the solid worldliness of Bunce's restaurant.

'And you knows the rest, miss,' said Joseph, fiddling with the brass lid of the Victorian ink stand which dominates the teacher's desk at Fairacre school. His dark eyes were downcast, crescents of thick lashes brushing his dusky cheeks.

'And I 'ad my tea with you, and then we come 'ome,' he continued.

'I remember,' I said. I also remembered Mr and Mrs Willet's

conversation at the tea table, of which Joseph was obviously unaware.

'A pity we have to go back so soon,' Mr Willet had said. 'They say there's a good show on at the end of the pier.'

'Someone told me there's a juggler that keeps six bottles moving,' said Mrs Willet, 'and a dog, dressed up like a nursemaid, pushing a monkey in a pram!'

'There's twelve acts altogether,' said someone further down the table. 'I looked at the posters. Top of the bill is the midgets. Acrobats they are – six of 'em. Call themselves The Mighty Atoms, or some such name. "Appeared before all the crowned heads in Europe," the poster said. I bet they'd have been worth seeing!'

'I'm partial to midgets myself,' Mr Willet had agreed, before the conversation took a different turn.

I looked at the little gipsy boy before me. What was going on under that black thatch of tousled hair, I wondered? Did he really believe the yarn spun him by the fanciful midget? Or did he merely want to believe it?

And what should be my reaction to Joseph's disclosures? I doubted whether this was the time to tell him the cold truth – whether, in fact, he would ever want to know the truth. It seemed wiser, I decided, to say as little as possible at this stage. Joseph's feelings were still too raw to stand rough handling. If he ever wanted to know more, I felt that he would ask me, and then I should answer him with the truth.

At this moment, the problem was settled, or at least shelved, by the appearance in the doorway of Mrs Pringle. In one hand she held an upturned broom, in the other a dustbin lid. She looked, at first glance, like some squat Britannia, with trident and shield.

'You done?' she inquired glumly.

'Yes, indeed,' I said. Under the present trying circumstances, Mrs Pringle's appearance was almost welcome. I put the stack of papers on top of the ancient walnut piano, anchored them safely from the cross-draughts with *Hymns Ancient and Modern*, locked the drawers of my desk, and made my way out into the playground.

Joseph followed me, still looking thoughtful. Outside, by the doorway, Mr Willet was perched on a pair of rickety steps. He was drawing a bent stick along the guttering, collecting dead leaves, an old nest or two, twigs and odd slivers of slate, all of which impeded the flow of rainwater to the butt behind the school.

I stopped to hail him.

'Run home now, Joseph,' I said to my shadow. 'You shall pin your picture on the wall tomorrow morning. It's one of the best.'

His countenance became more animated, and he began to move off. Suddenly, as though remembering something, he turned again to confront us.

'And there *was* a little man!' he said earnestly. 'Honest, there was!'

'I know,' I assured him. We looked at each other for a moment. Then he smiled, and he set off at a brisk trot through the school gates.

'What's up with young Joe, then?' inquired Mr Willet, when the child was out of earshot. 'He bin in trouble?'

'Not trouble exactly,' I answered. 'I'll tell you all about it some day. Let's say he's finding life a bit of a puzzle at the moment.'

Mr Willet snorted, and dropped a noisome handful of muck into the bucket at the foot of the steps.

'Who don't?' he demanded.

12. HARVEST FESTIVAL

There are a number of people in Fairacre who maintain that far too much importance is given to Harvest Festival in our village. Mrs Mawne, our local ornithologist's wife, is one.

'I find something abhorrently bucolic about Harvest Festival,' she announced one day, looking round the chancel of St Patrick's church where the ladies of the village were busy festooning ledges and pillars with the fruits of the earth.

Miss Jackson too, I remember, voiced much the same sentiments. She came among us – mercifully for a short time – as infants' teacher at the school, and had a very poor idea of rural festivals, church or secular.

'Simply a survival of primitive superstitions,' was her comment. 'An act of propitiation to malevolent tribal gods, bound up with fertility rites and other ceremonials of earlier civilizations.' Miss Jackson's dicta were always couched in high-flown language of this sort, and very tedious it became.

Luckily, such people are in the minority. For most of us in Fairacre, our Harvest Festival is a well-loved and well-supported institution. It is, after all, a public thanksgiving for the fulfilment of a year's hard work in the fields and gardens, and a brief breathing space before tackling the next year's labours.

Mr Roberts, the local farmer, gives a mammoth Harvest Home supper in his biggest barn at this season, but naturally it is the farm workers and their friends who attend this jollification. The service at St Patrick's caters for the whole village, for chapel-goers join church-goers on this occasion, and the church is always crowded.

'Far more crowded, in fact,' sighs the vicar, 'than for any other of our church festivals. I sometimes wonder why.'

I think I could tell him. Here is something tangible, something vital, the fruits of the earth – in turn, the fruits of man's labour – lying in splendid array, as living witness of God's and man's work together. A good harvest means food, security, life itself. A poor one, not that many years ago, could mean starvation – and memories are long in the country. It is easier to comprehend the things of the flesh than the spirit, and although one can sympathize with the good vicar's attitude, it does not mean that the praise and honour rendered to the Almighty at Harvest Thanksgiving are any less meritorious.

On the Friday afternoon before Harvest Festival Sunday, I took the schoolchildren across to St Patrick's as usual. Every year we decorate the pews and other allotted portions of the church, and we guard this privilege jealously. On Saturday the ladies of the village come with armfuls of flowers and greenery to do their share, but they always find that the Fairacre children have done their part first.

Usually we tie little bunches of corn to the pew heads, and arrange marrows, shiny apples, onions, giant potatoes, and any other contributions which will not wither or fade, along the ledges and window sills which we know by ancient custom are 'ours'.

It was a bright windy afternoon as we made our way across to the church. Somewhere in the village an energetic gardener was having an autumn bonfire, and great billows of blue smoke hung gauzy veils between us and the distant downs. The smell of the burning leaves had that whiff of sadness which an autumn bonfire always brings; a reminder that summer is over and that soon we shall be head-bent against the gales of winter. I thought briefly of that Devon school, but this time with no regrets. This, I thought, looking at my straggling flock bearing their harvest tributes, is the place for me!

On the south side of St Patrick's, the creeper was glowing scarlet and bronze against the grey flints. On the graves chrysanthemums and Michaelmas daisies made a brave show, and over the lych-gate, where Mr Willet began his story of Sally Gray last winter, a many-berried bryony trailed its bright loops and coils. In the vicarage garden, adjoining the church-yard, I could see dahlias, pink and yellow, as big as soup plates; and on the telephone wire, which stretched from the lane to the chimney stack of the vicar's study, a row of swallows chattered together – no doubt of the journey so soon to be undertaken.

St Patrick's was very peaceful after the wind outside, and soon the children had decked the pews, the steps of the font, and the allotted window-sills. They wandered about admiring their efforts.

'I reckons it looks real good,' said John, squatting down at the foot of the font. 'Tidy and careful!' He gazed with appraisal at the neatly-spaced apples before him.

''Twould look better with a marrer in the middle,' said Ernest, surveying it.

'A marrer!' echoed John, shocked. 'Much too big! Them apples is *exactly* the same size, and four inches apart!' He whipped from his sock a yellow school ruler to prove his point. His expression was scandalized.

'A marrer!' he repeated, with infinite disgust. 'That'd properly put the kibosh on it!' He gave Ernest a withering glance, replaced the ruler in his sock, and moved away in high dudgeon, every inch an outraged artist.

We returned to the school, wind-blown and much refreshed. Mrs Pringle had already arrived to clear up the mess. To give her a surprise we had already swept the floor clean of bits of straw and other debris from our harvest preparations. If we expected praise from our curmudgeonly cleaner we were to be disappointed.

'Hm! And so I should think!' was Mrs Pringle's comment, when an innocent infant drew her attention to the unusually clean floor. 'Pity it ain't done every day!'

She limped heavily across the room towards the infants' class room, and did not hear Ernest's regrettable, but justified, remark to his neighbour.

I did. But I don't mind confessing that I turned a deaf ear.

On Saturday afternoon I made my way across the church-yard again. This time I was carrying an armful of foliage for the ladies of the village to use in their part of the church decorations. Luckily, I am not required to assist on this occasion. It is considered that I have done my share with the schoolchildren the day before, so that my visit is usually brief.

Mrs Partridge, the vicar's wife, and Mrs Mawne were standing back, surveying two large stone vases which flanked the altar. Doubt was writ large upon both faces.

'It isn't so much the *form*, dear, as the *colour*,' said Mrs Partridge earnestly. 'That mass of peony leaves near the base looks far too dominant, to my mind.'

'Rubbish!' retorted Mrs Mawne, who had obviously put the peony leaves there. 'It's just a good splash of colour, repeated, if you notice, in the left-hand top of the set. Personally, I feel it is perfect for *form*. I just rather wondered if that spray of yellow golden rod which you've just added, isn't the tiniest bit jarring.'

Mrs Partridge looked hurt. She is one of the keenest members of the Caxley Floral Society, and has won several diplomas for flower arrangements of a somewhat sparse and austere nature. A few spiky leaves, and one or two tulip heads, balanced in five stones from the vicarage rockery, were much admired last year by those who know about such things.

'Such economy of line!' breathed the judge, making a little box of his fingers and peering at the arrangement through the gap. And Amy, who was present on that occasion, said that it well deserved first prize for 'inspired asymmetry'.

'She deserves first prize for keeping the thing upright,' I said. 'One good cross-draught and the lot'd capsize.'

Amy informed me coldly that I lacked the right approach to flower arrangements, and regretted my mundane outlook on Beauty and Higher Things. I was unrepentant.

Mrs Partridge, on this occasion, rose to the defence of the golden rod.

'It is freely acknowledged,' she told Mrs Mawne, 'by both Eastern and Western authorities on Floral Art, that a touch of yellow, in any arrangement, adds the vital spark of life and sunshine to the whole. It is closely connected with the fact that yellow is one of the primary colours – and the most dominant one at that!'

She advanced militantly upon the stone vase with yet another spray of the offending plant. Mrs Mawne's mouth took on a grim line, and I deposited my armful thankfully on the chancel floor and fled outside.

I get quite enough sparring with Mrs Pringle from Monday to Friday. On Saturdays and Sundays I like a little peace.

Mr Willet was working in the churchyard. He was armed with a bill-hook and was taking vigorous swipes at the long grass which grew beneath the hawthorn hedge dividing the graveyard from the vicarage garden.

He straightened up as I approached, resting one horny hand on the small of his back.

'Not so young as I was,' he said, puffing out his stained walrus moustache. 'Bending double, after three helpings of my wife's treacle pudden, don't seem as easy as it used to.'

The sun was warm. It was a mellow September day, with the elm trees turning a pale gold against a pellucid blue sky. Mr Willet's ruddy face was beaded with sweat. He had rolled up his shirt sleeves, and his muscular hairy arms were smudged with grass stains and blotched with pink where the nettles had stung him. Nevertheless, he appeared unperturbed.

He seated himself on the low flat lid of a tomb, and I sat down beside him. It was comfortable and warm with the sunshine which had been pouring on it since daybreak. Among the moss and lichens which covered the stone was the inscription; 'Jno Jeremy – Gent of this Parifh.' I felt sure that he would have no objection to our presence.

'Fred Hurst's grave's coming on a treat,' said Mr Willet approvingly. He had put the bill-hook on the stone beside him, and his two tired hands drooped between his knees. His eyes, however, were bright as they surveyed his domain.

I followed his gaze. Certainly, a fine strong growth of green grass, neatly clipped, covered poor Fred's resting place. But it was the older grave beside it that caught my eye.

'What's that on Sally Gray's mound?' I asked.

Mr Willet looked a trifle shame-faced. 'Well, to tell you the truth, it's a little rose-bush – one I took as a cutting from ourn in the garden. Seemed a pity for it to go to waste, and the poor old dear hasn't got nothing growing along her. I put it in soon after I told you the tale about her. Remember?'

I nodded. The tale of Fairacre's flying woman had certainly intrigued me.

'Funny how we all likes a story,' ruminated Mr Willet, watching a red admiral butterfly settle on some Michaelmas daisies. 'Don't matter if you really believes it or not – as far as I can see. I mean, half of you believes, let's say, but the other half doubts, and in the end it's the half that wants to believe in the story that wins.'

'What's put this in your mind?' I asked lazily. A pigeon cooed from a tree nearby, and the air was so soft that I found the two together peculiarly soporific. If Mr Willet's sturdy bulk had not been beside me, I should like to have stretched out flat upon Jno Jeremy's warm stone, and had a gentle doze.

'That business of Joe Coggs,' answered Mr Willet. 'I bet he really knew that little chap under the pier was a midget. Yet you see, he sticks to it it was the Lord of the Seas, or some such.'

'It's difficult to know,' I murmured.

'When you're that age,' continued Mr Willet, 'these 'ere fairytale ideas get hold of you real strong. Witches and that.'

He stopped suddenly and there was a pause. I felt myself slipping from reality to the world of sleep. The pigeon's cooing sounded fainter and fainter.

'We 'ad one in Fairacre,' said Mr Willet's voice, startlingly close at hand.

'A pigeon?' I asked, struggling to sit upright.

'Tch! Tch!' tutted Mr Willet. 'A pigeon! Who was talking about pigeons? What I said was – we 'ad a witch once in Fairacre. At least they said she was.'

'And when was this?' I asked, now fully awake.

'When I was a nipper. Same age as young Joe, come to think of it. Proves what I was saying. You want to believe anything out of the ordinary when you're a kid. Take me, for instance.'

'Did you believe she was?' I queried, scenting a story.

'Me? I was positive. And I went out to prove it, what's more.'

He took out a short-stemmed pipe from his trouser pocket, and a small tin of tobacco.

'May as well 'ave one as I tell you the tale,' said Mr Willet, with mischievous sidelong glance. 'You ain't busy, I suppose?'

'Never too busy for a story,' I assured him, watching him fill his pipe.

Within two minutes, with the fragrant blue smoke wreathing his head, Mr Willet began.

Mr Willet was about seven at the time, he told me. He and his brothers and sisters lived in a cottage on the way to Spring-bourne, and walked daily to school at Fairacre.

There were four children of school age, and a baby of two at home. The four Willet children carried a rush basket with them, containing a substantial midday meal. A large propor-tion of it was bread and butter, but a finger of cheese apiece, a hard-boiled egg, or a slice or two of cold fat bacon, added relish and nourishment and old Mrs Willet made sure that fruit in season and a mammoth bottle of buttermilk accompanied her little family daily.

The schoolmaster at that time was Mr Hope. He was a clever, rather sad fellow, who wrote poetry, and occasionally read it, too, to his pupils. They were not, it seemed, particularly appreciative and, in fact, looked upon their headmaster as 'a bit loopy'. Tragedy touched the Hope family when their only daughter, much the same age as young Willet, died at the age of twelve. After that, Mr Hope found consolation in drink, and before long was asked to leave the district.

But while young Willet was in his class, Mr Hope taught well. He read many stories to them, chiefly the classic tales of adventure, the myths of Greece and Rome, some stirring passages from Scott or Henty, and so on. But now and again, conscious that the younger members of his class were finding difficulty in following some of the excerpts chosen, he took down the fairy books of Andrew Lang and read them a tale of enchantment and fantasy.

It was thus that young Willet – Bob to his family – became acquainted with the supernatural. He had heard of ogres and giants, of wizards and witches before, but now they became much more real to him. He entered, it seemed, into a knowledge of their ways, became conscious of their powers and of the infringement of such powers upon an ordinary mortal's life. He began to look at grown-ups with a slightly suspicious eye. Could it be that among them was a wizard? Or a witch? Circumstances combined to persuade him that there was such a one – and very near at hand.

About a quarter of a mile from the Willets' cottage, the road to Springbourne dropped suddenly downhill into a hollow. The ground here was marshy, and trees and flowers, foreign to the surrounding downland, made it seem a strange and slightly eerie place. Here, at the foot of the hill, was a small ramshackle cottage known as 'Lucy's'.

Lucy had lived there for many years. At the time of the story, she was a bent old woman in her eighties, a fearsome sight with sparse grey locks and one formidable eye-tooth which had grown so long that Lucy had difficulty in accommodating it comfortably in her mouth. It protruded over her lower lip and gave the poor old crone a most sinister appearance.

Fairacre was not at all sure about Lucy, and never had been. She and her husband, Seamus Kelly, had been brought from Ireland by Sir Francis Hurley who lived at Springbourne Manor. The Kellys had been brought to his notice one day when he was visiting friends in Ireland. He had mentioned that he was in need of a coachman with a real understanding of horses, and Seamus Kelly was warmly recommended.

The couple were duly installed in rooms above the coach house at Springbourne and gave great satisfaction until one sad day when Seamus was involved in an accident. He had taken the carriage and pair to Caxley Station to meet Sir Francis who was returning from London, when one of the magnificent bays took fright as the train drew in, and bolted. Seamus was thrown, the wheels passed over his back, and his spine was permanently damaged.

Everyone agreed that Sir Francis behaved with the utmost generosity. All medical care was lavished upon the unfortunate man and he spent many months in a convalescent home by the sea, at his employer's expense. Finally, he was given a pension and the small cottage in the hollow for the rest of his days.

Lucy, who had been a somewhat scatter-brained lady's maid, also had to retire from service to look after her crippled husband. Luckily, she was a strong woman, more than able to tend the garden and look after hens and two goats, as well as running the house and acting as nurse.

Seamus's temper, always violent, grew worse as he grew older. Lucy gave as good as she got, her Irish tongue uttering the most blood-curdling oaths, which scandalized the Fairacre worthies whose swearing was limited to a paucity of curses of Anglo-Saxon origin. Lucy, they agreed, was a wild one! To hear the way she went on made you wonder if she was right in the head! I mean, they said, we know she's *Irish*, but even so!

One winter's day, when the mist from the hollow shrouded the little house, Seamus gave a great cry from his bed. Lucy, milking the goat in the nearby shed, set down her pail and ran in. There, his face tipped towards the smoky ceiling, lay her husband, his blue eyes wide open in death.

After that dreadful day, Lucy had lived alone, with only her pets for company. Three cats had lived inside the cottage, and their numerous progeny had been dealt with by Seamus, keeping the numbers within bounds. Many a Fairacre cat had started life at Lucy's, and very fine specimens they were.

Now, with Seamus gone, Lucy did nothing about the kittens, and the number grew to a score in no time. It was true that she still gave one away, now and again, to anyone in need of a cat, and gratefully received the basket of plums or bowl of chitterlings which might be given in return, but the fact remained that there were far too many cats in the house.

Lucy did not seem to worry. She did not seem to worry about anything after Seamus's death. It was as though, with her sparring partner gone, she lacked the will to live. She neglected the house and her person, and Fairacre tongues wagged even more feverishly about Lucy's feckless ways.

'A dirty ol' saucepan on the kitchen table, as large as life, and her eating out of it with a wooden spoon! It's the truth, my dear! I saw it with my own eyes!'

'And it's my belief she hasn't had a good wash since her poor husband went. She don't waste much on soap, I'll be bound!'

'As for that black skirt she wears, it's time it was burnt. She bought it up the Jumble a good eight years ago, that I do know, and she's had it on, day in and day out, ever since!'

So spoke the good wives of the village, and among them was young Mrs Willet. As Lucy's closest neighbour she particularly felt the shame of such a slut in the neighbourhood. Newly married, with a cottage as spruce as endless scrubbing and polishing could make it, Mrs Willet was already spoken of as a paragon of cleanliness. She was to be honoured as such all her days.

Time passed. Lucy continued to exist on the pension granted by Sir Francis, and now administered by his heir, Sir Edmund. Only the minimum repairs were done to the cottage to keep it weatherproof. Lucy neglected the property to such an extent that it was hopeless to do more.

She was seen very little in the village. She now began to mutter to herself and her animals, emerging when dusk began to fall and when she would not be bothered by the sight of any neighbours or casual passers. It was at this stage of Lucy's decline that young Bob Willet became convinced that she was, without any doubt, a witch.

He had said as much to his older brother Sidney as they walked home from school one summer's day. Mr Hope had read them a Russian folk tale with a description of Baba Yaga, the witch, which seemed to young Bob a faithful portrait of Lucy Kelly who lived so perilously near them.

Perhaps he half-hoped for a decisive denial from his brother. If so, he was disappointed.

'Might be,' was Sidney's perfunctory comment. At that moment he was engaged in swishing the heads from a bed of stinging nettles, and was clearly too engrossed to give the matter of Lucy Kelly much attention. Bob did not press the point, but it seemed to him that Sid too considered it a possibility. It was alarming, to say the least of it.

In the days and nights that followed, Bob listened with growing terror to any conversation about their elderly neighbour. He did not like to speak of his fears to Sid, but he did mention it, as casually as he could manage, to another boy of his own age.

Ted Pickett, Bob was relieved to find, took his remarks quite seriously.

'She might be,' said Ted slowly. 'You see, you can't tell, unless you know she flies on a broomstick.'

'Well, she don't do that,' said Bob flatly.

'Or has a black cat.'

'She's plenty of they,' said Bob, feeling a little shaky.

They sat in silence for a little while. Then Ted began again. 'The way to find out is to go down her place when the moon's full. That's when witches fly. I know that for a fact, Bob. I read it in a school book.'

'What time?' asked Bob practically.

'Any time it's real bright,' replied Ted. 'On the night it's true full moon.'

'Come with me?' asked Bob.

'Not likely!' answered his friend. 'I'm real frightened of anything like that,' he added with disarming honesty. A play-fellow rushed up at this point, carrying the limp body of a long-dead grass snake. In the pleasurable few minutes follow-ing, Ted forgot the witch for ever.

Not so Bob. He could think of nothing else. He was frightened of the idea, but none the less fascinated. In school, when his mind should have been on the intricacies of punctu-ation or the problems of fractions, it roved instead to Lucy Kelly's cottage. What spells could she weave? Could she really fly? How could he find out if she really were a witch or not? Was Ted's test the true one?

As the month wore on towards the night of the full moon, the boy's tension mounted. He had made up his mind that he would go alone, if the night were fine and bright, to see for himself just what went on at Lucy Kelly's cottage.

Full moon, according to the almanac pinned on the kitchen wall, was on September 17th. The day was cloudless and still. From the hot schoolroom, young Bob could hear the harvesters working away under ideal conditions. Already many of the corn fields bore rows of stooks, the sheaves sagging together with the weight of a fine harvest.

The boy half-hoped that the weather would change, and that nightfall would bring such rain or tempest as would mean a postponement of his plans. But the weather held. At half past eight, he mounted the creaking stairs to the bedroom under the thatch, which he shared with his brother Sidney. Outside, the world was still bathed in golden light, and the swallows dived joyously through the air, snatching the flying insects that hung in the sunshine.

Bob had intended to stay awake until all the household was abed, but fresh air had made him drowsy and he was asleep before he knew it. Luckily, he was roused by the sound of his father and mother going to bed. It was nearly dark, but a great golden moon, low on the horizon, gave promise of a bright moonlit night.

Bob's heart thumped at the thought of the adventure ahead. He was not quite sure what he was going to look for. Certainly a broomstick, and perhaps evidence of actual flight by old Lucy. If she did fly, as Ted Pickett had said, then this was just the sort of night for her jaunting.

He listened to the sounds of the household. Sidney lay on his back, as always, snoring slightly. Bob knew that he had nothing to fear there. Once Sid was asleep, nothing – short of screaming in his ear – would wake him. The two girls, in the tiny slip room at the back of the cottage, slept as heavily as his brother. Only the youngest child roused occasionally. He slept in his parents' room, and if he should wake up, it was reasonable to suppose that his parents would calm him without having to leave the bedroom. Bob reckoned that he could leave the house and return without much trouble.

He heard the clock at St Patrick's, across the fields, strike eleven, and waited a little longer. Midnight was supposed to be the time that witches chose for their flying operations, as Bob well knew. Then he slipped from his warm bed, dressed with shaking fingers, and crept fearfully downstairs.

The creaks and groans from the ancient staircase brought his heart into his mouth, but no one stirred. He made his way through the kitchen and let himself out by the back door.

The night was mysteriously beautiful. It was scented with corn, warm earth and garden flowers. The moonlight was so bright that young Bob could have read by it, had he been of such a mind.

He slipped through a gap in the back hedge, out of sight of his parents' bedroom window, and gained the lane. It was white in the moonlight, and dropped away to the hollow which was his destination.

His boots seemed to make a dreadful amount of noise on the gritty road. A cat shot across his path – one of Lucy's, he guessed – and frightened the wits out of him. By the time he reached Lucy's, he was bathed in sweat.

There was no gate. Bob crept on tip-toe up the overgrown path with one wary eye upon the upstairs window. It was tightly shut, as indeed were all the others downstairs, Bob noticed. It was as quiet as the grave, and in the light of the moon, the little grey cottage seemed to merge into the crepuscular background of the silvery willows and dead grass surrounding it.

At the side of the house was a lean-to shed made of wood, which had once been tarred, but was now weathered to a ghostly grey. If Lucy really had a mount then this would be its stable, Bob decided. He crept quietly towards it, intending to enter, but froze in his tracks long before he gained the lean-to. For there, propped outside the door, as large as life, was a stout broom, or besom, made of birch twigs.

Bob was almost sick with fright. Was it waiting there for Lucy to ride shortly? Or was it simply an innocent garden besom, such as his mother used to sweep their garden path? Who could tell?

He decided to creep right round the cottage, listening for any movement of Lucy within. He passed by the broomstick, almost expecting to see it pulsing with hidden life, and was relieved to gain the shelter of the side wall. Here was crouched a tabby cat, sitting sphinx-like and motionless – only the glittering of its moonstone eyes showing that it was alert and wakeful.

The boy padded along the back of the house where the shabby thatch was so low that it pricked him through his jersey as he grazed by the edge. Stinging nettles and docks made a rank and painful jungle here, and he was glad to reach the side of the house where the hens had pecked a bare patch. A little window looked out on this side and Bob peered within.

As far as he could see, it was Lucy's primitive larder. A dish or two stood on the shelves, and some onions were hanging from a hook. There seemed to be little more, except for cobwebs.

The front of the house was in full moonlight. Two small windows, cracked and grimy, glinted in the moon's brilliance. Through one Bob could see little, for a tattered curtain obscured his view, but he heard the sound of a cat jumping to the floor, as though he had been observed, and the cat was making for cover.

All around him was silence. His heart had ceased to thump so dreadfully, but he still sweated with fright and the nape of his neck felt tight with terror. As he edged along to look into the remaining window, the clock of St Patrick's struck twelve, and the boy froze with renewed horror. Now was the witch's hour!

As the last clear note died away into the warm stillness, Bob looked into Lucy's living room. Moonlight lit the dishevelled apartment, and at first sight it appeared empty. Then suddenly, in the shadow beneath the window, Bob saw a dark figure roll from a low couch or mattress hard against the wall. He shrank back, out of sight, his mouth dry with fear.

Lucy was clad in her daytime black, her grey hair looked wilder than ever in the light of the moon. Her crazy eyes and one long tooth glinted from the shadows as she stumbled, muttering, about the room.

She snatched a black shawl from the tumbled bed and flung it round her shoulders. From a peg on the door she clawed an old black trilby hat of the long-dead Seamus's, and clapped it on her eldritch locks. Then, with purposeful haste, she emerged from her door and made her way towards the lean-to.

But before she reached the broomstick, Bob Willet had fled.

'So you never found out,' I commented, as Mr Willet finished.

'I found out one thing,' said Mr Willet grimly. 'And that was not to go scaring folk at night. My dad heard me coming in and caught me on the stairs. I got a cuff on the ear as made me see stars as well as moon that night, I can tell 'ee.'

He paused for a moment, contemplating that distant night encounter.

'Looking back now, I'd lay a wager the poor ol' gal was making for her privy in the lean-to, but that warn't in my mind at the time, as you can guess.'

He rose stiffly from the gravestone and picked up the bill-hook.

'Well, best get back to work, I s'pose. But it makes you think, don't it? You see, I reckons I was as keen to believe in my witch, as little ol' Joe is to believe in his King of the Sea. It's a sort of *hunger*, if you takes my meaning.'

' "More things in heaven and earth, Horatio",' I quoted.

Mr Willet looked a little startled. 'I wouldn't know about Horatio,' he said reasonably. 'I'm only telling you my opinion.' And he resumed his onslaught on the long grass.

The next day Amy came to tea. She was elegant in a new brown and white dog-tooth check suit which I much admired.

'You could have bought it for yourself,' said Amy. 'It's been in the window of Bakers in Caxley High Street for over a week.'

'I haven't been to Caxley for three weeks,' I said. 'Nor anywhere else, come to think of it.'

Amy pursed her lips impatiently. 'Are you ever going to get yourself out of this rut?' she demanded. 'You were excessively naughty about that Devon job, and all because you didn't want poor little Lucy Colgate to come here.'

'Poor little Lucy Colgate,' I pointed out with some warmth, 'weighs over eleven stone, and is the last person on this earth needing anyone's pity – great, smug, insensitive lump of self-congratulation that she is!'

'Now, now!' warned Amy. 'You see what I mean? You are getting positively *warped* living alone here – a mass of neuroses – coveting my suit, and now picking poor Lucy to bits.'

'Let's have some tea,' I said. 'It might sweeten me.'

She followed me into the kitchen, and watched me stack a tray.

'My cousin tells me,' she said, 'that there is an excellent post going at a comprehensive school in her town. I think she said there are four thousand pupils and two swimming pools.'

'Good luck to them!' I said. 'But I prefer thirty-six pupils and two buckets of drinking water. And who knows? I may live long enough in Fairacre to see water laid on to the school! No, Amy, "I won't be druv!"'

Later, we walked across to our Harvest Festival. It was a perfect evening of mellow September sunshine. Through the west window, the golden sun lit the nave and burnished the sheaves of corn and all our offerings of fruit and flower.

Mrs Pratt was bumbling happily at the organ, improvising a voluntary until such time as the vicar and choir entered. As this was an important festal day in Fairacre, and the church was suitably crammed, there would be a procession from the west door down the nave.

Suddenly there was a scuffling noise behind us, the west doors were thrown open, and the sunlight streamed in. Bathed in its golden light the choir and the vicar slowly made their way eastward while we scrambled to our feet.

Come, ye thankful people, come!
Raise the song of harvest home!

we sang fortissimo.

Mrs Pringle, foremost among the contraltos, swayed past me, lowing powerfully. Mr Willet was not far behind, holding his own among the basses. Ahead, several of my pupils, unnaturally clean and holy, raised their voices in song.

It was good, I thought suddenly, to be taking part in something which had happened in this church for many years, without fail, an act of thanksgiving for the harvest which surrounded this ancient building on every side. Just so did Sally Gray, Fred Hurst, poor Job the Fairacre ghost, Mrs Next-Door and a host of others who now lay so quietly outside these walls, rejoice together, as we did, for mercies received. I looked about me. Amy, friend of many years, stood by my side. In front of me I could see Elsie Blundell and her husband. Two pews ahead was Isobel Annett with Malcolm, my godchild; sitting with them was dear Miss Clare. My eye roamed to the chancel where the choir was now in place and still singing lustily under the attentive eye of George Annett, their choir-master. Mr Willet's honest face was red with his exertions, and I remembered, with affection, the story of his midnight adventure.

How right he was, I thought! We do all need a story, as he said. There is a hunger in us which needs to be assuaged. With what avidity I have listened to my neighbours' accounts of tales of long ago, and with what unfailing curiosity I observe the happenings of today!

Here, around me, are all the folk of Fairacre, both the quick and the dead. The story of the village goes back a long, long time; and it still goes on. Every hour that we live, the story unfolds, now tragic, now comical, but always and everlastingly absorbing.

Can you wonder that we are never dull in Fairacre?

The Fairacre Festival

For Anne,
with love from her godmother

On the first night of October a mighty wind arose and smote the countryside around Fairacre. The violence of that wild night took almost all by surprise. Only the exceptionally weatherwise, such as Mr Willet, had any inkling of the devastation which lay in store, and even they admitted, as they surveyed the wreckage the next morning, that it was 'a durn sight worse'n they'd thought it would be'.

We had enjoyed a week of mellow sunshine at the end of September. Butterflies clung decoratively to the Michaelmas daisies, wasps lurched drunkenly from ripe pears to ripe plums, and the schoolchildren at Fairacre School were more comfortable in their cotton frocks and thin shirts than they had been on many other occasions during a changeable summer.

Harvest Festival was celebrated on the last day of September and, as usual, we helped to deck the ancient church of St Patrick's with 'all things bright and beautiful'. Coral-berried bryony from the school hedge wreathed the font. At the foot lay mounds of apples, pears and marrows. Carrots, parsnips and onions lined the ledges, and two fine sheaves of corn gleamed and rustled in their time-honoured place, one on each side of the chancel steps. The ladies of the parish had put their natural talents, and the expertise learnt at the local floral society, into the handsome flower arrangements, and it was generally maintained by the congregation that the church had never looked so magnificent.

Monday morning dawned as benignly as ever. I watched the

children, summer-clad and relaxed, as they drank their morning milk, and congratulated myself on postponing the lighting of the two tortoise stoves. Far too often, in the autumn term, I have asked my curmudgeonly school cleaner, Mrs Pringle, to light these monsters, only to experience a spell of humid weather in which we have all sweltered in the classrooms. Mrs Pringle never lets me forget these unfortunate errors.

'Remember last year?' she demands belligerently, massive jaw out-thrust. 'You would have it. Said the children was cold, and up I come with paper, with sticks, with matches, although my leg was not what it should be –'

'But it *was* cold,' I begin, but am swept aside.

'I fetches the coal, fetches the coke, goes down on me hands and knees for a full quarter of an hour to get the stoves to draw – and what happens?'

I don't bother to answer. This, I know from experience, is a rhetorical question. Sometimes I think what a wonderful actress the stage has lost in Mrs Pringle. Her looks are definitely a drawback, but she has a fine sense of drama and puts plenty of punch into her lines.

'We gets a hot spell. All my work's for nothing, and the coke's got to come out of us ratepayers' pockets. What's more, the children's pores are left hanging open for all the germs to get in as soon as they goes out into the cold playground!'

This year, I told myself, on that fair Monday morning, I had behaved in an exemplary manner. Tomorrow would be October the second, and after that the lighting of the stoves must surely be considered acceptable by my task mistress.

But, by midday, I was beginning to have doubts. The sun went in, the temperature dropped sharply, and the children began to rub their goose-pimpled arms. By the time they ran home in the afternoon, a cold wind had sprung up, snatching the yellow leaves from the plum tree in my garden and sending me scuttling to light my sitting-room fire.

As darkness fell, the force of the wind increased. It roared in the elm trees towering above the school. It screamed round the school house, spattering leaves against the window and sending the dustbin lid clanging across the garden. The little house shuddered at its onslaught. Safe by the leaping fire, with a pile of exercise books to mark and the cat asleep by my feet, I gave the elements scant attention.

But later, in bed, I became anxious. Never before had I heard the wind quite so violent in Fairacre. I remembered the doleful tales about elm trees which Mr Willet never tired of telling me. If one of those hefty branches fell across my roof it could be pretty damaging. And what about the roof tiles? It seemed incredible that anything could withstand the fury of the wind tonight. Strange creaks and groans seemed to come from the loft above me and an ill-fitting window let in a piercing draught accompanied by an ear-splitting whistle.

I pulled the bedclothes up round my ears, thanked heaven that I was a schoolteacher and not a sailor, and slept amidst the uproar.

*

Throughout the night the wind wreaked destruction. In the streets of Caxley it wrenched slates from roofs and toppled a dozen chimney-pots into the gutters. A flying tile broke the plate-glass window of Howard's Restaurant in the market square, and a poor unfortunate man, cycling head down against the onslaught on his way to night shift, was blown from the towpath into the cold waters of the Cax, and there drowned.

Just outside Caxley station a telegraph pole fell across the line, throwing all into confusion, and on the road to Beech Green a tree had crashed, tearing down the telephone wires in its fall. But Caxley, tucked in its hollow, came off comparatively lightly. It was the windswept villages on the downs which bore the full brunt of the wind's savagery and it was Fairacre which suffered the most shattering blow.

On a little knoll of high ground between the vicarage and St Patrick's a cluster of ancient elms stands, cradling a rookery in the topmost boughs. We, in Fairacre, admire the way that these lovely old trees form a background to the church. Rosy-purple in spring as the buds swell, providing dense shade in full summer, turning to clear gold in the autumn and spreading a black lacy tracery against the winter skies, they are a constant pleasure to the eye.

But Mr Willet has never been one of their admirers.

'One of these days,' he has said, on many occasions, 'them dratted elms is going to cause trouble. Got no proper root growth, has elms. All spread out too near the surface for my liking. A good wind up top and over they goes.' And he was to be proved right.

About two o'clock the fury of the wind was at its height. Its screaming woke me. The loose window shuddered and thudded, and the roaring outside was terrifying. It must have been this particular gust which caught the tallest of the elms nearest the church and sent it toppling. The topmost branches swept St Patrick's stubby spire, and bent the proud weather-cock until it drooped head-down from its twisted stay. The heavy branches came to rest across the nave, scattering tiles and damaging the roof for which the church is famed. The massive trunk lay athwart the graveyard and the old roots, torn from the turf, writhed above a huge gaping hole.

I did not hear the crash; nor do I think anyone else did. The noise was so continuous that it was impossible to pick out any particular incident. But the vicar said later that he awoke at that time and was conscious of some extraordinary commotion at the heart of the storm, and confessed frankly that he had felt frightened.

When light returned, the damage was discovered, and in no time at all a bevy of villagers came to survey the wreckage. Mr Willet was first on the scene, and with commendable magnanimity forebore to say: 'I told you so!' It was he who broke the news to Mr Partridge, the vicar, who was shaving when the bell of the back door rang.

'Bad news, sir,' Mr Willet shouted up to the frothy face which appeared at the bathroom window.

'The greenhouse?' queried the vicar, holding the window against the wind.

'No, sir. The church. Tree across it, sir.'

'Oh, my dear Willet!' cried the vicar, his face puckering in distress. 'What a terrible thing! I will be with you directly.'

The window slammed, and within five minutes the vicar and his wife joined Mr Willet at the scene of the disaster. Several workmen, on their way to their labours, had propped their bicycles against the flint churchyard wall, and stood shaking their heads at the confusion.

'We must get help from Caxley,' said Mrs Partridge decisively. 'There's no one in Fairacre with the equipment to shift that enormous thing.'

'We must indeed, my dear,' agreed the vicar distractedly. There were tears in his blue eyes as he paced from one position to another assessing the appalling damage to his beloved St Patrick's. 'I suppose a crane or some such piece of machinery will be necessary, Willet? I can't bear to think of the wreckage we shall discover when the tree is lifted. I must go inside at once and make sure that everything is safe.'

'I'll come inside with you,' said Mr Willet. 'You wants to watch out that none of them timbers is busted.'

They entered the church while more villagers arrived to inspect the night's work. Here was drama in plenty! The schoolchildren were pleasurably excited by it all, and to a certain extent so were their elders, but there was in addition a shocked solemnity in the face of this tragedy, and thin-lipped Mrs Fowler from Tyler's Row put into words the unspoken thoughts of all when she asked of the villagers at large:

'And who's going to pay for this lot, may I ask?'

It was a question which was to perplex Fairacre for many a long month.

Meanwhile, the work of clearing up the mess began. It was impossible to telephone to Caxley as the Post Office men were busy all the morning repairing the line at Beech Green, but Mr Mawne, churchwarden and member of the Parochial Church Council, set off for Caxley at the vicar's behest.

Henry Mawne is a comparative newcomer to Fairacre, a retired schoolmaster and a keen ornithologist. He and his wife take their fair share of responsibilities in village matters and the vicar, in particular, relishes the friendship and support of this quiet man. His competent handling of church accounts is a source of great comfort to the vicar whose grasp of financial details is hopelessly vague. Mrs Partridge confided once to me that her devout and erudite husband is under the impression that ten pennies make a shilling, and that this fundamental misapprehension is at the root of his difficulties. Certainly parochial affairs have been much more businesslike under Henry Mawne's administration.

As Mr Mawne expected, the plant hire firm had most of its

equipment spread about the country that morning, but a crane was promised for the afternoon and two men set off at once from Caxley to start cutting away branches and to clear the site for the rescue operation. He returned to find the vicar in conversation with his Bishop at the county town, the telephone lines in that direction having miraculously escaped damage. He had already been in touch with the Rural Dean, he told Henry Mawne, when he replaced the receiver, and the diocesan architect would be along as soon as possible to look at the damage.

'But the best news of all, my dear Henry,' cried the vicar, 'is from Jock Graham, who arrived just after you had gone, to say that he will act as our architect without any payment. Isn't that a magnificent gesture?'

'It is indeed,' agreed Mr Mawne. He did not care for this elderly Scot, recently retired, but realized how much this generous offer would mean to the parish.

'You see,' went on the vicar. 'I gather that all the expenses will have to be found by Fairacre. The diocesan people have just made it clear that there can be no money forthcoming from them. It's a parish responsibility. I suppose we must expect a bill of a hundred pounds or so?'

'I should prefer to wait until the diocesan architect has had his look,' said Mr Mawne cautiously, 'but from what I saw this morning, I should say we'd be lucky to get away with anything less than two thousand.'

'*Two thousand?*' quavered the vicar. Horror and stupefaction showed in his face. 'It's impossible, Henry!'

Henry Mawne rose from his seat and patted the vicar's shoulder kindly. 'Cheer up, Gerald,' he said. 'I'm probably hopelessly wrong, but I don't want you to get a shock later on. I think you'll find the bill is going to be a great deal more than a few hundred pounds, that's all.'

'But we can't pay it,' protested the vicar helplessly. 'Fairacre can't possibly raise anything more than a hundred at the outside!'

'I'm aware of that,' said his friend.

'And even that amount,' went on the vicar despairingly, 'means a succession of whist drives, fêtes, jumble sales, coffee mornings and all those terrible, terrible affairs. You realize that, Henry?'

'Only too well, Gerald,' replied Henry Mawne, doing his best to suppress a shudder.

The vicar rose from his chair and began to pace distractedly round his desk, his hands clasped behind his back and his brow furrowed. Mr Mawne watched him sympathetically from the doorway. It seemed hard to leave his stricken friend in his present distress, but there was much to be done.

Gerald Partridge stopped suddenly and faced him.

'It is a challenge, Henry! This is something sent by Providence to test us, to strengthen our faith. We must, and shall, restore St Patrick's!'

'That's the way to take it,' agreed Mr Mawne, touched by this brave display of resolution. Closing the study door gently behind him, he returned home through the wind.

When school dinner was over, I made my way to the church to see the extent of the damage. The men were busy clearing the worst of the mess from the churchyard, and I went inside by the west door.

Several people had volunteered to tidy up. Mr and Mrs Willet were there, the two sisters, Margaret and Mary Waters, and various other women.

'Got my washing on the line and come straight up,' said one.

'Had to find my poor hens first,' said another. 'The hen house blew clean off their backs, and they was everywhere from the fir tree to the coal-hole.'

Tales of the night's wrecking flew back and forth as they plied brooms and dustpans.

'The top half of Mr Roberts's hay stack went whirling by our roof.'

'Our Nelly lost three tea towels off the line. And the cat! He *would* go out and it's her belief he's been blown out of the parish.'

Somehow, I suspected, listening to these exchanges, the damages grew at each recital. We enjoy a bit of excitement in Fairacre, and the drama of this wild night would certainly go down, suitably embellished, in local history.

There was a great deal of plaster on the floor of the nave, and the pews were white with dust. Mr Willet was collecting the rubble in a wheelbarrow in the aisle. A dark patch gaped above, in the beautiful hammer-beam roof, but no daylight showed through. Hopes were running high that the damage was only superficial, but more would be known when the surveyor had inspected it.

The pulpit was badly scratched and one of the chandeliers had bounced from its hook, at the time of impact, and lay shattered on the floor.

'No loss!' remarked Mrs Mawne to me in an aside audible

to all. 'Hideous Victoriana! Pity the rest didn't come down too!'

Afternoon school was a somewhat distracted affair. The children are always excitable in windy weather, and this fascinating disaster added to their general fidgetiness. Hoping to channel their feelings into some positive and useful work – as exhorted to do by all good educationists – I set them to write an essay on the night's storm.

'And you can illustrate it too,' I added, hoping for a prolonged period of peace in the classroom.

'With crayons?'

'Yes, with crayons.'

'Won't be much good. 'Twas all dark. Shan't want no colours.'

'Then you can simply use your lead pencil,' I retorted loftily. Disgruntled muttering from the malcontent's desk I ignored pointedly.

An unusual quietness fell upon the room, broken only by laboured breathing as the pangs of composition gripped them, and the stutter of crayons depicting rain. I wandered to the window and gazed out. A drift of dead leaves rustled against the foot of the school wall, and a mat of ivy flapped loosely above it, wrenched from its anchorage by the gale.

The vicarage garden seemed bare of leaves, and through the gaps in the denuded shrubbery I could see several of the helpers making their way home. This, I told myself, certainly brings people together – nothing like a common foe to unite a community.

At that moment, young Tom in the front row raised his hand. His parents are fiercely evangelical, and he is uncomfortably well behaved and a trifle smug.

'How do you spell "Wrath-of-God"?' he inquired earnestly.

'How do you intend to use the phrase?' I asked guardedly.

He turned his attention to the paper before him and read slowly. ' "Our chapel was not hit in the night, but the church was. My mum said it was—"' He paused and looked up hopefully.

I spelt out the desired phrase. My sympathy went out to those working for Christian unity, and I made a mental note to have a lesson on 'loving thy neighbour as thyself', before the end of the week.

It looked as though Fairacre might profit from it.

2

Before Monday came round again, much had happened in the village.

In the first place, Fairacre had put itself to rights as best it could. Broken branches were sawn up into neat logs and stacked inside wood-sheds. Shrubs and standard roses were lashed to new stakes. Slates and tiles were hung again, thatch patched and hen-house roofs replaced and weighted with size-able flint stones, in case of future gales.

Nelly Potter's cat returned, none the worse for a night out. Mr Roberts, the farmer, retrieved some of his scattered hay, and Mrs Pringle, discovering a child's apron blowing on the hedge, recognized it as one of little Vanessa Emery's and returned it graciously to the child's scatter-brained mother.

'Nearly tore to shreds it was by the time the wind had done with it,' said Mrs Pringle to me, before school one morning, 'but I don't suppose it'll ever see needle and thread in that house. Proper muddler that woman is! Half-past nine when I called in, and she still in her dressing-gown!' Mrs Pringle drew an outraged breath at the very thought, and picked up a cinder which was marring the glossy jet of the stove's surround.

'Still, I will say,' she conceded, as she straightened up with an ominous creaking of whalebone stays, 'that she give me a very nice smile and thanked me for my trouble.'

'Good,' I said absently, rummaging in my drawer for a paperclip.

'*Which*,' boomed Mrs Pringle pointedly, 'is a lot more than some people do!'

And with a pronounced limp she made her way to the lobby.

Mr Willet had cleared up the mess in the school playground, and had continued the good work, in his capacity of church sexton, in the graveyard next door. Luckily, the ancient headstones had escaped injury, for the tree which caused most of the trouble had lodged against the roof of the church, and had been lifted clear by the crane without much difficulty.

The damage to the fabric of the church was Fairacre's most serious problem. Providentially, it was less than had been feared at first. The stout ancient roof beams had stood the blow well, and only three or four would need to be replaced. But much retiling needed to be done to the spire and the nave, and the belfry wanted a stonemason's attention.

'And can you give us any idea of the expense?' asked the vicar anxiously as he, Mr Mawne and Jock Graham accompanied the diocesan architect and his young assistant on the tour of inspection.

The architect peered over his half-glasses and looked solemn.

'Mr Graham will go into figures of course, but I should say, at a rough estimate –'

'A *very* rough estimate,' chimed in the assistant, speaking as one who has often been caught out and hoped to miss the unpleasant experience this time.

'As a *very rough* estimate,' agreed the architect, looking coldly at his colleague, 'somewhere in the region –'

'Only *in the region*,' interjected the assistant sternly.

'Of about one thousand eight hundred pounds to two thousand.'

'*About*, of course, *just about*,' echoed his companion. 'One can never be sure what one will find once the work is in hand, as I am sure Mr Graham will agree. One doesn't want to be too hasty in suggesting a figure.'

'So I noticed,' observed Mr Mawne drily.

His face wore a small satisfied smile. This was the sum he had suggested in the first place to his friend, the vicar, and it was some comfort in this bleak hour to know that he was not far out in his estimation.

The vicar's rosy face, however, showed no sign of pleasure, simply stupefaction and distress. He was quite beyond speech.

'We'll go back and report our findings,' said the architect kindly, tucking his half-glasses into a splendid gold-tooled case. 'And, if Mr Graham wishes, I'll send you the names of some reputable contractors who specialize in church repairs who will, of course, give you a detailed estimate when they have had a look at your little bit of trouble here.'

The vicar opened his mouth as though stung into speech, thought better of it, and said nothing. They crossed the churchyard to the black Humber at the gate.

'I shouldn't worry too much, my dear sir,' said the architect with misplaced heartiness. 'Could have been much worse, you know. Think of Coventry Cathedral. Now there *was* some damage!'

The car drove off, watched by Mr Mawne, Mr Graham and their stricken friend. As it rounded the bend to the village street, the vicar found his voice.

'I don't like to seem uncharitable, but I hope that I may never see that man again! "Our little bit of trouble" indeed!'

'Take no heed of his havering,' rumbled Jock Graham.

The vicar's lips quivered suddenly. 'But what are we to do? What are we to do?'

Henry Mawne rose to the occasion. 'We will call an emergency meeting of the Parochial Church Council and put on our thinking caps,' he replied firmly. Together they shepherded Gerald Partridge to the haven of his vicarage, and a much-needed cup of coffee.

The Parochial Church Council, all twelve of us, turned up in full force on Friday evening. We met in the vicarage dining-room which was still faintly redolent of the curried lamb and baked apples on which Mr and Mrs Partridge had recently dined.

There were present the vicar, in the chair, Mr Mawne and his wife, Mr Roberts, the other churchwarden and our local farmer, Mr Graham as honorary architect, Mr Willet and myself, all from the village. Mr Basil Bradley and Major Gunning represented Springbourne, which is also in the living of Fairacre's vicar, along with three rather prosperous younger men, who commute daily to the City, thus making up our full complement.

Basil Bradley produces a novel each year and is much thought of in the district. He is called upon to open bazaars and fêtes, and is much in demand as a speaker at various functions, twice rising to the dizzy heights of chief speaker at local Women's Institute group meetings. Since the death of his formidable mother, who guarded his goings-out and comings-in zealously, he has lived alone in a pretty cottage enjoying his freedom. He is a remarkably handsome man, with the ashen fair hair which slips imperceptibly over the years into silver, and the gentle manners born of many years of willing servitude to his tyrant. Men dislike him. Women dote on him, and do their best to get him married. Somehow, I do not think that they will ever be successful.

Major Gunning is as martial as his name, and has a garden full of well-disciplined plants as upright as himself. His paths are straight. His standard roses line them like a guard of honour. A row of poplars stands sentinel upon his skyline. No daisies spangle Major Gunning's lawns, no groundsel mars the beds. And should any pink or poppy droop its pretty head out of its appointed place, then summary execution must be expected.

It was he who spoke first after the vicar had explained the dilemma.

'Open an Appeal Fund. Stick up a good bold board outside the Church, and send notices to every man-jack in the parish.'

'Humph!' snorted Mrs Mawne beside him. 'That won't bring in much!'

'And have you any suggestions?' asked Major Gunning, bristling.

'Plenty,' snapped Mrs Mawne, slapping her gloves down on the table challengingly. 'First of all –'

'Address the chair,' put in Mr Mawne.

His wife twitched round exasperatedly and faced the vicar. 'Mr Chairman, I think determined and regular money-raising efforts should be started at once. A weekly whist drive, a weekly dance, a weekly raffle, a weekly coffee morning –'

'But, my dear Mrs Mawne,' pleaded the vicar, 'where is the money to come from?'

'I'm telling you. From all these activities!'

Basil Bradley took upon himself the thankless task of explanation. 'But where, I think our Chairman means, will *the people* get the money? Their wages will remain at the same level. They can't afford to go to so many weekly functions.'

'Thank you,' said the vicar simply. 'That is the position exactly. We must try to think of attracting outside help. The parish itself has no riches.'

A gloomy silence fell while we all pondered this sad fact.

'D'you mean that there is no help at all from some body or other?' demanded Mr Roberts at length. 'You know – Ecclesiastical Commissioners or the Diocese, or Friends of Friendless Churches? Something o' that?'

'St Patrick's isn't a *friendless* church,' said the vicar defensively. 'It's a very much-loved church.'

'Yes, indeed. Yes, indeed,' agreed Mr Willet warmly.

'But I'm afraid we have only ourselves to rely on,' went on the vicar. 'The Bishop was deeply sympathetic, but made it quite plain that the parish is solely responsible for these repairs.'

'I think Mrs Mawne's suggestions are on the right lines,' I volunteered. 'If all the village organizations make a particular effort it means that we shall raise quite a decent part of the whole by our own exertions.'

'We could map out a programme,' said Mr Roberts. 'What about a traction engine rally in my big meadow?'

'And a folk-dancing display by the village school?' said Mrs Mawne. I could have made a tart retort, but forbore.

'And a bumper Fur and Feather Whist Drive this autumn?' said Mr Willet.

'I should be very pleased to open my garden next summer,' offered Basil Bradley. 'And provide tea. I've just mastered Chelsea buns.'

'How very clever!' cried Mrs Mawne turning towards him. 'Now they are things which I simply *cannot* manage. Cream horns, almond slices, Victoria sandwiches, gingerbread – I flatter myself I can cope with anything like that, but yeast cookery is my Waterloo. How much sugar do you put in with your yeast?'

The chairman, seeing his meeting dissolve, as is so often the case in village affairs, banged loudly on the table.

'Please, please, ladies and gentlemen! Miss Read and Mrs Mawne have both made the suggestion that we see how much can be raised by superhuman efforts in the village by traditional methods. Can anyone add to this idea?'

A rumbling noise from under Mr Willet's tobacco stained moustache gave warning of wise words to follow. Little did we think, as we waited, that we were witnessing the birth of a momentous brainchild.

'What's wrong with having all these things – or most of 'em, say – in one week next summer? A festival, like. We hears a lot about the Edinburgh Festival and all their goings-on up there. And there's that chap, Britten, at the Aldwych –'

'Aldeburgh,' put in Basil Bradley.

'Same thing,' said Mr Willet airily. 'He has a festival by the seaside. Mr Annett's been. He said 'twas a real slap-up affair. Well, what I'm getting at is this. Why can't we have a Fairacre Festival?'

We all gazed at Mr Willet with respect.

'It's a wonderful idea, Willet,' said the vicar. 'Quite wonderful! But do you think people would come?'

'Why not?' demanded Mrs Mawne. 'If they go to Edinburgh, to that perishing cold climate, not to mention the reeking smoke which they admit themselves, then why on earth shouldn't they come here?'

'Perhaps not quite in the same numbers,' said Basil Bradley. 'After all, Edinburgh has wonderful concerts and ballets and what-have-you – but I'm sure we could have a Fairacre Festival which would be successful on a more modest scale.'

'Damn good idea,' announced Mr Roberts. 'One great glorious burst of fête, jumble sale, concert, whist-drive, bingo, dancing and everything else. If we advertise it well, the money will come rolling in.'

'We might have *Son et Lumière*,' said Major Gunning, 'with St Patrick's as the background. Tell the parish story, you know.'

'Not all of it,' said Mr Willet cautiously. 'There's some things best kept quiet. Take that affair of Ted Grimble's grand-dad now –'

'Yes, well –' the vicar broke in hastily. 'Perhaps we are getting away from the point. Could we have a show of hands for Mr Willet's excellent proposal?'

We were all agreed. It was decided to meet again to plan not only the Fairacre Festival for next summer, but also to arrange other money-making efforts, starting immediately.

It was while we were congratulating ourselves, and Mr Willet in particular, on our cleverness, that Henry Mawne spoke up.

'Before we go, I think we should be realistic about these ideas. They will raise a few hundred, I feel sure, and we might raise a few more by donations. But I don't think we can hope to raise even half by these methods.'

'But what else can we do?' pleaded the vicar.

Mr Mawne screwed his propelling pencil slowly, making the lead emerge further and further. He studied it intently as he spoke.

'You said earlier that the parish had no riches. It's not quite true. I hardly like to suggest this but I'm going to. We have, as you all know, locked in the bank and used only at the great church festivals, a valuable old chalice of solid silver and impeccable workmanship. One recently fetched over two thousand pounds. It was not as fine as ours.'

We gazed at Henry Mawne in silence. We were all, I think, a little shocked by his suggestion. To tell the truth, I had not realized the value of the chalice, and had certainly forgotten its existence whilst we had been debating ways and means. The vicar looked horrified and Mrs Mawne surveyed her husband with as much disgust as she would have displayed had he suggested slaughtering her dachshund for lunch.

'Impossible!' she exclaimed.

'Unthinkable!' cried Major Gunning.

'That's not ours to give away,' observed Mr Willet austerely. ''Twas given to the church to celebrate Queen Anne's reign. Some relation of old Miss Parr's, so they told us at school, gave it over two hundred and fifty years ago. It belongs to the parish.'

The vicar found his voice. 'Willet is quite right, Henry. The chalice is beyond price, and is in any case only ours on trust. It belongs to St Patrick's.'

'So did its roof,' said Henry Mawne. 'I know the idea is distasteful, but there you are. Is it right to keep such a valuable object locked away, while rain comes through the roof and the church deteriorates? St Patrick's also belongs to the parish. Which is of more use?'

Surprisingly, it was Basil Bradley who came to Henry Mawne's support.

'It has been done before. My uncle's church in Cumberland sold a most beautiful silver paten some years ago. It went to a new church somewhere in Massachusetts where it is very much prized, I can assure you.'

'I daresay,' replied the vicar, a shade frostily. 'But I cannot entertain the thought of selling our own silver.'

'I'm only suggesting,' said Basil Bradley steadily, 'that it may be some comfort to know that if the appeal and the Festival do not raise the money then at least we have the chalice behind us, as it were.'

'Quite wrong!' said Mrs Mawne forcefully, jamming on her gloves. 'The chalice must remain here for future generations.'

'Absolutely!' growled Major Gunning.

'Let's hope it won't come to that,' said Mr Roberts. 'We'll do our best to get the cash in every other way possible.'

And on that note, the meeting ended.

Later that night, the vicar lay sleepless, watching the moonlight wavering upon the ceiling above his head. Somewhere, far away, a stoat yelped shrilly. The leaves of the Virginia creeper rustled by the open window, and near at hand his big silver watch ticked companionably from the bedside table.

All was as usual in the peaceful room, but still sleep evaded him.

His thoughts turned again and again to Henry's appalling suggestion. How could he have conceived such an idea? It amounted almost to betrayal. The whole idea was monstrous. He simply could not think what Henry meant by putting forward such an outrageous scheme. It was bad enough to have had such thoughts. To put them into words made the matter even worse! The poor vicar tossed restlessly, and remembered the beauty of the ancient chalice with piercing clarity.

How heavy and smooth it was to handle! How comforting

was the sturdy stem, the beautiful moulded base! How warm and glowing the red wine looked in its polished depths! To the vicar, and to his flock, Queen Anne's chalice, as it was known, was a precious part of the Christmas and Easter communion service. And had been, the vicar reminded himself, for generation upon generation of Fairacre folk. Lips, dusty-dead two hundred years and more, had sipped the wine from this cup. Squire and servant, man and maid, the virtuous and the villainous had knelt beside each other awaiting pardon and peace from the chalice.

And they would do so still, the vicar told himself resolutely. They would do so still!

He turned over his pillow, thumped it soundly as though he trounced the Devil himself, and was asleep in three minutes.

3

The autumn was wet, windy and unseasonably warm. The children squelched into school from muddy lanes and the puddle-filled playground, incurring the wrath of Mrs Pringle daily.

Scaffolding was beginning to shroud the stumpy spire of St Patrick's and the damaged area of the nave, and the Appeal Fund board made a new feature in the village. So far the hand of the clock on the board stood only at one hundred and twenty-three pounds, but as we all pointed out to each other, it was a wonderful beginning.

The weathervane had been removed and the cock awaited regilding. On the day it was brought down to ground level Mr Willet put his head round the school door.

'If you've got a minute to spare,' he said deferentially, 'you might like a close look at the 'ol weathercock. He's come to roost in the churchyard, afore he gets a new lick of paint.'

The children began clamouring at once, only too glad to leave their English exercises.

'We'll come straight away,' I told Mr Willet, rising in readiness to quell the stampede to the door. When we had attained some semblance of order we made our way decorously to the churchyard. Near the south door, propped against a convenient flat tombstone, stood St Patrick's weathercock. It was surprisingly large with an expression of great ferocity.

'It's bigger'n our baby,' breathed Joseph Coggs with awe, stroking its cold head with a grimy hand.

'Weighs a fair bit, too,' said one of the workmen. 'Plenty of good metal in him.'

The children surveyed it admiringly and a few of them seated themselves on the damp tombstone beside it.

'Get up! Don't sit there!' I said a trifle sharply, more concerned with internal chills than irreverence, I must confess.

'Old Tom wouldn't mind, miss,' said Mr Willet peaceably. 'A loving sort of man by all accounts, specially to children – or so his stone do say.'

I stood rebuked in the face of such tolerance. A few yellow leaves fluttered down upon the sodden grass, and a wren skittered up and down the hawthorn hedge by the lych gate. Sunshine, so seldom seen in the last few drenching weeks, flooded the scene with amber light.

'We'll go for a walk before going back to school,' I announced, amidst general rejoicing. Thanks were given to Mr Willet and the workmen, affectionate pats to the weathercock, and then we set off to profit from sweet country air and exercise, in the forlorn hope that they would sharpen our wits for the work awaiting us in the schoolroom.

As Christmas approached, the money-raising activities increased in the village. The Fur and Feather Whist Drive was well attended, and the usual display of turkeys, ducks, hens, pheasants and hares adorned the platform in the village hall. Almost thirty pounds was raised by this mammoth effort, and only the collapse of the trestle table bearing the coffee cups marred the success of the evening.

'And it's my belief,' Mrs Pringle told me the next morning, 'that Mrs Emery's ugly great dog pushed the legs along. No business to let an animal into the hall at all. Nothing but a bag of fleas and smelling worse than Mr Roberts's pigs! As I told her straight.'

Mrs Pringle is a great one for 'telling people straight' and makes much trouble in doing so. Sometimes I feel like quoting to her a prayer learned in childhood which says: 'Let me not mistake bluntness for frankness,' but I doubt if such a frail dart would penetrate my school cleaner's rhinoceros' hide. And as she herself is so fond of saying: 'You can't teach an old dog new tricks.' I have learnt to leave well alone whenever possible, for Mrs Pringle makes a formidable foe, and I have to meet her daily.

We spent the latter weeks of the term preparing a school play, in which every child from the smallest five-year-old to

Ernest, a hefty eleven-year-old, had a part. Miss Clare, who once taught the infants' class at Fairacre, emerged from her retirement at Beech Green to help to dress the children and to play the accompaniment to their songs. The parents packed the school to overflowing, and apart from such expected crises as a measles suspect, two sore throats, a burst knicker elastic and a hitch in the curtain-pulling equipment, it all went splendidly. Two performances of our masterpiece netted ten pounds for the fund, and we were well content.

'A Gigantic Christmas Bazaar' widely advertised by posters on barns, trees and gateposts, as well as a notice in the *Caxley Chronicle*, was perhaps a trifle larger than the usual Christmas Bazaar which Fairacre organizes, and we all bought knitted tea-cosies and gingham aprons for each other's Christmas presents, and little boxes of homemade fudge which we fully intended to give away too, but ate ourselves as it was quite irresistible and, as we told ourselves, might not keep. The Appeal Fund was larger by twenty-six pounds at the end of the afternoon.

Nevertheless, the hand moved very slowly towards the target of two thousand pounds. After morning service on Christmas Day, a little knot of us stood outside the church, in the bleak east wind, exchanging Christmas greetings and discussing the progress of the Appeal. The hand pointed to a little under four hundred pounds, and with the best will in the world it was hard to be very optimistic.

'I suppose it's not too bad for a beginning,' said Miss Margaret Waters to her sister Mary. 'After all, it's only a few weeks since it happened.'

'I'd like to see it nearer the thousand,' said Mr Willet, standing next to her. 'We've had in the best part of the donations, from all accounts. Once we gets into the New Year, somehow it won't seem so urgent. People soon forgets, you know.'

Mrs Pringle, emerging after her stentorian boomings in the choir, heard the last part of Mr Willet's remarks.

' "Forgets" is the word, Mr Willet. Why, in the old days, this money would've been found in next to no time. The gentry – who *was* gentry then, let me say – would have put their hands in their pockets and settled it at once.'

'There ain't the money about,' agreed Mr Willet. 'At least, not to the same extent. It's spread over a few more, that's all, and them as earns it sticks to it. You can't blame the gentry. The tax man gets it off of them, and there's nothing left for things like the church spire.'

We gazed dolefully aloft at the roof, now bristling with scaffolding. No bells had rung a Christmas peal this year, because of the damage in the belfry. St Patrick's wore a forlorn and battered air. Without its golden weathercock the little spire looked unusually truncated.

'Ah well!' said Mr Willet, turning up his coat collar against the wind, 'mustn't lose heart, you know, specially on Christmas Day! Maybe the New Year will bring us all a bit of luck. And there's always the Festival to look forward to!'

'Yes, indeed,' said Mary Waters, snatching at this comfort. 'There's always the Festival!'

We set off on our several ways determined to be of good cheer, despite the nagging little doubts which pierced our defences as keenly as the bleak east wind about us.

The Christmas holidays slipped away with their usual speed and the spring term began in a flurry of snow. The children, of course, greeted it with rapture. Mrs Pringle looked upon it as yet another cross to bear. She went about her duties tight-lipped and with the limp which becomes more marked when she feels more than usually 'put upon'.

Luckily, the snow was light, nothing more than a shower here and there, powdering the black branches of the elms and the roofs in the village. But the weather was bitterly cold and even I, a poor weather prophet, knew that we should get more snow before long.

On one freezing evening, the Festival Committee met in my sitting-room. Thanks to Mrs Pringle's administrations, it presented an unusually tidy appearance. Piles of exercise books, test papers, infant apparatus and the general flotsam and jetsam found in a schoolmistress's room had been carted up to the spare bedroom, and although I despaired of ever finding any of it in order again, it was wonderful to entertain my guests in such immaculate splendour.

The Committee was formed by most of the Parochial Church Council and one or two other energetic people who had some organizing ability and bright ideas. I must confess that I had envisaged an evening making a list of the usual entertainments known only too well to Fairacre, and possibly deciding on the days on which to present them. It was exciting therefore to have Basil Bradley's bombshell exploded at the outset.

'This is really Major Gunning's idea,' he began, glancing across at that upright figure. 'You remember that he suggested that we might have *Son et Lumière* with St Patrick's as the background. Well, I've been talking to a friend of mine who has helped to produce this sort of thing, and he's willing to stage it and produce it for us.'

Congratulatory murmurs broke out on all sides.

'And if you would allow me,' went on Basil Bradley, looking modestly at his fingers, 'I should really love to write the story and er – record it for you.'

'That is indeed most generous,' said the vicar. 'Most generous.'

We all agreed warmly.

It was Mrs Mawne who rushed in where angels feared to tread, and said, 'But all that wiring and amplifiers, and setting up seats and things in the churchyard – surely that's going to be horribly expensive?'

'I thought, if the vicar agreed, it would be much more practical to have it inside the church, with the lights changing on the chancel and altar. Then, of course, we should be independent of the weather.'

'And have seats,' cried Mrs Mawne, seeing the light.

'And have seats,' agreed Basil Bradley gravely.

'I can see no objection to having the performances inside,' said the vicar. 'After all, the churches were always used for the early miracle plays, and it seems fitting that the story of our parish should be told in the building which has seen almost all its history. I think it is a splendid idea.'

'The only thing is,' said Basil Bradley, warming to his theme in the midst of such general approval, 'it is hardly worth setting up all the paraphernalia for less than a week. Do you think we can expect enough support?'

'Why not?' asked Mr Mawne. 'We'll advertise it well. People can bring parties from miles away. They're much more likely to come if they know it will be inside the building.'

'Oh, I do agree,' said his wife firmly. 'What with gnats, and the wind, not to mention the odd thunderstorm, outdoor evenings are more of a penance than a pleasure.'

It was at last agreed that the *Son et Lumière* arrangements would be for every evening of the Festival Week, and would, in fact, be the major part of the whole project which would take place in July.

'And do you really think we shall cover our expenses?' persisted Mrs Mawne.

'There will be no expenses,' said Basil Bradley. 'My friend John is giving his services, and the electrician's bills and so on will be my own contribution to the Fund.'

'It is uncommonly generous,' repeated the vicar. 'A really wonderful gesture. I am sure we are most deeply grateful.' And with this we all concurred.

Major Gunning cleared his throat so martially that we all jumped to attention, or as nearly as we could in a sitting posture.

'I've taken the liberty of speaking to a young cousin of mine . . . by way of being a singer. You may have heard of her. Jean Cole.'

'Jean Cole!' exclaimed Mrs Mawne, looking at Major Gunning with new respect.

'Jean Cole!' echoed Basil Bradley, turning pink with excitement. 'I'd no idea she was related to you. The most beautiful contralto voice in existence today! She was superb in *Aïda* at Covent Garden last year.'

'I have all her records,' said the vicar. 'The Bach arias are my particular favourites.'

Major Gunning bowed his head politely in acknowledgement of the adulation, but his tobacco-stained fingers, drumming on the edge of the table, showed his impatience.

'Yes, well . . . top and bottom of it is that she would be willing to give us a tune—'

Basil Bradley winced.

'To come here? To Fairacre?' breathed Mrs Mawne incredulously.

'As I was saying,' continued Major Gunning with a touch of asperity, 'Jean said that she could come and sing in the church during, or after, the *Son et Lumière* performance, if it would help. Not the Monday, though. She's flying back from Berlin that day, after a tour.'

There were delighted cries from the company. The vicar broached the delicate subject which was in all our minds.

'It is indeed the most generous offer. It would mean a great deal to our efforts. But your cousin is – er – much in demand. We must offer her some – er – recompense for the honour she is doing us. Can we . . .?'

'She'll come,' said the major briefly, 'for nothing. I'll see to that.'

If this sounded a trifle ominous, it was soon forgotten in the general delight.

'It's too good to be true,' cried Mrs Mawne. 'The most encouraging news of the evening!'

And with that we all agreed.

The rest of the programme was settled provisionally. The *Son et Lumière* would take place after dark each evening, beginning about nine. The Festival would begin with a splendid service in the church on the Sunday, at which the Bishop had promised to come and bless our endeavours.

'And all denominations in the area will be invited,' said the vicar.

'Bet they don't all come!' whispered Mr Roberts to me in a horribly penetrating whisper.

'They will be invited,' repeated the vicar reprovingly.

Various functions would take place during the week, a mammoth jumble sale, a gargantuan whist drive and so on, organized by various bodies in the village, and the week would culminate with a magnificent fête in the vicarage garden on Saturday afternoon, to be opened by someone who would be 'a real draw', as Mr Willet said, followed by a dance in the evening.

'Shall we have enough going on to warrant a *whole week*?' asked Mr Willet doubtfully.

'The *Son et Lumière* will be the main thread,' explained the vicar, 'and our other festivities will be hung like jewels, as it were, upon this chain.'

'Very nicely put,' commented Mr Mawne, a trifle drily.

'Yes, it turned out rather more poetically than I intended,' replied the vicar, rather surprised and pleased with his flight of fancy. 'I really should make a note of it for a future sermon.'

By this time the hands of the clock stood at ten o'clock. I went into the kitchen to prepare coffee, and the meeting ended with much animation and hope, on the part of the Fairacre Festival Committee, before they set off to face the wintry night.

4

'No, I never!'

'Yes, you did then!'

'I never, I tell you! I never done it!'

'We knows you done it all right, don't us?'

A chorus of self-righteous voices greeted this ungrammatical exchange which floated through the schoolroom window one bright morning. Sometimes I wonder why I trouble to correct the children in the classroom, knowing full well that they will relapse into their mother tongue as soon as they escape from my clutches.

The accused appeared to be Joseph Coggs. I could recognize his hoarse, husky croak easily above the manifold sounds from the playground. He is fairly popular with the other children who do not seem to be bothered by his poor clothes and his gipsy background. What he had done to deserve their united attack I was soon to know.

''Twas there all right yesterday,' said one, belligerently.

'Funny thing you havin' a wooden dagger the same evenin',' shouted another, mockingly.

'My cousin from Caxley give it to me,' growled Joseph. 'He got it off of some kid up the street.'

'Likely, ennit?'

'What, same colour an' all?'

The voices grew shriller, and I was in half a mind to leave my marking to investigate when I heard Mr Willet's hearty voice.

'What's going on then?'

A dozen voices clamoured together, and the gist of the story was that the hand of the clock had vanished from the Appeal Fund and Joseph Coggs 'had bin and pinched it'.

'You want to watch your tongues,' announced Mr Willet sternly. 'And stop picking on Joe. I took the hand away, if you must know, to put another coat o' paint on it. Put that in your pipes and smoke it, you young know-alls.'

His heavy footsteps passed on, leaving an uneasy silence.

'See?' cried Joseph triumphantly.

'Well, how was we to know?' muttered one of the crowd. 'Your dagger was the spittin' image of that hand.'

'Always on at us to look out for folks breakin' the law,' grumbled another, 'and what thanks do us get for trying?'

'Come on up the coke-heap,' shouted someone cheerfully. 'The bell'll be going before we've had a game.'

And the drama ended in a wild confusion of yells and scrunching coke, enjoyed by accusers and accused alike.

The hand of the clock which had been the cause of this fracas was moving far too slowly towards the target for Fairacre's peace of mind.

The most dramatic leap forward, in these last months, had been caused by an anonymous gift of one hundred pounds. Naturally, rumours as to the identity of this generous benefactor were legion.

'I wouldn't put it past the vicar himself,' said one.

'Or Mr Mawne?' queried another.

'That'll be the day,' said Mrs Pringle sourly, when she heard this suggestion. 'Them Mawnes don't part with money that easy. Best end of neck served up as chops in their house, so my niece Minnie tells me.'

One of the infants thought it might be 'a fairy'. This pretty fancy was soon dispelled by the realists who were slightly older.

'Don't talk soft!' implored her brother Ernest, shamed before his fellows in the playground.

'No such thing as fairies,' added Patrick scornfully. 'And if there was, how d'you think they'd lug a hundred pounds up to the vicar's? They ain't no bigger'n my thumb.'

This irrefutable argument settled the matter in this instance, but the anonymous donor still remained a fascinating mystery. It was one which was never solved.

Even more exciting than the anonymous gift was that Peter Martin, the pop star and idol of the young, had agreed to open the fête on the Saturday and to sing at the dance in the evening, accompanying himself on the famous guitar. He was going to prove a tremendous draw.

'The weather really won't matter,' said the vicar, beaming. 'People will come from miles around just to see him. A very *personable* young fellow, I believe.'

Mrs Pringle's niece Minnie expressed the general reaction to the news. 'Ain't it just wonderful? We'll be breathing *the very same air*! To think of him coming to this place! All Caxley'll be there. You ever seen him, miss?'

I said that I had not had that pleasure yet.

'Beautiful hair, he's got. Long and that, all thick down to his shoulders. And his clothes costs a fortune, and he don't drink nothin' but champagne!'

She sighed ecstatically. A visitation from the entire heavenly host, I thought somewhat tartly to myself, could not occasion more reverent adoration than this one glamorous star. Nevertheless, I too rejoiced. Think how it would swell the funds!

Work on the roof progressed steadily, and the sound of hammers and saws formed the background to our own school activities. These included now, in the last weeks of the spring term, preparations for the entertainment which was to be our contribution to the Fairacre Festival.

Only teachers who have dealt with these affairs can truly assess the heart-burnings and headaches which accompany something which the outsider considers a simple, and even a pleasurable, undertaking.

The only other member of the staff is the infants' teacher. For years Miss Clare, now retired and living at Beech Green, ruled the infants, and most of the adults in the village learnt to read, write and calculate under her benevolent eye. Miss Gray followed Miss Clare, but left to marry our neighbouring schoolmaster, Mr Annett, who also acts as choirmaster at Fairacre. Then came Miss Jackson, a stormy young woman straight from college whose departure I viewed with relief.

Since then we have had a succession of 'supply' teachers, some good, some ghastly but, for the last year, the infants have been in the charge of Mrs Bonny, a buxom widow, who manages them very well. All goes swimmingly if she is able to work in her own way, and I interfere as little as possible. Unfortunately, any sort of mild suggestion throws the lady into a defensive and resentful mood, as if one were casting a slur on her abilities. Coming to an amicable arrangement about the concert was an operation fraught with hazards, I found.

My first idea of a play in which the whole school could take part fell upon stony ground.

'Why can't the babies sing their nursery rhymes?' demanded Mrs Bonny plaintively. 'I've spent hours teaching them, and their mothers would love to hear them.'

Both facts were true. The daily chorus – one might be forgiven for saying 'caterwauling' – had penetrated the partition between our classrooms with painful clarity. And the mothers of these young choristers would dote on Mrs Bonny's efforts with them. I agreed resignedly.

'But nursery rhymes won't take very long,' I said, trying not to sound too relieved. 'We'd better have some other items.'

Mrs Bonny promised to consider the matter, and within two days the floorboards of the infants' room were reverberating with one of those galumphing folk dances from mid-Europe which involve much clapping and stamping. The clapping and stamping are no doubt performed in unison in the country of the dance's origin, but it certainly was not in Fairacre's infant room. Next door we were sorely tried. It was almost a relief to return to the nursery rhymes, and to listen, wincing, to:

> 'Ickory, dickory dock
> The mou-house run up the clock
> The clock struck ONE
> The mouse run down –

Here there followed a succession of claps as each child took its time to register the need for action, and then, triumphantly they would bellow:

'Ickory, dickory, dock.

Mrs Bonny would then praise them loudly, point out the aspirate at the beginning of 'Hickory' and the necessity of singing 'ran' instead of 'run', and the same thing would be repeated *ad nauseam*.

Our own efforts were little better. I had dramatized *The Princess and the Swineherd*, which gave everyone a chance of appearing on the stage, but doubted if the words would ever be learnt. Ernest, the only possible swineherd-cum-prince, became so sheepish about performing a chivalrous bow that I threatened to demote him to a courtier, although we both knew that there was no one else really capable of taking the part. Sometimes I despaired of ever getting Fairacre School to take part in the Festival, and wondered gloomily if the sale of Queen Anne's chalice might not, after all, be a better way of raising the money.

I did not, of course, voice these treacherous sentiments, but Mr Lamb, our village postmaster, spoke about it when I went to buy the school's savings' stamps one afternoon some weeks later.

'Of course, it's not plain sailing, this selling the church silver. Has to be a Faculty or something, the vicar tells me. A lot of chit-chat goes on evidently before permission's given. I can't see us being allowed to part with it. And, to tell the truth, I don't think anyone in Fairacre wants to see it go.'

He handed me the stamps and with them three or four photographs in colour.

'Your brother's family?' I asked, looking at them. Mr Lamb's brother George left Fairacre for New York after the war and runs a catering business there. He left before I took over the school but regularly corresponds with our Mr Lamb who shows us the photographs, and tells us all about his brother's successes when we visit the Post Office. He is very proud indeed of this younger brother, now the father of three husky boys who beamed from the photographs.

'Just a chance he may be over,' said Mr Lamb, taking back the photographs and inserting them carefully into his wallet. 'Some business trip, he says. They're chartering a plane, it seems, and if he can manage it, he'll be over here for a fortnight.'

This was good news. As I sauntered down the village street, enjoying the sunshine, I hoped, for Mr Lamb's sake, that his brother would be able to return to Fairacre. It was my guess that he would not find it much changed even though he had been absent now for over twenty years.

The question of the sale of the chalice was in everyone's mind. None worried quite as deeply as the vicar. He woke, on these bright summer mornings, to the chorus of the birds in his garden and then, after the first few moments of pleasure, the familiar little cloud cooled the sunshine of his waking moments and was with him for the rest of the day. He refused to do anything about negotiations for the sale of the precious chalice. He steadfastly hoped and prayed that enough would be raised by the Festival, and that this step, so repugnant to him, might never be necessary.

Mr Mawne did his best to make his friend change his mind, but he remained obdurate.

'I refuse to discuss it,' said the vicar one evening, pink with rare impatience.

'But, my dear Gerald, you simply can't bury your head in the sand like an ostrich. At least, find out the facts. Let's see if we can try for permission. Time's running out, you know. The bills are going to be pretty formidable, and can you honestly believe that the Festival will raise enough to pay them?'

'I have no doubt that the Lord will provide,' repeated

the vicar stubbornly. His friend raised his eyebrows, looked helplessly at Mrs Partridge, but forbore to reply.

The chalice had last been used at Whitsun, and not one touching the ancient mellow silver and gazing into its gleaming depths failed to feel a pang. Would this be the last time that Fairacre's treasure, with its blessed contents, would be offered to them? The service was a paean of praise. Red and white roses nodded on the altar. Sunshine poured through the windows, gilding the arum lilies at the chancel steps. Country voices had made the glittering brass vibrate with Whitsun hymns and Mrs Pratt, at the organ, had pulled out all the stops and flooded the church with mighty splendour. The thought of the possible loss of the chalice was the one touch of frost among the bursting glory of Whit Sunday.

As the Festival drew closer, our fears for the chalice became sharper. Somehow we simply must make the Fairacre Festival a success, we told each other! We did not say, in so many words, that Queen Anne's chalice was at stake, but the unspoken thought was constantly with us.

It was Mrs Pringle, usually the harbinger of doom, who brought a rare touch of comfort to Mr Partridge at about this time. He had called at the school with the list of hymns which he hoped I would teach the children, when Mrs Pringle clattered in bearing a battered pail in one hand and a scrubbing brush in the other.

'Bit late leavin', ain't you?' she remarked sourly. 'Clock wrong then? I was going to give the lobby a scrub out but no use doing it till the children have cleared off. Love's labour lost, that'd be!'

The vicar, who is used to this sort of thing, smiled benignly.

'You're going to have a churchful on the Tuesday, then. You was lucky to get that Miss Cole to sing,' she continued conversationally, setting down the bucket with a clang. 'My sister's girl, what works at the coach station in Caxley, says there's three coach loads booked already to come over.'

The vicar's smile grew wider. 'What splendid news, Mrs Pringle!'

'And no end of Women's Institutes have rung up about it, and the Mothers' Union and some Young Farmers.'

'A really *wide* audience!' commented the vicar rapturously.

'It takes all sorts to make a world,' conceded Mrs Pringle graciously. 'But it do look hopeful, I must say.'

'It does indeed,' replied the vicar, gazing affectionately upon my school cleaner. 'It does indeed.'

She bent to pick up the bucket and then took up her customary militant stance. 'Well,' she demanded, with a return to her usual truculence, 'do them children go now or not? This 'ere water's getting cold.'

'I'll send them through the other way,' I said meekly. 'We won't hold up your scrubbing any longer.'

This was no time for petty warfare, I felt. Mrs Pringle, messenger of hope, should have her way.

5

The posters were up everywhere in the countryside. They blazed from barn doors, from gateposts, from tree trunks and in the windows of many a village shop. One made a bright blue corner on the Appeals' board. Across the village street, between The Beetle and Wedge and the Emerys' house, a banner fluttered, bearing the words:

FAIRACRE FESTIVAL
JULY 9–15

Bunting was draped across our house fronts, and those of us who owned a flag had it in readiness to hoist on the Sunday which was to be the first day of the Festival. The cross of St George, freshly laundered by Mrs Willet, would soon be flaunting itself above the church spire upon which the regilded weathercock perched again.

Inside the church the electricians were putting the final touches to the wiring and lighting. Jock Graham, the retired architect who had so nobly offered his services, became extremely agitated by the ladders lodged among the timbers of the hammer-beam roof. He was unduly sharp with Mr Mawne who had dropped in one morning to see how things were progressing.

'I'll not be responsible,' he rumbled, rolling his r's in Doric splendour, 'for any damage to that historic roof. A lot of tomfoolery to rig up lights so near the timbers. Those men have no idea of the pricelessness of the work around them.'

'Oh, come now,' protested Mr Mawne. 'They are used to this sort of thing. I believe they were employed at Winchester Cathedral. Or was it Salisbury?'

'It wouldn't be allowed in Scotland,' Mr Graham assured him.

'That I can well imagine,' remarked his companion drily. The hint of sarcasm inflamed Jock Graham still further.

'A decent God-fearing kirk would be ashamed to turn itself into something no better than a theatre. I'd no idea, when I offered my sairvices, that this sort of thing would be countenanced.'

'I see nothing offensive about it,' retorted Mr Mawne. 'It is an act of praise.'

'It's commaircial!' boomed Mr Graham, his sandy eyebrows bristling. 'It wouldn't happen in Scotland, I tell ye!'

'I really can't think,' replied Mr Mawne, with maddening detachment, 'why so many of you Scotsmen bother to come south if you dislike it so much. Personally, I'm all for Scottish nationalism, and I'd rebuild Hadrian's Wall for good measure, once I'd got all you immigrants back on the right side of it.'

'Ye'd no get far without a stiffening of good Scots' blood among ye,' thundered Jock Graham. 'A weakly unprincipled set of shilly-shallyers, lacking pairpose and integrity!'

The workmen, high above, had ceased their labours and were watching this passage of arms with intense interest.

The two men faced each other. Mr Mawne's pale face wore a supercilious smile. Mr Graham's, suffused to an unbecoming shade of purple, was thrust close to his antagonist's. At this dramatic moment, Basil Bradley arrived on the scene.

'I can't tell you how relieved I am that I've already recorded the script,' he croaked huskily. 'My tonsils are absolutely aflame. I can't think why I've succumbed so easily at this time of year. I swear by orange juice for breakfast – nothing more – just fresh orange juice!'

'Ye'd do better on a braw fresh herring and a plate of salted porridge,' thundered Jock Graham. He brushed past the two men and marched, head erect, down the aisle to the west door.

'Whatever's got into him?' asked Basil Bradley, bewildered.

'Scotch blood,' said Mr Mawne cryptically. ' "Scotland for ever!" I mean "Scotland for aye!" '

'Oh dear,' croaked Basil Bradley, extracting a small tin from his pocket. 'Ah well, it makes one quite glad to have been born in humble Bayswater, doesn't it? Have a black-currant lozenge, Henry.'

Jock Graham was not the only Fairacre resident to be in a state of tension at this time. The vicar, facing the Bishop's visit, was anxious about the service, and also about the safety of the church fabric. What a terrible thing it would be if something should fall upon that stately figure! Despite reassurances, the vicar was not wholly at ease.

Mrs Partridge, whose privilege it was to entertain the Bishop to lunch, and possibly to tea, was busy planning a meal which would do honour to their distinguished visitor and yet be simple enough to prepare and serve single-handed. Cold salmon and salad had seemed a good choice until she remembered that the Bishop was extremely short-sighted and far too handsome a man to relish wearing glasses at lunch time. And just suppose that a fish-bone appeared? It would, without fail, be on the guest's plate. Perhaps cold beef? Or leg of lamb left in a slow oven during the service and mint sauce made beforehand? Mrs Partridge continued to cudgel her brains, and to long for the days when the vicarage had a resident cook and two kitchen maids.

Mr Annett, the choirmaster, was worrying about the new anthem. The choir of St Patrick's had left him in no doubt that he had bitten off more than they could chew.

'This 'ere modern stuff ain't got no tune to it,' protested Mr Willet. 'What's wrong with a bit of Bach or Handel?'

'It's a very good thing to make a change,' Mr Annett snapped back, secretly conscious that the new anthem was beyond their powers, but too proud to admit it. 'As Browning said: "A man's reach should exceed his grasp." '

'Browning never 'ad to tackle this lot,' pointed out Mr Willet, peering closely at the sheet of music. 'If there's anything I 'ates it's five flats.'

They had struggled on with their unfamiliar burden, but no matter how often they practised, Mr Annett realized that the anthem would turn out to be a hesitant dirge rather than the outpouring of praise which the composer had intended. Too late to do anything now, he told himself, as the great Sunday approached. But the thought gave him little comfort.

Basil Bradley, afflicted with his feverish cold, was suffering agonies of self-consciousness about the script which he had written, and his recording of it. He had checked all his facts most carefully, but there was always the possibility of a mistake. How dreadful if he had made some blunder! There was that episode about the nun being given shelter in the vestry during the eighteenth century. Should he have omitted it, perhaps? There were some very dubious rumours about the incumbent at that date, and the Bishop might take exception to the publicity, guarded though Basil's account had been of the affair. Really, creative work was terribly exhausting, thought poor Basil, as he gargled hopelessly before the final rehearsal.

A spell of unbroken sunshine preceded Festival week and we in Fairacre prayed that it might continue. It grew so hot that the children took many of their lessons outside, in the shade of the elm trees. Rehearsals of the infants' contributions also took place in the playground, which afforded some relief to our class, when it was working inside, and considerable interest to proud mothers who clustered at the gate to watch their offspring bounding around in the folk dance.

The Princess and the Swineherd still had many faults. Ernest had overcome his shyness with such success – terrified of handing over the part to someone else – that he now played the Prince with a swashbuckling impudence which was, to my mind, quite as offensive as his former interpretation of the part. However, I was now resigned to the shortcomings of my production and simply concentrated on getting the cast word-perfect, which was no light matter.

Mr Willet, as sexton, was concerned about the tidiness of the church and the churchyard.

'Slummocky lot, them builders,' he told me. 'Drops their paper bags everywhere. Bread crusts and cheese rinds and old potato crisps scattered all over the churchyard. Them mice are getting as big as foxes.'

'It will look splendid on Sunday,' I assured him. 'Especially if this weather lasts.'

We looked across my garden to the meadows at the base of the downs. A heat haze veiled the distance, but nearer at hand a herd of black and white Friesian cows, the pride of Mr Roberts, stood knee-deep in tall grass. Not one moved. They might have been painted there, against the hot motionless beauty of hills and empty sky, so still they stood.

'Well, let's hope it does,' agreed Mr Willet. 'Don't want it to break yet awhile. It'll end in thunder, or my name's not Willet.'

He turned to look at St Patrick's. The scaffolding had been

removed from the spire but still clad the square tower containing the belfry and part of the nave.

'Wish we could have rung in the Bishop with a fine peal,' he said regretfully. 'But there it is. All six o' they bells is up against the church wall waiting to go aloft again as soon as it's safe for 'em. I likes to go and look 'em over now and again. I've got a soft spot for them bells, particularly Old Bess. They say she was cast in the field behind The Beetle and Wedge, sometime in the 1560s.'

'The children don't want the bells to go back again. They've been over to see them – under my eagle eye, let me say – lots of times, and they've copied the inscriptions.'

' "*Sanctus, sanctus, sanctus*",' gabbled Mr Willet, swatting a gnat on his freckled forearm. ' "*In piam memoriam Caroli Fowler. Requiescat in pace*". Fowler, notice? Still a good few Fowlers in Fairacre. Wonder if any of them cast Old Bess?'

He bent to pull up a dandelion from my border, and straightened up with a sigh.

'I do truly hope this Festival puts the old church on its feet. There's a lot at stake, Miss Read. A lot at stake!'

Sunday dawned bright and beautiful. I took my breakfast tray into the garden among the dewy pinks and roses. A robin perched hopefully on the lilac bush nearby, a beady eye cocked for crumbs.

The Union Jack hung motionless from the school flag pole. High above it, on St Patrick's church the cross of St George waited for a breeze to spread it out in its full red and white magnificence.

It was already blissfully hot although the clock said only nine. By ten to eleven, when I made my way to church, the heat was almost oppressive. We were all in our best summer finery and I felt quite sorry for the Bishop, magnificently accoutred in a splendid gold and white cope which must have been uncomfortably warm.

We sang the most exultant hymns, beginning with 'Praise my soul the King of Heaven' as the choir processed from the west door up to the chancel, with their choirmaster, George Annett, at their head. Several of my pupils had undergone their weekly metamorphosis from scruffy urchins to well-scrubbed cherubs, and with hair plastered down with a wet brush and their eyes modestly downcast upon the polished boots peeping demurely from beneath their cassocks, they gave an impression of youthful sanctity which did not deceive those of us who knew them during the rest of the week.

The new anthem was tackled with dogged effort and Mr Annett gave noble support with a resonant voice which led his struggling choir valiantly. When it was over, I noticed Mr Willet mopping his brow and moustache with obvious relief.

The Bishop gave the sermon and spoke of the part the church played in parish life, the disaster which had befallen it, and praised the efforts of our small community to repair the damage.

'God will bless your work,' he promised us. 'This is a festival in every sense. It is an expression of praise for past mercies and a re-dedication of ourselves to service.'

He made a brave and unforgettable figure in our ancient pulpit, and his words were as inspiring as his presence. When the benediction had been said, and Mrs Pratt broke into a triumphant voluntary on the organ, we all felt that Fairacre was embarked upon a venture which was bound to succeed.

We emerged into the hot sunshine, blinking like owls in the dazzling light. Around us the rose bushes gave out a voluptuous fragrance. Above us an aeroplane left a white trail in the cloudless sky. Bumblebees lumbered from clover-head to clover-head on the grassy mounds of our Fairacre forefathers. It was indeed high summer.

'And real Festival weather!' said Miss Margaret Waters, gazing happily about her, beneath the brim of her old-fashioned straw hat.

'After all this looking forward,' said her sister, 'it's hard to believe that it's actually started.'

It was a thought we all shared as we made our various ways homeward to Sunday dinner.

At last, the Festival had begun!

6

Amy my old college friend, drove over from Bent to the first performance of the *Son et Lumière*.

It was to be a very grand affair. Several local landowners were bringing parties of guests and we humbler folk were busy looking out our best evening attire. It was not easy to find something splendid enough for the occasion, decorous enough for churchgoing and warm enough to counteract the chill of an evening in St Patrick's draughty pews. I had plumped for safety in my plain black frock, and had looked out my one fur piece, a useful stole, for despite the heat of the last few days, which had degenerated into an ominously still stuffiness, the age-long coolness of the church's interior would take some combating.

Amy, *soignée* in a most beautiful frock of blue silk, looked me over critically.

'You really *shouldn't* wear black, my dear, with your skin. It kills any sort of glow you have. Why not wear a deep red dress, or a brown?'

'Because I haven't got one,' I said flatly.

Her eye travelled, without relish, down my full length and lingered sadly at my feet.

'Those heels are definitely out,' she pronounced.

'Not in Fairacre,' I replied with spirit. 'In fact, they've only just *come in*! I paid a great deal of money for these shoes, my girl, and I intend to get plenty of wear out of them.'

Amy shuddered delicately, and fingered her one splendid adornment, a glittering diamond brooch on her shoulder. It was, I knew, a present from James, her husband, and marked his return from a particularly protracted business trip to the Bahamas. There are many such absences from home, about which I have my private suspicions, as no doubt Amy has too, but they certainly result in the most beautiful presents for his wife, and she has enough sense not to cross-question James too closely.

We sat down to my carefully prepared meal of cold chicken and salad. I was secretly rather proud of the salad for I had remembered to cut the radishes into water-lily shapes in the dinner hour and had left them soaking all the afternoon. The tomatoes and cucumber had come from Mr Willet's green-house, and the lettuce from my own garden. The hard-boiled eggs, winking goldenly from among the greenery, had come from Mrs Pringle's hens and the fine chicken was lately one of the members of her flock.

Amy ate heartily, I was glad to see.

'All so deliciously fresh,' she commented, and I preened myself at this unaccustomed compliment – prematurely, as I might have known. 'But I really think the latest way of dishing up a salad is better. Just a bowl of green stuff tossed in the very best olive oil and vinegar, and tomatoes freshly sliced in a separate dish salted and peppered and with a *soupçon* of chopped chives or parsley, of course – for those who like *coloured* salad mixed with green. I find that most people these days consider radishes rather too coarse a flavour, and there's so much medical argument about hard-boiled eggs that I don't serve them, I must admit.'

'You'd better bring your own nose-bag next time you come,' I told her. I've known Amy too long to worry about her criticisms and can well recall the hearty relish with which she attacked college bread and margarine spread with thick-cut Scottish marmalade, not to mention a truly repellent dish of minced meat in a suet crust which, with juvenile flippancy, we christened 'Boiled Baby'.

However, she approved graciously of my coffee, and as soon as we had finished we set off to the church.

'Looks like thunder,' commented Amy, eyeing the

darkening sky. There was a sullen coppery look about the piled clouds, and not a leaf stirred in the airless heat.

'Let's hope it waits until we're safely home again,' I answered, as we joined the queue at the south door.

It was good to see St Patrick's so full. Seldom had the ancient hammer-beam roof looked down upon such a glittering assembly. We had all done our best to make this a splendid occasion. I studied the attire and coiffures around me. There were several new hats, worn by those who felt unable to attend church unless so crowned, and among them was one upon Mrs Pringle's locks. It was entirely new to me. Where was the faithful old number adorned with dangling cherries? Where was the navy-blue, decorated with white feathers, which had first seen the light at her niece Minnie's wedding? No doubt safely lodged on top of the wardrobe at home. I hoped so. I missed those two old friends, but studied the new creation with interest. It was of green straw, formidably brimmed, and garlanded with plastic anemones which looked suspiciously like those given away recently with packets of soap powder. It was exceedingly handsome, I thought, and proof of Mrs Pringle's support of the Festival.

In the front pews sat our local gentry, elegant in silks and velvets, their hair blue-rinsed, silver-streaked, or discreetly tinted. Occasionally, wafts of delicious perfume floated back to us, as a stole was rearranged or a handbag was opened.

The nave was shadowy, but a shaft of golden light illuminated the chancel and altar. Mrs Pratt, at the organ, played some gentle melody, vaguely familiar, which I guessed must be by Haydn or Mozart.

St Patrick's clock struck nine. The music stopped and the vicar appeared at the chancel steps.

'You are about to hear the story of Fairacre,' he told us, 'and in particular the story of this lovely old church. But before it begins, let us pray that we may see it restored to its former beauty, so that those who come after us may cherish it as we have done.'

We slipped to our knees and listened to the simple prayer. Then, with a susurration of silks and satins, we resumed our seats, eager for what might come.

The golden light which suffused the chancel changed to a dim blue. The cross glimmered upon the altar amidst the ghostly shadows. We shivered in awe. It was very quiet. Only, far away, a faint rumbling could be heard. It could have been distant thunder, or a farm vehicle out late upon its lawful business.

There was a faint crackling sound and then Basil Bradley's voice echoed strongly through the church.

'Long, long ago, so learned men tell us, the Romans may have passed this way. They did not settle here as far as we know. Among our downs water is scarce, and there are few natural defences against the elements or the enemy. The Romans left no signs of occupation here.

'But centuries later, when the next invaders came to Britain, they left their mark upon this place. Upon this spot, where now we are gathered, the Normans built a small, strong church of which parts still remain.'

At this point the chancel arch was thrown into prominence, a mellow golden light illuminating the angular stone carving. Few of Fairacre's parishioners had realized until this dramatic moment what unsuspected richness had lain in the shadowy chancel arch so high above them.

'The work was begun probably about the middle of the twelfth century –' A crackling noise interrupted the mellifluous voice, and was immediately followed by a burst of thunder which broke around us like machine-gun fire. We ducked involuntarily at the report, then, remembering ourselves, sat up and looked polite and attentive.

The church was plunged into darkness and the voice had

ceased. A little agitated whispering rustled round the congregation.

'Lord Almighty!' boomed Mr Roberts whose voice is as large as his generous heart. 'We've been and got struck!'

At this, commotion broke out on all sides. There was nothing panic-stricken about us. We are all used to storms, which can occur with horrifying ferocity but are soon over in Fairacre. What really worried us was the breakdown of the performance and the bitter disappointment of all those who had spent so long in preparing it.

The vicar, rising from his seat to direct and comfort his flock, suddenly saw, with amazing clarity, in his mind's eye Queen Anne's chalice. It seemed to float in mid-air, brilliantly clear at first, but gradually fading, as if it were passing away from him to distances unknown. The vicar's heart beat uncomfortably loudly, his throat grew constricted, but he put his fears from him and addressed his flock.

'Please remain seated, dear people. Candles will be lit at once, and would Mr Roberts be so kind as to step across to the vicarage and telephone the Electricity Board to see what can be done?'

'I'm on my way, sir,' called Mr Roberts, and the crash of strong footsteps confirmed this.

'Mark my words,' said Amy beside me. 'The *Caxley Chronicle* will tell us that this power cut was caused by a swan flying into the cable.'

'Perhaps it was,' I replied.

'Fiddlesticks!' snapped Amy. 'It was the storm!'

A jagged flash split the sky, to be followed by another reverberating thunder clap.

'It's farther off,' said someone hopefully.

'You wants to count, one, two, three, four, see? As soon as the lightning comes you starts counting and sees how many you gets to afore the thunder bangs out. That'll tell you how many miles off the storm be!'

I recognized the voice of this young know-all as Ernest, my Swineherd-Prince.

'You speak when you're spoken to,' said his mother, in a scandalized whisper. 'Piping up like that, and in church, too!'

A few scurrying figures flitted about the shadows bearing candles. There was a medieval beauty about their downbent heads and their curved hands sheltering the precious tiny flames from any draught, which was poignantly in keeping with the ancient building.

'Mrs Pratt,' announced the vicar, 'will play some music by Bach while we wait.'

We settled again against the hard pew-backs and let the sonorous chords flow over us. How many of our Fairacre forebears, I wondered, had listened to Bach by candlelight, as we were doing now? My mind began to wander. There was something wonderfully comforting in the thought that we shared so much in this building with those long-dead and those yet unborn. We were, after all, simply a link in a long chain stretching back for centuries and forward into eternity.

The candle flames stretched and wavered in the draught. A rumble of thunder rattled over the roof.

'I told you so,' whispered Ernest defensively. 'It's going away.'

At that moment, Mr Roberts reappeared. 'The power will be back at any minute,' he announced. 'A swan has flown into the cable, they say.'

Amy nudged me with such vigour that my side was quite sore.

'Thank you, Mr Roberts,' said the vicar. 'Let us sing a hymn together while we wait.'

After some whispering with Mr Annett, the vicar proclaimed: 'Pleasant are thy courts above', and we all dutifully stood in the twilit church and raised our voices. As we reached the last line, the lights came on again, and we sang 'Amen' with undue fervour.

We resumed our seats expectantly and Basil Bradley, looking slightly careworn, appeared at the chancel steps.

'I think we had better begin again from the beginning, ladies and gentlemen. We are so very sorry for this breakdown. Please bear with us, and let us hope that all is now plain sailing.'

There were sympathetic murmurs from the congregation, the lights went out and the blue spotlight lit up the altar once more. There was a preliminary crackle and then Basil Bradley's voice as before.

'Long, long ago, so learned men tell us, the Romans may have passed this way.'

We settled back, like children hungry for a story, and gave ourselves up to enjoyment.

It took a little over an hour for the tale to unfold, and so well had Basil Bradley told it and so beautiful had the lighting been, that we emerged from the experience filled with unbounded admiration tinged with awe.

Even Amy was impressed. '*Remarkably* good,' she said as we walked home. 'Really *outstandingly* good! It ought to bring hundreds of visitors.'

'Let's hope it does,' I replied. 'Two thousand pounds takes some finding.'

'I wonder if the national press will write it up,' mused Amy. 'It deserves it. You'll get people from all over the place if it's widely advertised.'

'We've done our best,' I assured her. 'It's been in all the local papers, I know.'

'I think I shall send a letter to *The Times*,' said Amy, climbing elegantly into her car. 'We want to cast the net *really wide*.'

She drove off and I returned to the school house. Distant voices in the lane and the sound of cars starting on their homeward journeys formed the epilogue to Basil Bradley's moving production.

A star, bright as a jewel, hung beside St Patrick's spire. It looked hopeful, I thought, as I prepared for bed. If the rest of the Fairacre contributions matched this evening's in splendour, our Festival must surely succeed, and more important still, Queen Anne's chalice would remain among those who loved it so well.

7

Next morning I began to realize just how far-flung the news of our Fairacre Festival had been.

There was a hearty banging on the classroom door during our history lesson and in walked a thickset man wearing a crewcut and a broad smile. The likeness to our Mr Lamb at the Post Office was unmistakable.

'Miss Read?' he began.

'George Lamb,' I said. 'How nice of you to look in!'

'Well, you see, I was raised in this place and I felt I just had to take another peek at this old schoolroom. Don't appear to have changed much since my time. Bit cleaner, perhaps.'

'You'd better repeat that to Mrs Pringle,' I told him. 'It'll make her day.'

I turned to the class. 'Stand up and say "Good morning" to Mr Lamb, who was once a pupil here.'

There were welcoming cries and smiles, all the warmer because any interruption to lessons is a pleasurable one.

'That's a Coggs,' exclaimed our visitor, pointing delightedly at Joseph in the front row.

'Quite right,' I said. 'He's Arthur Coggs's son.'

'Oh, I know *Arthur*,' replied George Lamb with some emphasis. I had no doubt that he knew a great deal about his old schoolmate's fondness for liquor and the resultant shindies in our village.

I settled the children to some work and accompanied our guest on a tour of the room.

'Not the same piano! Sakes alive, that must be going on for a century.'

'Eighty, anyway,' I agreed, fingering the walnut fretwork front, and the ivory keys, yellow with age.

'And still the same gaps in the partition,' he went on, bending down to squint through a crack into the infants' room. 'The things we poked through there you'd just never credit, Miss Read.'

'Mr Willet's told me,' I assured him. 'Stinging nettles, knitting needles, dozens of notes – yes, I can well imagine. It happens still, you know. Children don't change much.'

He ambled appreciatively round the room, touching the walls, peering from the windows, and ruffling the children's hair as he passed.

'I hear Miss Clare's still at Beech Green. I'm paying her a visit before I fly home.'

'She'll be so pleased,' I said truthfully.

'I owe a lot to her,' he said, suddenly grave. 'Taught us all proper manners and to think of others. She used to say grace before we went home at night. It went: "Bless us this night and make us ever mindful of the wants of others." I always liked that. "Mindful of the wants of others." Good words those.'

He gazed through the window as he spoke, his eyes fixed upon the men working upon St Patrick's belfry.

'They're getting on very well. They've almost finished,' I said, intending to release the tension a little.

George Lamb shook himself into the present again. 'Ah! Looks pretty tidy now. You been to the show there yet?'

I said that I had.

'I'm taking some of the chaps who flew over with me tomorrow night. All helps the funds. I owe a lot to Fairacre, and it'll give the fellows no end of a kick to see a building that's over eight hundred years old, and to hear Jean Cole too.'

He glanced at the square gold watch upon his wrist and grimaced. 'Best get back to the Post Office for my lunch, or I'll catch it,' he said. 'Goodbye, Miss Read. Goodbye children.

Hope you'll look back on your days at Fairacre School with as much pleasure as I do.'

I accompanied him to the gate. Above the elm trees the rooks were circling high.

'Sign of rain, eh?' he said. ' "Winding up the water", we used to say as kids. You know one thing, Miss Read? Everything seems a lot smaller in Fairacre than I remember it except St Patrick's spire and them old elm trees! Maybe they've both been growing since I left here.'

Chuckling at his own fancies, he made his way back to the village.

On Tuesday evening came the eagerly awaited visit of Jean Cole.

Halfway through the recorded story of Fairacre there was an interval. A spotlight lit the chancel arch and the vicar led in the majestic figure of Major Gunning's cousin. She was resplendent in a long glittering black gown, and her appearance alone was enough to awe her country admirers, but when that glorious voice wrapped us in its warmth and beauty we were touched as never before.

She sang the aria from Handel's *Judas Maccabaeus*, to Mr Annett's accompaniment on the organ. It was a felicitous choice for it celebrated the restoration of the Sanctuary of Jerusalem. We sat in wonderment as the lovely voice soared and fell, and when finally she bowed and left us, we still sat silent and spellbound, whilst through my mind ran Shelley's lines:

> Music, when soft voices die,
> Vibrates in the memory –

I heard later that George Lamb was as good as his word, and that eight of his business friends had been among that evening's congregation.

After the performance was over, it appears, the vicar found them looking round the church in the company of the honorary architect, Mr Graham. He was busy pointing out the particular beauties of the building, and had a fascinated audience. The vicar joined the party and was moved to see the awed admiration with which the strangers viewed the ancient building.

'Back home,' said one, 'we reckon two hundred years as mighty old. It takes your breath away to touch a wall or a doorway this ancient.'

They wandered from vestry to belfry, from altar to side-chapel, and finally emerged from the west door and accepted the vicar's invitation to coffee at the vicarage.

'I can offer you Drambuie with it,' said the vicar with pleasure, as he handed round the steaming cups, 'or a liqueur called aurum, distilled from oranges, and brought from Italy as a present by some friends in the village.'

'Not for me,' said Jock Graham austerely, 'but I'll no refuse a good Scots liqueur like Drambuie.'

He was in a remarkably mellow mood. To have such an attentive audience was a joy to him. The villagers of Fairacre took their church very much for granted, but these strangers were perceptive and appreciative. Jock Graham's tongue wagged all the faster, as the Drambuie diminished sip by sip, and he extolled the unique attributes of the building he loved so well.

It was almost half-past eleven when at last the party broke up.

'I'd no idea it was so late,' said the vicar. 'Have you far to go?'

'We're booked in at Caxley,' said one. 'Two of us have business there tomorrow. The others are off to London on the early train, rustling up some more customers we hope.'

Farewells were made, and the vicar and Mrs Partridge turned back into the hall.

'What very nice fellows!' exclaimed Mr Partridge. 'George Lamb seems to have found some good companions.'

'And a wife who's interested in cooking,' added Mrs Partridge. 'He's going to ask her to send me a recipe for almond cookies.'

'Cookies?' repeated the vicar, his brow furrowed with perplexity.

'*Cookies!*' said his wife firmly. 'Biscuits to us. Really, Gerald, at times you are hopelessly insular.'

'I suppose so,' agreed the vicar rather sadly. Then his face brightened. 'But we've broadened our horizons tonight, my dear, haven't we? With our American friends, and prima donnas!'

Amicably, they mounted the stairs to bed.

The day came when Fairacre School presented its contribution to the Festival. We had decided to give two performances, one in the afternoon when mothers with young children could come, and one in the evening when fathers could attend.

We chose Wednesday for the simple reason that it is early closing day in Caxley and that the people of Fairacre would not be tempted to go there to spend their money. Thursday is market day, and three buses run from our village into Caxley on that busy day. We could not hope to compete with Caxley's magnetic pull on a Thursday. Besides, as Mrs Bonny pointed out reasonably, they would have more money to put in the silver collection *before* market day.

Excitement had mounted steadily during the Festival week and by the time Wednesday came it was at fever-pitch. The costumes and simple properties had been stacked on desks at the side of my room and Mrs Bonny's, for want of any other place to put them, and mighty little work had been done by the children with such attractions lying near by. Pens in hand, arithmetic exercises neglected before them, the children's bemused gaze turned constantly to the glamorous heaps of clothes. Here was a glimpse of another world. Our country children rarely go to the theatre. An annual visit to the panto-mime is about all that comes their way. Here, close at hand, were all the trappings of magic, the means of slipping from the everyday world of school to one of enchanting fantasy. It was little wonder that I had very few sums to mark each day. But a wise teacher knows when she is beaten, and I forbore to scold.

As soon as school dinner was demolished we set about arranging the seating. The partition was pushed back, the desks removed either to the playground or to one end to form the basis of the stage. Mr Willet, Mr Roberts the farmer, and Jim Farrow his shepherd, arranged the long planks across the desks, tried the curtains we had rigged up, and pronounced the stage ready.

Meanwhile, the children were putting the chairs in rows for the audience. These were new stackable beauties from the village hall, and we had been threatened with all sorts of penalties if any damage were done.

The din was appalling. The metal frames of the chairs clanged like an iron foundry. The men's voices, raised above the racket, were thunderous. The thud of their mallets as they knocked the planks into place reverberated among the pitch-pine rafters above. When at last the work was done, and the men had departed, Mrs Bonny and I took an aspirin and a cup of tea apiece in the hope of curing our headaches.

At two-thirty the schoolroom was packed tight. In the front seats were the vicar and the managers and a number of illustri-ous friends of the school. Parents, aunts and uncles, little brothers and sisters and numerous distant relations, whom I had never seen before, kept up a cheerful hum of conversation while panic grew steadily behind the stage curtain.

The first item was a collection of folksongs sung by the whole school. It was a tight squash to get all sixty-odd children on to the stage, and one scaremonger among the infants told everyone that 'them planks ain't safe', thus causing widespread terror.

'Anyone who wants to get off the stage can do so,' I said fiercely. 'But don't forget your mothers have come to see you.'

This quelled the riot a trifle, but Mrs Bonny and I had the usual fears to calm.

'S'pose us forgets the words?'

'S'pose there's a fire. Which door does we go for?'

'I feels a bit sick.'

'I forgets how the tune goes.'

'John Todd shoved me!'

'I never then!'

'Miss, there ain't enough room for us up this end. The wall's all coming off on my sleeve, miss. My *best* sleeve.'

At this moment, Mrs Bonny was obliged to take three of her youngest to the lavatory – an inevitable hold-up at any school function – whilst I applied my eye to the crack of the curtain to watch the audience. It really was a wonderful house, kindly and enthusiastic, and I only hoped we should not disappoint all those present.

At last all was ready. Mrs Bonny took her seat at the piano. United in the face of their common ordeal, the children grew suddenly silent. I hauled on the curtain rope, and we were off to a flying start.

The deafening applause which greeted every item was most gratifying. The infants, naturally, won the palm, and every time the curtain rose upon them there were loving cries of: 'Oh, aren't they sweet?' 'Look at our Billy!' 'The pretty dears!' 'Don't they sing lovely?' and the like. They certainly went through their paces magnificently, after initial bashfulness, and the folk dance nearly brought the roof – and the stage – down with energetic clapping and stamping.

This number ended the first half and we could hear the infants hard at it as my class prepared for *The Princess and the Swineherd* in the lobby. Ernest, usually so stolid, had become hilariously excited and was clowning about in his finery, reducing the girls to a state of helpless giggling.

The princess's skirt had been trodden on, and given way drastically at the gathers, so that I was obliged to do last-minute repairs with safety pins, with my hand inside her waist-band.

'Oh, miss, you tickles!' giggled Elizabeth, wriggling about like an eel. 'Oh, miss, your hands is cold!' Then a squeal. 'Oh, miss, you've bin and *pricked* me!'

'Stand still then,' I begged, snapping the last pin home. 'There, now you'll do!'

'It's pinned to my vest, miss.'

'And that's how it will have to stay,' I assured her flatly. 'We're on in five minutes.'

These words had a dual effect. Some children were, merci-fully, struck dumb. Others became panic-stricken and fussed even more vociferously. Luckily, applause and cheers broke out from the schoolroom at this stage, the infants came trooping back, flushed with success, and we were obliged to collect our senses ready for our big moment after the brief interval.

'The magic saucepan's bin and gone!' exclaimed Patrick dramatically. This was the highly necessary property round which the Princess and her ladies gathered to discover the meals being cooked all over the town. There was a frenzied scattering of costumes, searching under chairs and general confusion until one of the infants, flown with success, was discovered with it on his head from whence it was wrenched by one of his enraged elders.

'You might have had his ears off,' observed an onlooker dispassionately, but relief was so general that no one took much notice of this true statement.

After all the excitement I was prepared to find the cast both agitated and wordless, but all went well. Ernest's courtly bows were marvels of grace, and the only slight slip was the addition of 's' now and again, in true Fairacre fashion.

'We knows who's going to have sweet soup and pancakes! We knows who's going to have porridge and chops!' chanted the ladies exultantly. At least, I told myself philosophically, they did not say: 'Us knows', as they might so easily have done.

The applause at the end of the performance was deafening, and augured well for the repeat programme in the evening.

By the time the children and their parents had gone home, Mrs Bonny and I were dog tired. We tottered across to my house, and revived our strength with tea, tomato sandwiches and shortbread.

'Mr Willet says we've taken over seven pounds this afternoon, and it should be as much again this evening,' said Mrs Bonny, surveying her stockinged feet at the other end of the sofa. 'It should help the funds quite a lot.'

'It should,' I agreed. We lapsed into exhausted silence, and I guessed that her thoughts were running on the same lines as mine. Should we ever, in this small village, even with the herculean efforts we were making, ever come anywhere near the target we had so hopefully and bravely set ourselves?

Three hours later, much refreshed, we crossed the playground for our second house. Against a ravishing blue sky, the newly gilded weathercock flamed triumphantly on the pinnacle of St Patrick's spire. It was a heartening sight.

Resolutely we thrust our doubts from us, pushed open the heavy school door, and were engulfed once again by our teeming mob.

8

Our School Concert, which finally netted sixteen pounds for the funds, was one of the more modest efforts in Festival Week. It was on a par with the Mammoth Whist Drive, the Giant Draw and the Fabulous Flower Show. The *Son et Lumière*, with the added attraction of Jean Cole, was the backbone of the week, of course, and was so successful that it was decided to carry on for the next week as well, much to everyone's joy.

It was fortunate that it had done so well, for calamity hit Fairacre the day before the fête. The pop star Peter Martin, whose advent we had all awaited so eagerly, was involved in a car crash on Thursday evening, and was taken to hospital with two broken ribs and concussion.

We heard the news on radio and television that evening and were plunged into gloom. The vicar, good Christian that he is, forbore to express what was in most of our minds, simply saying: 'Poor young fellow! It is a mercy that his injuries are no worse!'

Jock Graham was more outspoken. 'This'll make a difference to the takings,' he observed dourly, reading the headlines in Friday's *Guardian*.

'He won't die, will he, miss?' asked a bevy of little girls round my desk. Peter Martin's injuries and the cruelty of Fate in thus snatching him from us were the playground topics of the day, and in fact, of the whole neighbourhood.

Lady Sawston, who lives locally, nobly agreed to step into the breach and to open the fête, but it was quite apparent that fewer people would attend now that our star attraction had gone. It was a sore blow indeed to our efforts.

The final item in the Festival's programme was the Gala Dance which was held in the Village Hall on Saturday evening and at which Peter Martin was to have sung. It was the culmination of our efforts, and the ladies of the Floral Society excelled themselves with shower arrangements on every wall bracket and a bank of massed flowers, contributed from Fairacre cottage gardens, across the width of the stage.

Homemade refreshments had been billed as one of the chief attractions, my own modest contribution consisting of two dozen sausage rolls and a rather handsome set of small savouries in aspic jelly, so ravishingly pretty – at least, in my own eyes – that I hoped that Amy might drop in unexpectedly and be impressed. Needless to say, she did not, and the only comment which I heard on their appearance came from Mrs Mawne, who remarked disparagingly to one of her helpers: 'Probably sent by the vicar's wife. She dabbles in aspic.' *Dabbles in aspic indeed*, I thought, smarting in silence. It is hardly surprising that Mrs Mawne is so generally detested.

I looked in during the last hour of the event. Faces were flushed, skirts whirling, you could have cut the air with a knife, and 'The Dizzy Beat' from Caxley lived up to its name, with enough tympani to drown the other three instruments.

It was a huge success, and I joined with zest the great circle for 'Auld Lang Syne', and wrenched other people's arms from their sockets with enthusiasm matching my neighbour's. After 'God Save The Queen', the company drifted away to the sound of car engines, roaring motor bikes and farewell cries, and I helped to wash up the debris.

Mrs Willet accompanied me home. It was lovely to be out in the cool night air. Someone had night-scented stocks growing in his front garden, and the fragrance was delicious. A half-moon lay on its back, cradled in the tree-tops, and an owl hooted from the vicarage cedar tree.

'A beautiful night,' said Mrs Willet. 'And a successful one. Do you think the vicar will know the result of the Festival Week tomorrow? Everyone's praying we'll have made enough to save the chalice, though they don't say much.'

'We'll live in hope,' I replied, opening my gate. 'We couldn't have done more anyway. That's one comfort.'

The vicar did not make an announcement the next day, but the hand on the Appeals' board shot round to one thousand and seven hundred pounds.

'Getting along now!' said the parishioners excitedly, as they made their way past the board. 'It's coming on, isn't it?'

'But not fast enough,' was Mr Mawne's comment to the vicar, after the service.

'I agree with you there,' said Jock Graham soberly. 'I've kept a tight eye on the money all the way along the line, and give Christie's their due, they've done a fine job at a reasonable price.'

'What is still outstanding?' inquired the vicar, leading the two to the vicarage for a glass of sherry.

'My estimate, a generous one, was two thousand. Christie's have had two lots of four hundred so far, the rest to be paid when the job is finished. That's twelve hundred to find. With luck we'll find the total is something under two thousand, and the rest can go into the Fabric Fund. We must have something behind us in case of further disaster.'

'God forbid!' exclaimed the vicar, his mouth working

piteously. He poured a sherry with a shaking hand, and they sipped in silence.

Mr Mawne broke it at last. 'It's no good, Gerald. You must go into this business of the sale of the chalice. It's all very well to be sentimental –'

'*Sentimental!*' cried the vicar, but his friend swept on.

'But the fact is that the chalice could be our salvation. Not only now, but as a hedge against future crises. After all, we could always have a replica made.'

'*A replica?*' echoed the vicar in anguish. 'But it wouldn't be the same!'

'Of course not,' agreed Mr Mawne soothingly, as though addressing a fractious child, 'but it would do as well.'

The vicar, too stunned to explain, shook his grey head sadly.

Jock Graham, unusually perceptive, spoke gently. 'It's a sore blow, I know, vicar, but it would be prudent to find out the possibilities. With any luck, it may never be needed, but it's only fair that the parish should know the position. We need another five or six hundred pounds to pay for this damage and to put the Fabric Fund on a sound footing. The Festival may bring in another sixty to seventy. There are the sums from the guarantors and the covenantors which will bring in another hundred or so, over a period of time. But it just isn't enough.'

The vicar put down his sherry glass carefully and looked from one to the other. 'Let me sleep on it,' he said. 'I'll give you an answer, one way or the other, early next week. It's a step I can hardly bear to contemplate.'

'Good man!' said Mr Mawne encouragingly, slapping his old friend painfully on the back, and the two men left the vicar to his own troubled thoughts.

'Simply pecking at your food, Gerald,' commented his wife, briskly removing the plates at lunch time. 'You worry far too much. You'll have another of your dizzy spells, if you're not sensible.'

'I'll have a walk this afternoon,' said the vicar meekly. 'Fresh air always calms me.'

The road to the downs above Fairacre peters out into a grassy track. Birds darted across the vicar's path, with cries of alarm. Rabbits bounded away with a flourish of white scuts, and at least four larks vied with each other high against the blue and white dappled sky. It looked so peaceful, so unchanging, much as it looked, thought the vicar with a pang, when the silversmith had finished his masterpiece, in the reign of Queen Anne over two hundred and fifty years ago.

He sat himself heavily on the springy turf and plucked a nearby harebell, twisting its wiry stem this way and that as he gazed at the village spread out below.

What should he do? He had had faith that his prayers would be answered, but God in His wisdom had seemed to withhold the easy way. There, below him, the villagers rested after their wholehearted efforts in Festival Week. The response had been wonderful, the village united as never before. There could be very little more expected from them. Henry Mawne was right. More help must come from another source, and the only possibility was the chalice. He must bring himself to approach the Bishop and to seek his advice. He owed it to his church and to his villagers. He had been selfish and weak in refusing to face the facts.

He sighed heavily, and the view below him grew suddenly blurred. Sad at heart, he struggled to his feet and made his way home.

The vicar slept little in the nights that followed. He had met Mr Mawne and Jock Graham and agreed reluctantly to consult the Bishop. It had taken him a week to compose a letter, and now he awaited a reply in an agony of spirit.

One morning he sat leaden-eyed before his breakfast egg, surveying the pile of letters. There was no word yet from the Bishop, but among the bills, receipts and circulars was a long blue air mail envelope, as gaudy as a peacock among sparrows. The vicar took it up first, savouring this rare foreign treasure.

'George Washington had a fine face,' he observed, studying the stamps closely. 'And what a good idea these little address tickets are! So much more legible than some unknown hand-writing at the head of a letter.'

'Who's it from?' asked Mrs Partridge, cutting to the heart of the matter.

'Oh, now let me see. "G. D. Lamb," it says, Lamb,' said the vicar ruminatively. 'Do we know a Mr Lamb in America, my dear?'

'Of course we do!' exclaimed his wife impatiently. 'George Lamb who was here during the Festival. That's probably the recipe for almond cookies he promised me. Do open it, dear, and *please* eat your breakfast. I want to clear the table. I'm having a coffee morning here today to raise more funds.'

The vicar obediently took a bite of toast and then slit the envelope. The letter was written in a firm hand in good copper-plate which owed its beginnings to Miss Clare's guidance, many years earlier.

Mrs Partridge watched her husband's eyes widen and his face grow pinker as he perused the paper in his hand. At last, bemused, he put it down, and rummaging in the envelope produced a cheque which he studied with stupefaction.

'Is my recipe there?' asked Mrs Partridge.

The vicar shook his head slowly, as if to clear it, rather than in answer to his wife's query. He seemed beyond speech.

'Has he sent something to the Fund?' asked Mrs Partridge, her glance falling on the cheque. 'How very, very kind of him!'

The vicar opened his mouth, and shut it again. He took a sip of coffee, and then found his voice.

'He has sent us a cheque for two thousand dollars.'

'*No!*' said his wife, thunderstruck. 'He *can't* have done! Not even Americans are as rich as that, and George only has a catering business which he built up himself!'

Without a word, the vicar handed the cheque across the table.

'It must be two thousand, because it's got it in words as well as figures,' said Mrs Partridge, studying the cheque earnestly, and speaking with great care as though she were explaining matters to herself. 'I simply can't take this in, Gerald.'

'It's not George alone, my dear. It appears that his good friends on the trip were most concerned to hear of our plight, and contributed very generously, and also got other people to do so. George says in his letter that two old ladies, whose parents came from these parts originally, gave a considerable part of the money, and so did some relatives of George's wife. Can you believe it, my dear? We have been gloriously blest.'

'It is absolutely wonderful!' said his wife huskily. 'In the face of such generosity one hardly knows whether to laugh or cry. Oh, Gerald, this will save the chalice, won't it?'

'It was my first thought,' confessed the vicar. 'I must telephone Henry immediately, and Jock, and then we must get in touch with the Rural Dean and the Bishop.'

He pushed back his chair and came round the table to kiss his wife. He looked, she thought, as though twenty years had fallen from him in the last five minutes. She watched him affectionately as he gazed once again at the cheque.

'How does one translate it into pounds?' he asked.

'Divide by three,' said Mrs Partridge promptly. 'That's somewhere near. Henry will know exactly.'

'But that means this is worth almost seven hundred pounds! It is quite incredible! To think that people who have never seen us or our little church should be so overwhelmingly generous! It does one's heart good.'

'The same sort of thing happened at Dorchester Abbey,' his wife reminded him. 'And there was a simply lovely service of thanksgiving with lots of Americans there. Remember?'

'Yes, indeed,' nodded the vicar. 'And there will be one here in Fairacre before very long, I can promise you.' He picked up George Lamb's letter and put it carefully, with the cheque, into his wallet. 'I shall do my telephoning, and write this morning to George and all his kind friends,' he said. 'But what I shall say, I really don't know. My heart is too full.'

The joyous news flashed round the Fairacre grapevine within hours, helped considerably by the partakers of coffee at Mrs Partridge's morning meeting. Villagers were incredulous at first, and then genuinely touched by the unexpected benefaction. Even Mrs Pringle seemed moved by the magnificence of the present, though she was grudging in her first pronouncements to me.

'That George Lamb must've done well for himself in New York. Been fleecing the customers, I shouldn't wonder.'

I was roused to wrath and told her that the idea may certainly have been George's, but the bulk of the money was from Americans who had never even seen St Patrick's, which made the gesture even more wonderful. Mrs Pringle had the grace to look a little sheepish as she spread a tea towel over the hot boiler to dry.

'Yes, that's true,' she conceded. 'I've always understood the Americans – for all their funny ways – had a feeling heart. And say what you like, Miss Read, it's a feeling heart that matters when you're in trouble. They tell me the vicar's already planning a thanksgiving service as soon as the repairs is done.'

'We'll all be there,' I promised her.

EPILOGUE

Exactly a year after the fateful night which wrecked the roof of St Patrick's, the bells were rehung in the repaired belfry.

Now all was completed. The spire and the roof presented their usual tidy aspect to the village. At last the scaffolding had gone. The workmen's huts had vanished, and the trodden grass of the churchyard was fast returning to its velvety greenness under Mr Willet's tending. The hand on the Appeal Fund board stood triumphantly at well over two thousand pounds thanks to the efforts of the folk of Fairacre and their friends near and far.

In his study, the vicar was composing the sermon he would be giving the next Sunday at the great thanksgiving service. On his desk stood Queen Anne's silver chalice reflecting the autumn sunshine in its mellow curves. The vicar touched its ancient beauty with loving fingers. In a few minutes it would be in the kitchen being cleaned by Mrs Partridge in readiness for its part in the festivities of the great day.

What hopes and fears had centred round this lovely thing during the past year, he thought! What a year it had been for them all in Fairacre!

He pushed aside his papers and went into the garden for a breath of air. It was a quiet, gentle day with no breath of wind, a contrast indeed with the fury of the first of October last year when disaster had struck.

He thought, with gratitude, of all the blessings which had followed – the united efforts of all in the village, the bravery, the generosity of everybody, particularly of those American friends who had forged an unforgettable link with this small unknown village, as a result of last year's storm. What friends Fairacre had made! What fun it had been!

He stooped to pick up a shred of paper which was lodged among the button chrysanthemums in the border. He smoothed it out and surveyed the lettering with a smile of intense happiness. Crumpled, rain-washed and faded, it was the final triumphant scrap of

THE FAIRACRE FESTIVAL

EVERY F...